THE
LIST

SIOBHAN VIVIAN

PUSH

SCHOLASTIC INC.

For Mommy, for a million reasons

This book was originally published in hardcover by PUSH, an imprint of Scholastic Inc., in 2012.

ISBN 978-0-545-16918-9

12 11 10 9 8 7 6 5 4 3 2 1   14 15 16 17 18 19/0

Printed in the U.S.A. 40
First Scholastic paperback printing, April 2014

The text type was set in Baskerville MT.
Book design by Kristina Iulo

"The perception of beauty is a moral test."

— HENRY DAVID THOREAU

PROLOGUE

For as long as anyone can remember, the students of Mount Washington High have arrived at school on the last Monday in September to find a list naming the prettiest and the ugliest girl in each grade.

This year will be no different.

Roughly four hundred copies of the list currently hang in locations of varying conspicuousness. One is taped above the urinal in the first-floor boys' bathroom, one covers the just-announced cast for the fall drama production of *Pennies from Heaven*, one is tucked between pamphlets for dating violence and depression in the nurse's office. The list is affixed to locker doors, slipped inside classroom desks, stapled to bulletin boards.

The bottom right corner of each copy has been dimpled by an embossing stamp, leaving behind the scar of Mount Washington High rendered as a line drawing — before the indoor pool, the new gymnasium, and a wing of high-tech science labs were added. This stamp had certified every graduation diploma before it was stolen from the principal's desk drawer decades ago. It is now a piece of mythic contraband used to discourage copycats or competitors.

No one knows for sure who authors the list each year, or how the responsibility is passed along, but secrecy has not impeded tradition. If anything, the guaranteed anonymity makes the judgments of the list appear more absolute, impartial, unbiased.

And so, with every new list, the labels that normally slice and dice the girls of Mount Washington High into a billion different distinctions — poseurs, populars, users, losers, social climbers, athletes, airheads, good girls, bad girls, girlie girls, guy's girls, sluts, closet sluts, born-again virgins, prudes, over-achievers, slackers, stoners, outcasts, originals, geeks, and freaks, to name just a few — will melt away. The list is refreshing in that sense. It can reduce an entire female population down to three clear-cut groups.

Prettiest.

Ugliest.

And everyone else.

This morning, before the first homeroom bell, every girl at Mount Washington High will learn if her name is on the list or not.

The ones who aren't will wonder what the experience, good or bad, might have been like.

The eight girls who are won't have a choice.

THE LIST

FRESHMEN

Ugliest:
DANIELLE DEMARCO —
Also known as Dan the Man.

Prettiest:
ABBY WARNER —
Bonus points awarded for overcoming family genetics!

SOPHOMORES

Ugliest:
CANDACE KINCAID —
Beauty isn't just skin-deep, btw.

Prettiest:
LAUREN FINN —
Everyone's hot for the new girl.

JUNIORS

Ugliest:
SARAH SINGER —
It's like she's trying to be as ugly as possible!

Prettiest:
BRIDGET HONEYCUTT —
What a difference a summer can make.

SENIORS

Ugliest:
JENNIFER BRIGGIS —
(Drumroll, please.)
The only four-peat in Mount Washington history!
Congrats, Jennifer!

Prettiest:
MARGO GABLE —
All hail this year's homecoming queen!

MONDAY

CHAPTER ONE

Abby Warner strolls around the ginkgo tree, one hand drifting lazily over the thick calluses of bark. A breeze nips at her legs, bare between the hem of her corduroy skirt and her ballet flats. It is practically tights weather, but Abby will avoid wearing them for as long as she can stand the chill. Or until the last of her summer tan fades away. Whichever comes first.

The spot is known as Freshman Island. It is where the more popular ninth graders of Mount Washington assemble in the mornings and after school. During springtime, nearly everyone avoids Freshman Island because of the putrid smell of the pale orange ginkgo bulbs that thud swollen onto the ground, expelling a pungent gas. This is a fine arrangement, though, because by spring the freshmen will nearly be sophomores, and will avoid anything that might identify them as younger.

Abby's parents dropped her and her older sister, Fern, off here what feels like hours ago, because Fern has some debate club thing. Or is it academic decathlon on Mondays? Abby yawns. She can't remember which. Either way, these kinds of mornings suck, because Abby has to get up *extra* early to have time to shower, do her hair, and put together something cute to wear. She does it all without turning on the light, so as not to wake Fern, with whom she shares the largest bedroom in the Warner home. Meanwhile, Fern sleeps until the last possible minute because she has no morning routine to speak of, besides brushing her teeth and cycling through a rotation of jeans and boxy T-shirts.

This morning, Fern had proudly put on a new T-shirt that she'd bought online. It had an ornate crest printed on the chest, proclaiming allegiance to a rogue sect of warriors from The Blix Effect, a series of fantasy novels all of Fern's friends are obsessed with. And in the car, Fern had asked Abby to give her two French braids, one on each side of her head, like the ones the female main character in The Blix Effect wears into battle.

Fern only ever wants Abby to give her two French braids, even though Abby can do a knot or an up-twist — hairstyles Abby feels are better, more sophisticated choices for her sixteen-year-old sister. But Abby never says no to Fern's requests, even though she finds it weird that Fern wants to dress in what is essentially a costume, because the braids do make Fern look better, or at least like she cares a little bit about how she looks.

School buses and cars begin to appear. One by one, Abby is warmed by her friends' hugs. They all spent the weekend sending pictures of potential dresses back and forth to one another for the homecoming dance on Saturday night. The dress Abby is completely in love with — a black satin halter with a thick white bow cinching the waist — is on hold in her size at a store in the mall. Her only hesitation is that none of her freshmen girlfriends seem to know how dressed up you're supposed to get for high school dances that aren't prom.

"Ooh! Lisa!" Abby says when her best friend, Lisa Honeycutt, comes walking over from the parking lot. "Did you show Bridget my homecoming dress? Does she think it's too formal?"

Abby's jaw goes slack with surprise. Even though she isn't sure what Lisa is talking about, it is clearly news to be excited about. Luckily, one of their other friends asks, "What list?" and then everyone turns to Lisa for an explanation.

As Lisa fills them in, Abby nods along, pretending that she isn't as clueless as the rest of them. Of course Fern hadn't bothered to mention this very important thing, just like Fern wouldn't have a clue about which dresses were right for the homecoming dance. Sometimes Abby wished that Bridget was her sister.

Okay. Lots of times.

Abby's friends take turns bouncing her around with congratulatory hugs, and each squeeze makes her heart flutter a little faster. Though the freshmen boys act uninterested in their celebration, Abby notices their game of hacky sack inch closer to where she is standing.

But it still hasn't sunk in. There are a lot of pretty freshmen girls at Mount Washington, and Abby is friends with most of them. Did she really deserve to be at the top of the pack?

It is a strange, foreign place for her to be.

"I'm sorry you girls didn't get picked," Abby says suddenly to everyone, and she partly means it.

"Please," Lisa says, pointing at her mouth. "Who's going to vote me prettiest of *anything* with these railroad tracks running across my face?"

"Shut up!" Abby cries, knocking into Lisa. "You're *so* pretty! Way prettier than me." Abby honestly thinks so. In fact, she is lucky to have made the list this year, because when Lisa finally gets her braces removed, all bets will be off. Lisa is at least five inches taller than Abby, with long black hair that always looks shiny and a tiny little mole at the top of her left cheek. She has a great body, with curves and boobs. Really, the only thing that isn't perfect about Lisa is her braces. And maybe her feet, which are kind of big. But people usually overlook that sort of thing.

"You are the worst at taking compliments, Abby," Lisa says with a laugh. "But this is seriously huge. Everyone in school will know who you are now."

Abby smiles. She's never been more excited about the next four years than she is right this minute. "I wish I knew who picked me so I could thank them." The idea of one girl, or maybe even a delegation, bestowing this honor on her is extremely exciting. She has friends, older girls, she didn't even know about. "So . . . where did you see the list?"

"I saw a copy on the bulletin board near the gym," Lisa says. "But they are everywhere."

"Do you think I could take one?" Abby wonders. She wants to keep the list someplace special. Maybe in a scrapbook, or a memory box.

"Definitely! Let's go grab one."

The girls hold hands as they run into school.

"So who else is on this list?" Abby asks. "Besides me and your sister?"

"Well, the ugliest freshman is Danielle DeMarco."

Abby slows down. "Wait. The list names ugly girls, too?" In the excitement, she'd missed that part.

"Yup," Lisa says, pulling her along. "Wait until you see it. Whoever wrote it this year put funny things underneath every-one's names. Like Danielle's called *Dan the Man*."

Abby isn't friends with Danielle DeMarco, but they are in the same gym class. Abby had watched Danielle kill it during the mandatory mile run last week. It was admirable, and Abby could have probably run faster than the crappy seventeen minutes she ended up with, but she didn't want to be sweaty for the rest of the day. Of course she feels bad that Danielle has been named the ugliest girl in their class, but Danielle seems tough enough to handle it. And, hopefully, Danielle will understand that there are other girls who could have been named the ugliest, too. Just like in Abby's case. It's truly the luck of the draw.

"What did it say about me?"

Lisa lowers her head and whispers, "It congratulated you for overcoming genetics," before letting out an embarrassed giggle.

Fern.

Abby bites the inside of her cheek and then asks, "Is Fern the ugliest junior?"

"Oh, no," Lisa says quickly. "It's that freaky girl Sarah Singer, who scowls on the bench near Freshman Island." Abby lowers her eyes and nods slowly. She guesses Lisa can see her guilt, because Lisa pats her on the back. "Look, Abby. Don't worry about the genetics thing. It doesn't mention Fern by name. I bet a lot of people don't even know you two are sisters!"

"Maybe," Abby says, hoping what Lisa says is true. But even if most of the kids at school don't know they're related, her teachers sure do. It has been one of the worst things about going to Mount Washington: watching her teachers realize, after the first week or so, that Abby is nowhere near as smart as Fern.

Lisa continues, "Anyway, Fern always gets the recognition. And every time she does, you're so happy for her. Remember last year, when you made me sit through that three-hour Latin poetry reading contest Fern competed in at the university?"

"That was actually a big deal. Fern got picked out of the whole high school to recite it, and she won a bunch of scholarship money."

Lisa rolls her eyes. "Right, right. I remember. Now it's your turn to get some attention."

Abby squeezes her friend's hand. Yeah, the genetics comment is kind of mean. But Lisa is right. It's not like Abby *herself* said it. And she *is* always cheering on Fern for her academic stuff. She never even complained once about those early-morning wake-ups or all the college visits they'd gone on this summer instead of a vacation.

Not out loud, anyway.

When they get close to the gym, Lisa jogs a few steps ahead. "Here it is," she announces, tapping the paper with her finger. "In black and white."

Abby finds her name near the top of the list. *Her name!* Seeing it makes the whole thing way more real, feel more earned. Abby is, officially, the prettiest girl in her freshman class.

She's not sure how long she stands there staring at it. But eventually Lisa pinches her arm. Hard.

Abby tears her attention off the bulletin board. Fern is marching down the hall with incredible purpose, her book-bag straps pulled tight over her shoulders, the tails of her French braids swinging side to side.

If Fern knows Abby is on the list, Abby certainly can't tell. Fern walks by exactly the same way she usually does at school — as if Abby doesn't exist.

Abby waits until Fern rounds the corner. Then she pulls the list off the bulletin board, using her pinky nail to ease out the staples, careful not to tear the corners.

CHAPTER TWO

From a block away, Danielle DeMarco realizes that she's missed her bus. It is too quiet, especially for a Monday. Nothing in the air but the typical morning sounds — chirping birds, the *click click click* of rising automatic garage doors, the tinny rumble of empty trash cans being dragged back up driveways.

Late to school, starving for breakfast, utterly exhausted. Not such a great way to start off the week.

But Danielle still thinks last night was worth it.

She'd been asleep for two hours when her phone rang. "Hello?" she asked, her word wrapped in a yawn.

"How can you be sleeping? It's only midnight."

Danielle checked that her bedroom door was shut. Her parents wouldn't like Andrew calling so late. They still referred to him as her *friend from camp*, despite the million times she'd corrected them. As if *boyfriend* was a tongue twister. Or maybe that was the thing they worried about, because Andrew was a year older. But for someone her parents lumped in the same category as her best friend, Hope, they certainly had a lot of rules about when, where, and how Danielle could spend time with Andrew.

That had been the hardest part about coming home from Camp Clover Lake, where they'd both worked as counselors this past summer. They'd lost the freedom to hang out when they wanted, talk when they wanted. There were no more nights of Andrew sneaking through the dark and scratching the screen in the window above her bed. No more taking the paddleboats out to the center of the lake and waiting until the breeze brought them back to the dock.

Summer already felt like a million years ago.

Danielle pulled her comforter over her head and kept her voice low. "Lights out, campers," she teased.

Andrew sighed. "I'm sorry I woke you. I'm just way too amped up to sleep. I've got tons of adrenaline stored up from the game and no way to get rid of it."

Danielle and Hope had watched from the stands that afternoon as Andrew was stuck in a perpetual warm-up routine on the sideline while the football field got torn up by other players' cleats. He'd bounce on his toes, do jumping jacks, or run a sprint of high-knee lifts to stay warm. After each play, Andrew glanced over at the varsity football coach, fingers laced around the face guard of his gleaming white helmet. Hopeful.

She felt terrible for him. It was the fourth game of the season, and he hadn't seen one minute of playing time. What would it have mattered, giving sophomores like Andrew a chance? Mount Washington was losing by three touchdowns at half-time. The Mountaineers hadn't won a single game.

"Well . . . I thought you looked cute in your varsity jersey," she said.

Andrew laughed, but Danielle could tell by the dryness that he was still upset. "I'd rather not get called up if I'm not going to see any playing time. Just let me start on JV. It's humiliating, standing on the sideline, doing absolutely nothing while we get our asses beat game after game. I could have had nachos with you and Hope in the bleachers for all it mattered."

"Come on, Andrew. It's still an honor. I bet there are a ton of other sophomores who'd kill to be on varsity."

"I guess," he said. "You know, Chuck got to play the whole second half. I wish I were big like him. I should do more weight room work and maybe try those nasty protein shakes he's always chugging. I'm way too skinny. I'm, like, the smallest guy on the team."

"You are not. And anyway, why would you want to be like Chuck? Yeah, he's big . . . but it's not like he's in good shape. I bet you could run circles around him." Danielle was pretty sure Andrew knew she wasn't crazy about Chuck. Andrew once told her that Chuck had a special shelf for his cologne bottles, which he displayed proudly, and wouldn't leave the house without a splash on. Chuck would even put some on before he'd go lift weights in his garage. According to Andrew, Chuck was really grossed out by the smell of sweat, even his own.

Andrew considered it. "That's true. The dude does eat crap. I don't think Chuck even knows what a vegetable is, unless it goes on his Big Mac. No wonder he can't get a girlfriend."

They both laughed at that.

It had taken Danielle a few weeks to understand the way Andrew and his friends acted around each other. The guys were super competitive, but especially Chuck and Andrew. Everything between those two was a rivalry — grades, new sneakers, who could reach the water fountain first. It seemed to Danielle like normal boy stuff for the most part, but every so often, Andrew would take some stupid "loss" really hard. Danielle was also competitive, and while she sympathized with Andrew's pangs of defeat, she also never pitted herself against her friends.

She didn't even want to think about how sucky it would have been if she or Hope hadn't both made the swim team.

That said, Danielle did take special pride in knowing that, when it came to the boys having girlfriends, she'd tipped the scales in Andrew's favor.

"Hey," Andrew said. "Guess what I found out today. Even if I don't play a single minute this season, I'll still get a varsity jacket."

"You'll look hot in it," Danielle said. It was kind of a silly thing to say, but she knew it would make Andrew feel better.

"I don't care about the jacket. It'll just be cool seeing you in it this winter."

"You're sweet," Danielle said, blushing in the dark. It *would* be cool to wear Andrew's varsity jacket, at least until she could earn her own.

"Will you stay on the phone with me a little longer?" he asked quietly.

Danielle fluffed up her pillow, and she and Andrew clicked through their respective televisions together, as if their remotes were in sync. They laughed at the bizarre late-night infomercials that populated the cable channels in the middle of the night. Spray-on hair. Home gym contraptions that could double for medieval torture devices. Skin remedies for swollen, zitty faces. Diet pills based on ancient Chinese secrets.

Danielle fell asleep with her cell pressed to her ear, images of *before* and *after* flashing in the dark. Her battery died around four thirty A.M. Her alarm died with it.

For love, or something pretty close to it, she missed the bus.

Danielle reaches for her phone to call home, when she spots a notebook lying open in the street, pages fluttering. She picks it up. Using it to shield her eyes from the orangey sun, she sees, at a distance of roughly three blocks, her school bus bouncing along to the next designated stop. She missed it, but not by much.

She lowers her chin and stares out the tops of her eyes.

A second later, she's running.

Her body isn't warm, and she worries about possibly pulling a muscle. Chasing down the school bus definitely isn't worth a stupid injury that might keep her out of the water. But after a few strides, Danielle slips into a comfortable rhythm. A pleasant heat ignites her pumping arms, her whirling legs.

The school bus stops for a car pulling out of a driveway. Danielle quickly closes the gap. "Hey!" she calls out when she gets close enough to recognize the students in the back windows. "Hey!"

But the kids are too busy socializing with each other to notice Danielle. The bus accelerates and a cloud puffs out from the tailpipe, stinging her eyes. She veers to the right and centers herself in the driver's side-view mirror. She shouts again over the roar of the engine. She bangs her fist against the side.

The bus slams to a stop. The kids look down at her, shocked. Danielle pushes a few wisps of brown hair out of her face as the folding door opens.

"You could have gotten killed," the bus driver barks.

Danielle apologizes in between heaving deep breaths. She climbs the steps, holds the notebook over her head like a trophy, and waits for someone to claim it.

After stashing her coat in her locker, Danielle heads straight to the cafeteria with Hope. She woke up too late to eat breakfast, and there is no way she can last until lunch without food. She passes up the student council bagel sale, because carbs make her sleepy and she's tired enough as it is. Hopefully there'll be something in the vending machines besides potato chips and chocolate bars. Danielle has been eating more and more since making the freshman swim team, her body always desperate for fuel. She wants to be careful to feed it well.

An older boy passes the girls as they enter the cafeteria. "Hey! Dan the Man!" he says, and slaps Danielle on the back.

"Was he talking to you?" Hope asks.

Danielle is too startled to react. She tries to get a look at the boy's face to see if maybe she knows him, but he disappears as quickly as he arrived. "Um . . . no clue."

The girls continue over to the vending machine. The entire glass front is covered over by papers. Danielle assumes it's an overzealous school club desperate for members until she pulls a sheet down and reads it.

Dan the Man?

Ugliest?

A cramp spreads inside her, contracting each and every muscle.

To be called ugly is one thing. Of course Danielle has heard the insult before. Is there a girl in the world who hasn't? And while she certainly isn't happy about it, *ugly* is something people say about each other, and say about themselves, without even thinking. The word is so generic, it's almost meaningless.

Almost.

But the *Dan the Man* thing is different. That hurts, even though Danielle knows she isn't a particularly girlie girl. Wearing dresses makes her feel weird, as if she's in a costume, pretending to be someone else. She only puts makeup on for the weekends, and even then only a little bit of gloss and maybe mascara. She's never had her ears pierced because she's deathly afraid of needles.

But Danielle still has all the essential girl parts. Boobs. Long hair. A boyfriend.

Hope rips down a list of her own and sucks in a big breath, the way she usually does before plunging underwater. "Oh, no, Danielle . . . What is this thing?"

Danielle doesn't answer. Instead, she stares at her reflection in the newly exposed square of vending machine glass. She hadn't had time to shower this morning, so she just threw her hair up in a bun. A haze of short brown strands spike up around her hairline. It shouldn't surprise her — bits of broken hair fill the inside of her swim cap after every practice — but it does. She tries to smooth them down with a suddenly clammy hand, but the strands pop right back up. She pulls off her elastic and shakes out her hair. It is dry and dull from chlorine and doesn't move like normal hair should. It suddenly looks to Danielle like a bad wig.

Danielle turns away from her reflection. She sees that the lockers outside the cafeteria also have papers taped to them. She chokes out, "Hope, I think these lists are hanging all over school."

Without further discussion, the two girls leave the cafeteria, split apart, and begin running, one on either side of the hallway. They tear down every copy of the list they pass.

Though Danielle is glad for something physical to do, it is also her second sprint of the morning without any breakfast. She searches deep down inside for the strength to keep putting one foot in front of the other, like a straw rooting around the bottom of a soda can. She makes it to the end of the hallway, and then runs smack into Andrew, who's standing with a few other sophomore guys from the football team.

Including Chuck.

"Yo! It's Dan!" Chuck calls out in a deeper-than-usual voice. "Dan the Man!"

The boys stare at her and laugh.

They've seen the list.

Which means that Andrew has seen it, too.

"Come on, Andrew," another boy says, giving him a big shove in her direction. "Go give Dan a kiss!"

"Yeah! We support gay rights!" shouts Chuck.

Andrew laughs good-naturedly. But as he walks toward Danielle and away from his friends, his smile slips into a look of concern. He leads her into a stairwell. "Are you okay?" he asks, careful to keep his voice quiet.

"Not bad, considering the sex change operation I apparently had last night," Danielle says, a desperate joke to break the tension. Neither of them laugh. She holds up the copies of the list she's torn down. "What is this thing, Andrew?"

"It's a stupid tradition. It happens every year at the start of homecoming week."

She stares at him. "Why didn't you warn me?"

Andrew runs his hands through his hair. It is still light from the summer, but his roots are growing in darker. "Because I never thought you'd be on it, Danielle."

This makes her feel better, but not much. "Do you know who wrote it?" Danielle doesn't have a ton of friends, but as far as she knows, she doesn't have any enemies, either. For the life of her, she can't think of one person who would hate her enough to do something this mean.

Andrew glances at the copies of the list in her hands and quickly shakes his head. "No, I don't. And look, Danielle — you can't go running around tearing these things down. These lists are everywhere. The whole school knows about it. There's nothing you can do."

Danielle remembers the boy who slapped her back in the cafeteria, the heat from his hand on her spine. She doesn't want to do the wrong thing. She doesn't want to embarrass herself any more than what is already happening. "I'm sorry," she says, because that's how she feels. For many reasons. "Tell me what to do."

Andrew rubs her arm. "People will want to see you looking upset. They'll want to see you react. Everyone still talks about this girl Jennifer Briggis and how she freaked when she got put on the list her freshman year. Trust me — doing the wrong thing now could ruin the rest of high school for you."

Danielle's chest gets tight. "This is crazy, Andrew. I mean, this is crazy."

"It's a big mind game. It's like we tell the kids at camp: If you pretend like the teasing doesn't bother you, it will eventually stop. So don't give anyone the satisfaction of seeing you upset. You need to be stone cold." He anchors his eyes on hers. "Game Face. Okay?"

She bites her lip and nods, fighting back tears. She knows Andrew can see them, but thankfully he pretends not to. Apparently, he has his Game Face on, too.

Danielle takes a second to compose herself and follows Andrew out of the stairwell, though a few steps behind.

Hope stands in the middle of the hallway looking around in a panic. She spots Danielle and rushes over. "Hurry up, Danielle. I grabbed every copy in this hall and in the science wing. Let's go check near the gym." She gives Danielle a huge hug and whispers, "Don't worry. I swear on my life that we're going to find out who did this and make sure they get what they deserve."

"Forget it, Hope," Danielle says. She drops the copies she's holding into a trash can.

"What? What do you mean?" Hope turns around to glance at Andrew, who has rejoined his friends. "What did Andrew say?"

"Don't worry. He said all the right things." Which is how Danielle feels, without question.

CHAPTER THREE

"What the f?"

Though it's posed as a question, the three words aren't delivered like one, with the last syllable ticking up to a higher, uncertain pitch. And yet Candace Kincaid is clearly confused by the copy of the list taped to her locker door.

She frees a strand of brown hair stuck in her thick coat of shimmery lip gloss, then leans forward for a closer inspection. She drags a raspberry fingernail down the list, linking the word *ugliest* and her name with an invisible, impossible line.

Her friends pop up behind her, wanting to see. They'd all come to school looking for the list today. Candace was so excited for its arrival, she'd barely slept last night.

"It's the list!" one says.

"Candace is the prettiest sophomore!" another cries.

"Yay, Candace!"

Candace feels the hands pat her back, the hands squeeze her shoulders, the hugs. But she keeps her eyes on the list. This was supposed to be her year. Honestly, *last* year should have been her year, but Monique Jones had modeled in teen magazines, or at least that's what she'd told people. Candace didn't think Monique was *pretty* pretty. She was way too skinny, her head was too big for her body, and her cheekbones were . . . well, freakish. Also, Monique only made friends with guys. Classic slut behavior.

Candace had been very happy when the Joneses moved away.

She pinches the corner, flattening the blistered embossment between her fingertips, and then tears down the list, leaving an inch of tape and a rip of paper stuck to her locker door.

"I hate to break this to you, girls . . . but apparently I'm the ugliest sophomore girl at Mount Washington," Candace announces. And then she laughs, because it is honestly that ridiculous.

Her friends share quick, uneasy glances.

"On the plus side," Candace continues, mainly to fill the awkward silence, "I guess we know for sure that Lynette Wilcox wrote the list this year. Mystery solved!"

Lynette Wilcox uses a Seeing Eye dog to lead her through the hallways. She was born blind, her eyes milky white and too wet.

So it's a joke. Obviously.

Only none of her friends laugh.

No one says anything.

Not until one of the girls whispers, "Whoa."

Candace huffs. *Whoa* is the absolute understatement of the year. She turns the list around and goes over the other names, expecting other mistakes that might explain what the hell is going on. Sarah Singer is definitely the ugliest junior. Candace has a faint memory of who Bridget Honeycutt is, but the girl in her mind is kind of forgettable, so she isn't sure she's thinking of the right person. Everyone in school thinks Margo Gable is gorgeous, so seeing her name as prettiest senior makes sense. And, of course, Jennifer Briggis is the obvious choice for the ugliest senior. Honestly, any girl *other* than Jennifer would have been a total letdown. Candace doesn't know either of the freshmen girls, which isn't a surprise because she's not the kind of girl who gives a crap about freshmen.

There's one other name she doesn't recognize. Weirdly enough, it is her sophomore counterpart. The prettiest to her ugliest.

Candace flicks the list with her finger and it makes a snapping sound. "Who's Lauren Finn?"

"She's that homeschooled girl," one of her friends explains.

"What homeschooled girl?" Candace asks, wrinkling her nose.

Another girl nervously looks over both shoulders to make sure no one else in the hallway is listening, and then whispers, "Horse Hair."

Candace's eyes get big. "Lauren Finn is *Horse Hair*?"

She'd thought up the nickname last week, when everyone was forced to run a mile in gym class and Horse Hair's horsey blond ponytail kept swishing back and forth as she trotted along. Candace had made a point of neighing as she passed Lauren because it was gross to let your hair grow that long. Unless, of course, you had layers. Which Lauren didn't. Her hair was cut straight across the bottom at her waist. Probably by her mother with a dull pair of scissors.

"Well . . . I think Lauren's pretty," another girl says, shrugging her shoulders apologetically.

Someone else nods. "She could use a haircut for sure, but yeah. Lauren's definitely pretty."

Candace lets out a pained sigh. "I'm not saying Horse Hair isn't pretty," she moans, though she'd never actually considered Lauren's looks. And why would she? This conversation isn't supposed to be about Lauren. It's supposed to be about her. "It doesn't make any sense that I'd be picked as the ugliest sophomore." Her eyes roll off her friends and on to other sophomores walking down the hallway. Candace sees, in the span of a few seconds, at least ten other girls who it should be. Ugly girls who deserve this.

"I mean, come on, you guys. This is total crap!" Candace gives her friends another chance to defend her, though she feels a little pathetic at having to bait them. "Pretty girls are not supposed to end up on the ugly side of the list! It, like, undermines the whole tradition."

"Well, the list doesn't *actually* say that you're ugly," someone gently offers.

"That's true," adds another girl. "The ugliest girls are *seriously* ugly. The list just says you're ugly on the inside."

It isn't the rousing defense Candace is hoping for. But as the words sink in, Candace nods slowly and lets a new feeling bloom inside her. So what if people think she is ugly on the inside? Clearly her friends don't believe that, or they wouldn't be friends with her! And pretty on the outside is what really counts. Pretty on the outside is what everyone sees.

One of the girls says timidly, "So . . . should we go discuss what we're doing for Spirit Caravan?"

Candace had announced this as the plan for the morning. Spirit Caravan happens on Saturday, before the homecoming football game. It's an impromptu parade where the students at Mount Washington drive around town with their cars decorated, beeping their horns and getting people excited for the game. This is the first year Candace and her friends can drive themselves, since a few, herself included, had gotten their driving permits over the summer. Candace has everything planned in her notebook, like whose car they should ride in (her mother's convertible, obviously), how it should be decorated (streamers, tin cans, soap on the windshield), and what the girls should wear (short shorts, kneesocks, and Mount Washington sweatshirts). Still, Candace stares at her friends slack jawed. "I can't say I'm in a very school spirit-y mood at the moment." The fact that they didn't pick up on this annoys her. "Let's table that until tomorrow, okay?"

One girl shrugs her shoulders. "But we only have until Saturday to figure things out."

Another adds, "We can't leave it until the last minute. We need to come up with a concept. We're sophomores now. We can't just, like, throw something together."

A *concept*? Seriously? Candace rolls her eyes. But it occurs to her, as her friends nod along with each other, that they are going to talk about the Spirit Caravan with or without her. It is the strangest feeling to have, even stranger than being called ugliest.

She quickly changes her strategy and rips her page of ideas out of her notebook. "Fine," she says, handing it off. "Here's what I'm doing. Figure out who's riding with me, because my mom's convertible can only fit five of us." She quickly does a head count. There are ten girls standing at her locker. "Maybe six, if you squeeze."

Candace opens her locker door and stares through the metal slats as her friends walk toward homeroom without her. Her eyes move to the magnetic mirror hanging inside the door. Something about her face seems off, imbalanced. It takes her a few seconds of close inspection to realize that she's forgotten to put eyeliner on her left eye.

Why didn't any of her friends tell her?

After digging in her makeup bag, Candace inches close until the tip of her nose nearly grazes the mirror. She gently pulls the corner of her left eye toward her ear and traces a creamy band of chocolate pencil, one of the samples her mother gave her, across the lid. Then she lets go, her skin snapping pertly back into place, and blinks a few times.

Candace's eyes are her best feature, as far as she is concerned. They are the lightest blue, like three drops of food coloring in a gallon of ice-cold water. People always commented on them, and even though Candace finds that predictability annoying, she of course still relishes the attention. How a salesgirl would suddenly look up from the register and say, "Wow, your eyes are amazing!" Or, better yet, a boy. Her eyes get more attention than her boobs, and that is seriously saying something. She is, after all, a true C cup without any of that ridiculous padding, which is false advertising, in her opinion.

A small sense of relief washes over her. List or no list, Candace Kincaid is pretty. She knows it. Everyone knows it.

And that is all that matters.

CHAPTER FOUR

L auren Finn and her mother agree the sedan still smells like Lauren's dead grandfather — a musty blend of pipe smoke, old newspapers, and drugstore aftershave — so they drive to Mount Washington High School with the windows open. Lauren splays her arms across the window frame, resting her chin where her hands overlap, and lets the fresh air rouse her.

Mondays are always the most tired mornings, because Sundays are always the worst nights. The anxiety of the coming week speeds Lauren up when she wants to be slowed down. She feels every lump in the old mattress, hears every creak and sigh of her new old house.

She is three weeks into this new life and nothing is comfortable. Which is exactly what she'd expected.

The wind whips Lauren's long pale hair like a stormy blond ocean, all but the section pinned with a tarnished silver barrette.

She found it last night, after the first hour of tossing and turning in the same bedroom, the same bed, where her mother had slept when she was a fifteen-year-old girl. The slender bar stuck out like a loose nail where the wood floor met the wall, its cloudy rhinestones blinking in the moonlight.

Lauren crept across the hall in her pajamas. Her mother's reading light cast a warm white glow out the seam of the open door. Neither of them had been sleeping very well since moving to Mount Washington.

Lauren cracked it wider with her foot. Pairs of caramel drugstore panty hose hung on the coils of the wrought-iron bed frame to dry after having been washed in the sink. They reminded Lauren of the snake skins shed in the warm dunes behind their old apartment out west. Their old life.

Mrs. Finn looked up from the thick manual of tax laws. Lauren weaved through unpacked boxes and hopped onto the bed. She opened her hands like a clamshell.

Mrs. Finn grinned and shook her head, looking a bit embarrassed. "I had begged your grandmother to buy me this when I started high school." She pinched the barrette between her fingers, examining the fossil of her youth. "I don't know if you've ever had this feeling, Lauren, but sometimes, when you get something new, you trick yourself into believing it has the power to change absolutely everything about yourself." The corners of Mrs. Finn's mouth pulled until her smile stretched tight and thin, turning it into something entirely different. With a sigh, she said, "That was quite a lot to ask of a barrette, don't you think?" Then Mrs. Finn threaded it into Lauren's hair, securing a sweep over her daughter's ear, and pulled the quilt back so Lauren could lie beside her.

Lauren hadn't experienced the feeling her mother had described, but one much more unnerving. Like with Randy Culpepper, who sat one desk away in her English class.

On her very first day at Mount Washington High, Lauren had noticed that Randy smelled strange. *Woodsy and sort of stale* was how she'd first categorized it, until she overheard in the hall that Randy was a small-time pot dealer who smoked a joint in his car each morning before school.

That Lauren now knew what an illegal substance smelled like encapsulated how much her life had changed, whether she'd wanted it to or not. She swallowed this secret, along with so many others, because knowing them would break her mother's heart. She could never confirm that things in her new school were as bad as she'd been told.

If not worse.

A while later, after Mrs. Finn had finished studying and turned off the light, Lauren stared into the dark and held on to her mother's words. Despite all these changes, she would stay the same girl. Before falling asleep, she touched the barrette, her anchor.

Lauren reaches for the barrette again as the sedan slips into a free space along the curb.

"How do I look? Like an accountant you'd want to hire?" Mrs. Finn turns the rearview mirror toward her and regards her reflection with a frown. "It's been so long since I've had an interview. Not since before you were born. No one's going to want to hire me. They're going to want some beautiful young thing."

Lauren ignores the sweat stains in the armpits of her mother's blouse, the small run in the panty hose that betrays the paleness of her mother's skin. Paler still is Mrs. Finn's hair, blond like Lauren's, but dulled by gray.

"Remember the things we talked about, Mommy. Focus on your experience, not the fact that you haven't worked in a while."

They'd done a mock interview last night, after Lauren's homework had been finished and checked. She'd never seen her mother so unsure of herself, so unhappy. Mrs. Finn doesn't want this job. She wants to still be Lauren's teacher.

It makes Lauren sad, their situation. Things hadn't been good the last year out west. The money left by Lauren's father was running out, and her mother cut back on the cool field trips they used to take to get a change of scenery from The Kitchen Academy — what they called their breakfast nook between the hours of eight and four. Lauren hadn't even known her mother had stopped paying rent on their apartment. Her grandfather dying and leaving them the house was a blessing in disguise.

"Lauren, promise me you'll talk to your English teacher about the reading list. I hate the idea of you sitting in her class for the whole year, bored to tears with books we've already read and discussed. If you're afraid to do it —"

Lauren shakes her head. "I'll do it. Today. I promise."

Mrs. Finn pats Lauren's leg. "We're doing okay, right?"

Lauren doesn't think about her answer. She just says, "Yeah. We are."

"See you at three o'clock. I hope it goes fast."

Lauren leans across the seat and hugs her mother tight. She hopes for that, too. "I love you, Mommy. Good luck."

Lauren walks into school, barely a force against the tide of students flowing from the opposite direction. Her homeroom is empty. The fluorescent lights are still off from the weekend, and the legs of the upturned classroom chairs spike four-pointed stars, encircling her like oversize barbed wire. She turns one over and takes a seat.

It is terribly lonely at school.

Sure, a couple of people have talked to her. Boys, mostly, after daring each other to ask her stupid questions about homeschooling, like if she belonged to a religious cult. She expected as much — her male cousins were just as goofy and awkward and annoying.

The girls were only slightly better. A few smiled at Lauren, or offered tiny bits of politeness, like pointing out where to put her dirty cafeteria tray after lunch. But no one extended herself in a way that felt like the start of something. No one seemed interested in getting to know her beyond confirming that she was that weird homeschooled girl.

It shouldn't have surprised her. It is what she was told to expect.

Lauren lets her chin rest against her chest. She pretends to read the notebook lying open on the small patch of desk attached to her seat. Really, though, she discreetly watches the girls filter into the room and take chairs beside her. She picked up the trick from Randy Culpepper, who used the same posture to sleep, undetected, in second period.

She doesn't see the girls' leader with them, the pretty one with the icy eyes. It's a rare sighting.

The girls are frantic, whispering like crazy. Stifling giggles and laughs. Completely consumed with whatever they're gossiping about. Until one notices Lauren watching them.

Lauren lowers her eyes. But she's not fast enough.

"Oh my god, Lauren! You are *so* lucky! Do you even know how lucky you are?" The girl puts on a big smile. Huge, even. And she runs on tiptoes over to Lauren's desk.

Lauren lifts her head. "Excuse me?"

The girl ceremoniously places a piece of paper on top of Lauren's open notebook. "It's a Mount Washington tradition. They picked you as the prettiest girl in our grade." The girl talks slowly, as if Lauren spoke another language, or had a learning disability.

Lauren reads the paper. She sees her name. But she is still completely confused. A different girl pats her on the back. "Try to look a little happier, Lauren," she whispers sweetly, in the same way one might discreetly indicate an open zipper or food stuck in her teeth. "Otherwise people will think something's wrong with you."

This throwaway line surprises Lauren most of all, because it completely contradicts what she's already assumed.

CHAPTER FIVE

Sarah Singer's plan is to break it to him fast, so there's no scene. Forget dressing it up, explaining things. That's only going to make it worse. She'll just say something like, *I'm done, Milo. Our friendship, or whatever the hell you want to call it now, is over. So go ahead and do what you want. Live your life! Become best bros with the captain of the football team. Feel up the head cheerleader, even though everyone knows Margo Gable stuffs. I'm not gonna judge you.*

That last part will be a lie. She'll totally judge him for it.

Sarah sits on her bench, nibbling the edges off a strawberry Pop-Tart. The tangy smell of smoke on her fingers sours the sweet. She forces down what's in her mouth and chucks the pink frosted center — her favorite part — into the grass, because all this sugar clearly isn't helping. Let the squirrels eat the crack; she needs to calm the hell down. She moves a tangle of tarnished necklaces off her chest and feels for her heart. It flutters like a hummingbird's, so fast the individual beats blur together and make a steady, uncomfortable hum.

She rips the cellophane off a new pack of cigarettes, lights up. A lift of wind carries away the smoke, but she knows Milo will smell it on her when he gets to school. He's like a police dog, trained to sniff out her vices. Last night, when she was hanging half out of his bedroom window, she smoked the third-to-last cigarette in her old pack and told him, after his depressing play-by-play of his aunt's final days of lung cancer, she'd seriously think about maybe quitting.

Remembering that now makes her laugh, puff out smoke signals. Both dissipate into the chilly morning air.

Last night, she talked a lot of shit.

But Milo . . . apparently he'd been talking shit since the day they met.

Whatever. Let him bitch about her smoking. It would be a relief to replace her anxieties with something simple and clear, like being annoyed with him.

Sarah watches two junior girls scurry along the sidewalk. Sarah knows who they both are, but what she thinks is: *All the junior girls at Mount Washington look the damn same.* The shoulder-length hair with highlights, the stupid shearling boots, the little wristlet purses to hold their cell phones, lip glosses, and lunch money. They remind her of zebras, keeping the same stripes so predators can't tell them apart. Survival of the generic. It's the Mount Washington way!

The two girls stop in front of her bench and huddle, shoulder to shoulder, each clutching a piece of paper. The smaller one hangs on her friend and chokes out a series of high-pitched laughs. The other simply sucks air in and out, a rapid fire of hiccupping wheezes.

Sarah's nerves can't take it.

"Hey!" she barks. "How about you ladies hold your little powwow someplace else?" She uses her lit cigarette as a pointer and jabs off in the distance.

It seems like a fair request. After all, these girls have the entire school to roam undisturbed. And everyone at Mount Washington knows that this is *her* bench.

She discovered it freshman year. It had always been vacant,

because it was positioned directly beneath the principal's window. That didn't bother Sarah. She wanted to be alone.

That is, until Milo Ishi came along last spring.

He'd been adrift on the sidewalk one random day, a new boy tossed around between currents of students who looked nothing like him. He folded his arms and tucked them tight underneath his chest, the chosen defensive posture for skinny vegan half-Japanese boys with shaved heads. Milo didn't look like Sarah, either, but maybe a more-evolved version. His sneakers were only available overseas. His headphones were expensive. His black eyeglass frames were crazy thick and probably vintage. He'd even gotten his first tattoo already — a Buddhist proverb scrawled on his forearm.

After a few minutes of watching, Sarah took pity on him and called out, "Hey, New Boy!"

Milo was terribly shy. Almost cripplingly so. He hated talking in class and broke out in hives whenever his parents argued. It was hard to get him to open up, but when he finally did, Sarah felt like she'd found a kindred outcast. She liked begging Milo to torture her with stories of his former life in West Metro, what going to an arts-focused high school in a city had been like. Milo said West Metro was a third-tier city, but to Sarah it could have been New York for how it stacked up against Mount Washington. At West Metro High, field trips were to fine art museums, there were no sports teams, and the drama club wasn't just a showcase for girls who aspired to be another Auto-Tuned voice sugaring the radio.

The bench is where they wait for each other before and after school each day, where they do their homework and split a pair of earbuds for the right and left sides of an illegally downloaded song. An oasis where two kids who once kept to themselves suddenly keep with each other.

Once, Sarah tried to carve their names in the bench, but discovered the wood was that new space-age treated stuff and broke the knife she'd nicked from the cafeteria after the third stroke. So she makes sure to have a black marker in her book bag to trace a fresh layer of ink over their initials whenever they begin to fade.

As Milo's bus pulls in, Sarah tucks the long front pieces of her inky black hair behind her ears. Milo had shaved the back of her head for her a few weeks ago, after he'd finished shaving his own, but it's growing in fast. That hair, pure and healthy, is soft, like a puppy dog's, and a golden brown that totally clashes with the dyed-black front. Her natural color. She'd almost forgotten what it looked like.

Milo, all lanky bones and sharp angles, walks toward her with a manga split open in front of his face. His knobby knees pop past the army green fringe of his cutoffs with each step. Milo claims he wears shorts no matter the weather. Sarah says that's because he's never lived through a winter on Mount Washington. She will give him such shit the first time she sees him in jeans.

She catches herself smiling and quickly resets her mouth with another drag.

"Yo," she says when Milo reaches the bench, and gets ready to let the ax fall.

Milo looks up from his manga. A grin spreads across his face, so deep his dimples appear. He says, "You're wearing my T-shirt."

Sarah looks down at herself.

Milo's right. This is not her black T-shirt. There are no white spots from bleaching her hair. She always strips it before she dyes it, so the new color sets as pure and saturated as possible. It's the only way, really, to make sure what's underneath doesn't show.

"You can keep it," he mumbles coyly.

"I don't want your shirt, Milo." In fact, if Sarah had other clothes with her, she'd change out of it right now. "Obviously I grabbed the wrong one last night. And I haven't done laundry, so I just threw it on again this morning." She clears her throat. Damn. She is already off her game. "Look. I want my shirt back. Bring it tomorrow."

"No problem." Milo falls next to her on the bench and goes back to his manga. From her seat, Sarah can see the page. An innocent school girl with doe eyes and a pleated skirt cowers in fear before a wild, snarling beast.

She moves her eyes and thinks, *Makes total sense.*

Milo's quiet for a few pages and then says, out of nowhere, "You're acting weird. You said you wouldn't act weird."

He is wrong.

"Let's not make this weird, okay?" is what Sarah had said when she'd come out of the small space between his wall and his dresser without her jeans. She left everything else on — her hooded sweatshirt, her socks, her underwear.

"Okay," he'd said, eyes wide, lying on a set of faded Mickey Mouse sheets, ones he'd probably had since he was a kid.

"No talking," she'd said, and dove under the covers.

The rest of her clothes came off shortly thereafter. Not her necklaces, though. Sarah never took off her necklaces. Milo climbed on top of her and his weight pressed the tiny metallic links into her collarbone.

She reached out to his nightstand and turned his stereo up as loud as it could go; it was playing one of the mixes she'd made when they'd first met. The vibrations shook the crap piled on Milo's dresser, buzzed the window glass. But even with the music blaring right next to their heads, Sarah could still hear Milo breathing, hot and fast in her ear. And every so often, a moan. A tender sigh. From her own mouth.

The memory of her voice fills Sarah's head now, like an echo, mocking her over and over.

She turns away from him. "I'm *not* acting weird. I just don't want to talk about last night. I don't even want to *think* about it."

"Oh," Milo says glumly. "Alright."

Sarah won't let herself feel guilty. This is all Milo's fault.

She takes a drag and blows the smoke down against his school bag. She knows his sketchbook is in there. She could reach in right now, flip to that page, and ask him straight up, *How come you never told me?*

That's what she goes to do. But she's drowned out by the girls standing near the bench.

They've doubled in size, from two to four. The girls scream with laughter, completely oblivious that there is a relationship about to implode right next to them.

Sarah feels the heat on her fingertips. Her cigarette has burned down to the filter. She flicks her fingers, sending the orange butt soaring in their direction. It bounces off one girl's fuzzy yellow sweater.

Milo puts his hand on her arm. "Sarah."

"You could have lit me on fire!" the girl who's been hit screeches, and she spazzes out, checking herself for burn marks.

"I asked you nicely to go somewhere else," Sarah points out. "But I'm not feeling nice anymore."

The girls shift their weight in one unified huff.

"Sorry, Sarah," one says, shaking the paper. "This is just *really* funny."

"That's how inside jokes usually are," Sarah snarks back. "Funny to those inside, annoying as shit to the rest of the world." Milo laughs at her barb. It makes her feel marginally better.

After sharing plotting looks with the rest of her group, another girl steps forward. "Well, here," she says. "Let us clue you in."

As soon as the paper is dropped in her lap, Sarah realizes what it is. That damn list. It makes her want to barf year after year, watching how the girls in her school evaluate and objectify each other, tear girls down and build others up. It's pathetic. It's sad. It's . . .

. . . her name?

It's like she's trying *to be as ugly as possible!*

Sarah looks up. The four girls are gone. It's like a sucker punch to the gut, the surprise worse than the hurt itself, and no chance to hit back.

"What's that?" Milo takes the paper.

Milo transferred in last spring to Mount Washington, so he doesn't know about the shitty tradition of the list. Sarah's head hurts, watching him read it. For a second, she thinks about explaining, but ends up chewing her fingernail instead. She says nothing. She doesn't have to. It's all right there, on the stupid fucking paper.

His mouth puckers. "What kind of asshole guys would do this?"

"Guys? Please. It's a coven of secret evil sluts. This happens every year, a masochistic prequel to the homecoming dance. I swear to god, I can't wait to get the hell off this mountain." She means it for so many reasons.

Milo reaches into Sarah's back pocket. His hand is warm. He grabs her lighter. After a few clicks, a flame hisses up. He holds it under the corner of the list.

It's nice, watching the list burn until it's nothing but char. But Sarah knows that there are copies hanging up all over school. Everyone will be staring at her, wanting to see her embarrassed, belittled. The tough girl knocked down, forced to admit that she does care what they think of her. When the paper breaks into tiny pieces of flaming ash, she grinds them out with her sneaker.

I'm such a dumbass, Sarah thinks. Believing that she could do her thing and they could do their thing, both sides coexisting in a fragile but still-functioning ecosystem. It started every morning on the bus. She'd plop herself in the front seat, put up her hood, tuck her headphones into her ears, and sleep with her head against the window. It was easier to completely tune out than to overhear girls talking the cruelest shit about each other one day and pledging themselves as BFFs the next.

The phoniness is what sickens her most about the girls of Mount Washington. Their charade of undying friendship and love is as badly acted as the high school musicals, yet everyone plays along and pretends that in twenty years, their cheap FRIENDS FOREVER charm necklaces won't have a bit of tarnish.

Other girls have been knocked out of favor, the same way she had back in seventh grade. But Sarah is the only one who never tried to get back in, and she knows it makes them hate her even more.

Evolution provides clues to the clueless. Animals bear the kinds of markings and bright colors that show how dangerous, how poisonous they are. Sarah has taken great pains to make sure everyone won't think she wants to be like them.

The maddening thing is that she *could* have tried. She could have made the decision to shop at their stupid stores, to buy the ugly boots and the teeny purses, to bounce along to their crappy music.

If they think she's ugly for trying to be different, that's fine by her.

Mission accomplished, in fact!

"Forget it," Milo says. "Those so-called pretty girls are completely deluded. They're the ugly ones."

She stares Milo down. Had he said this yesterday, before she'd found out the truth about him, she could have believed him; she would have felt better. But today was today, and now she knew better. Whatever they had was over. It had to be. She can't pretend Milo is something he's not.

But Sarah *is* glad he's here right now. Glad for the moment, anyway. Because she needs Milo's help.

She hoists her book bag onto her lap and pulls out her black marker from the front pouch. "Do me a favor. Write *UGLY* as big as you can across my forehead."

Milo shrinks back. "Why would I do that? Why would you want to do that?"

Sarah stutters for an answer, and settles on, "Do it, Milo."

He swats the marker away. "Sarah, we had *sex* last night." He's all earnest. It's infuriating.

"Milo! You do not want to piss me off right now! I'd do it myself but I'd write it backward. Please."

He groans, but he climbs onto his knees and pushes the hair up off her forehead.

The marker drags across her skin. As Milo writes the word, she glances up at the windows in the second-floor bathroom. There are girls staring down at her; they know where to find her, so they're checking to see if she's heard yet. Sarah salutes them with her middle finger. "Make it as big as you can," she tells Milo.

The spicy scent of the ink makes her woozy. Or maybe it's the anticipation. Milo caps the marker, and the click is like a movie clapboard. The show's about to start.

"For the record, I am totally *not* cool with this," Milo whispers as they enter the main door of Mount Washington.

"Then don't walk with me," she bites back. "Seriously. Don't." She gives him the chance to leave, to take the easy out.

Milo opens his mouth, then thinks better of it. "I'm walking with you," he says. "I walk you to class every day." His eyes go again to the word on her forehead, and the corners of his mouth sink.

It makes Sarah's throat tight. She can't fucking deal with Milo right now. So she starts walking, fast. The speed flutters her hair off of her forehead, so people can see the word. And they do. They see it.

But only for a second. Once the people in the halls see what she's done to herself, they quickly find another place to set their eyes. Their shoes, their friends, their homework. They'd rather look at anything but her.

The list is so powerful, its judgment so absolute, and yet no one wants to deal with it in black Sharpie on her face.

Fucking cowards.

But knowing this doesn't make Sarah feel better. In fact, it makes everything worse. Not only do they think she's ugly, but they want her to be invisible, too.

CHAPTER SIX

Bridget Honeycutt is halfway to school when her sister, Lisa, starts begging to put on a little bit of her lipstick.

"No way, Lisa. I wasn't allowed to wear makeup until sophomore year."

"Come on, Bridge! Please! Please! Please! Please! Mom won't know."

Bridget puts a trembling hand on her temple. "Fine. Whatever. Just . . . be quiet, okay? I have a serious headache."

"You're probably just hungry," Lisa says, and then reaches into the backseat for Bridget's purse. She rummages until she pulls out a slender black tube.

Bridget watches from the side of her eyes as her sister flips down the visor. Lisa traces her lips with the stub of peachy pink, presses them together, and blows a kiss at Bridget.

The pink makes Lisa's braces look extra silver, but Bridget doesn't say that. Instead she says, "Pretty."

Lisa touches up the corners of her mouth. "I'm going to wear red lipstick every single day when I'm your age."

"Red won't be good with your skin," Bridget tells her. "You're too pale."

Lisa shakes her head. "Everyone can wear red. That's what *Vogue* says. It just has to be the *right* red. And the right red for girls with dark hair and pale skin is deep cherry."

"Since when do you read *Vogue*?" Bridget wonders aloud,

thinking of the rainbow that the spines of Lisa's horse books make on the shelf over her bed.

"Abby and I bought the September issue and read it cover to cover on the beach. We wanted to be prepared for high school."

"You're scaring me."

"Don't worry. Besides the red lipstick thing, we didn't learn much. But we did get ideas for homecoming dresses. Abby will be happy you like the one she wants. It's a red-carpet knock-off." Lisa pouts. "I hope I find something nice, too."

Bridget wipes away a smudge of lipstick left on Lisa's chin. "I said I'd take you shopping this week. We'll find you a dress."

"Do you think Mom will let me wear makeup to the dance? I was thinking that if I ace my Earth Science quiz, I'd show her the grade and then ask her. Isn't that a great plan?"

"Maybe . . . if Mom didn't already expect you to get As."

"I guess I could sneak it on once I get there. I'll just have to make sure no one takes any pre-dance pictures of me." As Bridget parks the car, Lisa sets the lipstick on the dashboard and grabs her things. "See you later!"

Bridget watches Lisa sprint across the yard toward Freshman Island, weaving in and out of human traffic, her overstuffed book bag slapping against her legs, her long black ponytail stretching down her back. Lisa is growing up so fast, but there are plenty of glimmers of the little girl that shine through.

It gives Bridget hope for herself. That there's still a chance to be the girl she was before last summer.

She turns off the car and sits for a few minutes, collecting herself. It is quiet, except for her deep, measured breaths. And the voice in her brain, calling out instructions that reverberate inside her hollow body.

You have to eat breakfast today.

Eat breakfast, Bridget.

Eat.

This is her life every morning. No, every meal, every bite chewed to a monotone mantra, mental cheerleading needed to accomplish a task that would be no big deal to a normal girl.

She picks up her lipstick and drags a finger through the thin layer of dust on her dashboard. Bridget wants to feel proud that she's been doing much better. Eating more. But the victories feel bad, if not worse, than her failures.

A girl Bridget knows taps hello on the glass. Bridget lifts her head and manages to smile. It's a fake one, but her friend doesn't notice. No one does.

It's scary how fast things got messed up. Bridget thinks about this a lot. The timeline of her life had been linear and sharp and direct for most of her seventeen years. Until something went jagged.

She could trace it back to, of all things, a bikini.

Every summer of Bridget's life began and ended the same way — with a trip to the Crestmont Outlet Mall.

It was the halfway point between Mount Washington and the beach cottage where the Honeycutt family spent the entire summer. The family stopped at the Crestmont outlets to eat lunch, fill the gas tank for the second leg of the drive, and shop for clothes. In June, Bridget and Lisa stocked up on summer things. And then, on their way back to Mount Washington in

August, they'd search for back-to-school deals on cardigans and wool skirts.

With summer vacation beginning, Bridget's shopping bags were full of new tank tops, shorts, a jean skirt, and two sets of flip-flops. The only thing missing was a new bathing suit.

The bikini she'd worn last year had sprung an underwire, and the tankini from the year before was too small for her chest, so she'd given it to Lisa. Snipping the tags off a brand-new bikini was akin to the ribbon cutting of a store or breaking ground on a building site. The Grand Opening of Summer.

Bridget was determined to find one. She flew in and out of stores.

"We should get going, Bridge, if we want to make it before dinner," her mother said with a sigh from a few steps behind. She wiped some perspiration from her top lip with a napkin from the food court. "Your father and Lisa are already back at the car, probably dying of heat. You can get a suit on the boardwalk tomorrow."

Bridget knew better. The boardwalk shops only stocked two kinds of bathing suits: fluorescent triangles that belonged in *Playboy* or frumpy flowered one-pieces for grandmas.

It was now or never.

The Crestmont Outlet Mall had opened a few new stores since she'd last been there, and Bridget came to a stop in front of one she recognized. It was a surf shop, complete with longboards that doubled as the cash stand, beaded curtains on the dressing room doors, and twangy songs vibrating through the glass window. The same store was in the mall back home, only the clothes there were full price.

As soon as she walked in, she spotted a sherbet-y orange gingham bikini with a white eyelet lace ruffle. It was the last one, it was her size, and it was marked an additional 50 percent off. She ran into the dressing room while Mrs. Honeycutt reminded her daughter to leave her underwear on, lest she catch an STD.

Bridget frowned as she pulled the bottoms up. They were surprisingly tight. The elastic cut into her legs. Maybe it was her underwear? She took them off and tried the bottom on again, but the fit wasn't any better. Her belly rolled a soft, fleshy wave that crashed over the ties at her hip. The top was similarly ill-fitting. The shoulder straps dug into her skin, and when she managed to test the limits of elasticity on the chest strap, poof! Back fat!

Bridget had never considered herself overweight before seeing the fabric stretched across her. But the reflection in the dressing room mirror startled her. She panicked, remembering her friend's End of School pool party last week, how she'd walked around the whole day in her old bikini without even a T-shirt on, in front of boys and girls, completely clueless as to how awful she'd looked.

She checked the size tag, expecting an error. But it was no mistake. The bikini was the same size as the other new clothes she'd bought. Her size.

This is an outlet mall.

That's why the clothes are cheap.

Because they're irregular.

Imperfect.

Defective.

Even though Bridget knew this, she couldn't quite hold on to the idea. It was slippery, sliding right out of her as she rushed back into her clothes. She clipped the suit back onto its hanger. Sadly, it was still a cute bikini. So very cute. Or it would be, if she were maybe five or so pounds lighter.

Bridget smoothed her hair as she stepped out of the dressing room. Mrs. Honeycutt stood by the register impatiently, her credit card already out, chatting with the salesgirl. The waist of Mrs. Honeycutt's navy linen pants swelled underneath her sleeveless white shell, the skin on her bare arms taut and overstuffed and about to split, like hot dogs left too long on the grill. Her mother never wore shorts. Her mother never swam in the ocean. She stayed in the air-conditioning in those wide-legged pants.

All of her aunts said that Bridget looked exactly like her mother had as a teenager. Staring at her, Bridget realized she had no memories of her mother being thin.

Bridget placed the bikini on the counter, careful not to look at it or anyone else while her mother paid.

As she walked back to the car, Bridget rationalized her decision. Everyone did it. Bought clothes that fit a little too tight, with the hope they would be inspiration to lose a few pounds. It would be a reward for good behavior. The bikini became a test. A test Bridget hoped to pass by the end of the summer.

And just like that, a new part of her mind lit up as she became acutely aware of all her bad habits. It dinged like a warning alarm when Lisa tore open a bag of Old Bay potato chips for movie night, or when Bridget got too close to the dish of salt water taffy her mom kept filled on the kitchen counter. Bridget's brain continued to evolve over the months, rewiring her cravings for boardwalk soft serve with the challenge to run another mile to the next pier, brainstorming excuses to skip out on Dad's amazing tuna fish sandwiches, until it commented not only on everything she put inside herself, but every piece of food she even thought about eating. It wiped away any memory she ever had of being pretty, and made it a goal, something she might be lucky enough to accomplish one day if she worked hard enough.

By the Fourth of July, she'd aced the test. With flying colors.

But even after she'd fit into that beautiful bikini, Bridget hardly wore it. Instead, she practically lived in her jeans. At the end of summer, they were so loose that when Bridget pulled the waistband flush against her hip, there was enough room to fit her whole fist on the other side.

The return trip to Crestmont Outlets at the end of summer provided her with a new wardrobe at a low, low size. But deep down Bridget knew this wasn't a good thing. At least that part of herself was still working. She wasn't totally gone.

Bridget's stomach rumbles.

As she climbs out of her car, she tugs on the hem of her tan cable-knit sweater, attempting to bridge the gap of skin between it and the waist of her jeans. The skinny space in her waistband four weeks ago has shrunk. Or rather, Bridget has expanded. She can only fit a few fingers now. Not her whole fist, like before.

You weren't healthy before.

You had a problem, but now you've got it under control.

On her way inside the school, her dark hair whips in her face, the sweet scent of coconut shampoo blowing across her with the breeze. It is too sweet, too rich. Her stomach twists on itself. Change jingles in her pocket. Enough for a bagel with cream cheese. She'd counted it out after passing on the bowl of cereal Lisa had poured for her. She shouldn't have said no to the cereal. Especially when she'd only picked at last night's dinner.

Prove that you're fine, Bridget.

Eat a bagel with cream cheese.

Eat it all before homeroom!

Every Monday, student council sets up a huge banquet table practically in front of Bridget's locker. There are huge paper bags filled with bagels, economy-size tubs of cream cheese and butter. Bridget takes careful steps matched with careful breaths. The smell is overwhelming. The yeasty, spongy sourdough. Charred bits of garlic. The sweet stink of bloated raisins suspended in bread. Her stomach squeezes, only not in hunger.

Don't you dare, Bridget.

Bridget is Dr. Jekyll and Mr. Hyde. Two sides of herself, always arguing. She is tired of the fight, the constant struggle between a muddied version of good and evil, where right feels wrong and wrong feels really good.

"Bridget!"

One of Bridget's friends steps out from behind the bagel table, fingertips glistening with buttery residue. "Have you seen the list?" The girl smiles wide, a few poppy seeds black between her teeth. "You're the prettiest girl in the junior class!"

In spite of herself, Bridget gasps. All the bagel smells fill her up like helium inside a Thanksgiving Day Parade balloon. And in a flash, the guilt, the sadness, and the depression she'd felt the whole way to school vanish and are replaced by warmth.

Bridget Honeycutt made the list?

Impossible.

Someone else hands her a copy. Bridget reads aloud, "What a difference a summer can make." She looks up and blushes.

You know why.

You know what's different.

"Here!" her friend says. "Have a celebratory bagel on the house!" The girl takes a serrated knife and slices a bagel in half. Seeds and crumbs sputter off the blade and drop to the floor. When the table is packed up and put away, there will still be crumbs everywhere in the hallway. Bridget will feel them squish and pop underneath the soles of her shoes on the way to first period. Big, like gravel. Like boulders.

"Do you want butter or cream cheese?"

"Neither," Bridget says. She pushes her hair back. It is damp around the edge of her scalp.

"Oh. Well . . . congratulations again!"

"Thanks," Bridget says quietly, taking the bagel in her hand. She can't believe the weight of it.

Bridget walks into homeroom. She is shaky from the shock of it. Never, never in a million billion years would she have dreamed this would happen to her. Sure, when school started, she was taken aback by all the compliments she got. How fit she was looking. How thin! And now, to be on the list. To be the prettiest junior in the whole school. It is confirmation that there'd been something wrong with her before. That she *had* needed to lose weight.

It is terribly confusing.

Eat.

After putting down her book bag, Bridget steps over to the trash can and presses her fingers into the still-warm flesh of the bagel. She pulls out clumps of soft dough, then drops them like pennies into a wishing well until the shell of the bagel is all that's left. She wants to throw that into the trash, too.

When she looks up, she sees Lisa running with Abby Warner down the hall. Lisa beams at Bridget, so unbelievably proud of her big sister. The lipstick Lisa had put on in the car has faded. It's barely noticeable.

Bridget is light-headed. As right as things felt mere seconds ago, she knows better. Inside, she knows how wrong this is. She hates herself for knowing better, for robbing herself of one good feeling. One moment of being happy with herself.

Eat, Bridget.

Just five bites.

They can be little ones.

Bridget manages two.

It is not something she wants to celebrate.

CHAPTER SEVEN

Jennifer Briggis makes her way through the morning hall-way traffic, head down, silently counting off the twelve green linoleum floor tiles she'll cross before reaching her locker. The kids lining the walls keep their voices low, but Jennifer still hears every word. Most of her classmates don't actually talk to Jennifer, just whisper about her, and all those hushed conversations over the years have done a strange thing to her ears. They've become tuned in to pick up what everyone's saying, whether she wants to or not.

"Have you seen the list yet?"

"Is Jennifer on it? Oh my god, I bet she's on it again. Oh my god!"

"Do you think she knows what today is? She *has* to, right? I mean, how could she *not* after the last three years?"

"Twenty bucks says if she's the ugliest senior, she barfs again. For old times' sake."

Every conversation orbits the same central question: If this year's list decrees it, how will Mount Washington's undisputed queen of ugly accept her crown?

Jennifer has thought about little else since last year's list named her the ugliest junior and effectively knocked down the second-to-last domino in this impossible chain of events. Despite the muddy feelings she had about her particular situation, a clear *either/or* presented itself.

Senior year would arrive, and either Jennifer wouldn't be on the list . . . or she would.

But that's not what captivates Mount Washington High this morning. Four lists or three or two or even one can't change what is widely accepted as fact: Jennifer Briggis is clearly, certifiably, undeniably ugly. But Jennifer knows that what everyone in the hallway salivates for is her reaction. That'll be the *real* show. And the expectations for something big, something messy, aren't beyond her control, like being pretty or being ugly. They are, in fact, her fault.

When Jennifer was put on the list her freshman year, she became an instant legend. No one, in the history of ugly girls, had reacted so unattractively.

Jennifer had sunk to the floor in front of her locker and bawled unabashedly until her entire face was shellacked with a mixture of tears, snot, and sweat. The list, damp and twisted in her fists, was reduced to soggy pulp. Blood vessels burst in her cheeks and in the whites of her eyes.

She'd barely survived the worst summer of her life, and now this?

The freshmen collectively backed up and gawked in horror, the way one might upon seeing a dead body. Except Jennifer was very much alive. A gasp for breath turned into a choke, and then she vomited on herself. The metallic smell of it filled the hallway, and people ducked into classrooms or pulled their clothes up over their noses to avoid it. Someone ran for the nurse, who extended rubber-gloved hands to help Jennifer to her feet. She was led to a cot in a dark corner of the nurse's office.

Jennifer couldn't stop crying. She wailed so loudly, the science classes heard her even with their doors closed and the teachers lecturing. Her misery vibrated against the steel lockers, turning the halls into one big tinny microphone that broadcast her suffering to the whole school. The nurse eventually sent Jennifer home, where she spent the rest of the day in bed, feeling bad for herself.

When she returned to school the following morning, no one would look at her. She found some vindication in the school's collective avoidance, but mostly Jennifer felt lonely. She knew for sure that her old life was officially over. Despite having played it cool for an entire summer, praying that things would return to normal, the list had ruined everything. She would never get back what she'd lost after the way she'd acted. The only thing she could do was move on.

It proved a difficult task. Before Jennifer, the prettiest girls were the ones remembered and the ugliest girls faded into the shadows. But Jennifer bucked that trend. No one would forget her.

Sophomore year, the second time, Jennifer was on her way to a fresh start and the previous year's list was a distant memory, at least to her.

In 365 days, Jennifer had gained some confidence, having successfully auditioned for chorus, and had grown friendly with a couple girls who also sang soprano. They were nothing special, not even well known in the chorus/band circle. Their clothes weren't particularly cool, and they never wanted to do the things Jennifer suggested — preferring to rent old musicals and collectively sing along with them rather than, say, trying to get into a party. But Jennifer knew that beggars couldn't be choosers. Nothing would be as good as it had been. She'd just have to live within her means.

The morning of the sophomore-year list, Jennifer rode the bus completely aware of what day it was, but without a thought that she might make the list again. In fact, she couldn't wait to see who had been picked for her grade. She had her hunches. Nearly every one of her chorus friends would have been a likely choice.

This time, after she spotted her name, Jennifer remained in school the entire day. She cried a little, alone in the bathroom, but she didn't throw up or make a scene, which were marginal improvements. Her friends did their best to console her.

Junior year, when Jennifer saw her name on the list, she laughed. Not because it was particularly funny, but because it was so ridiculous. She didn't delude herself — she knew she wasn't going to be named prettiest. But wasn't it only fair to pass the ugliest torch along to another girl?

She didn't cry, not once. Her chorus friends comforted her again, of course, but more intriguing were the random students who sought her out to personally apologize. They never said what they were sorry for, but Jennifer had a pretty good idea; no one should have to be the ugliest girl three years in a row. It was too cruel, too mean. There were other girls who deserved to be picked, not only her. She was being unjustly singled out.

Though a big part of her was angry at this repeated indignity, Jennifer graciously accepted the supportive pats on the back. This, she noticed, made people relax around her. It eased their minds. The entire student body seemed to appreciate that Jennifer was taking this with grace. They were relieved that she wasn't going to make this awkward for them, like she had back when she was a freshman. There was no hysterical scene, no finger-pointing, no barfing. She was a really good sport.

It was clear to Jennifer what had happened. The list, for better or worse, did elevate her status at school. Practically everyone knew who Jennifer was, and that was more than the other ugly girls, her friends, could say.

The rest of junior year transpired without incident. Jennifer made halfway decent grades. She stopped hanging out with the chorus girls. She never really liked them much anyway.

After twelve green tiles, Jennifer pivots. She spins the lock left 10, right 22, left 11.

Jennifer steels herself and clicks open her locker. The entire hall watches as a white paper falls softly to the floor and lands inches away from her feet. She sees the embossed stamp of Mount Washington High. Certified truth, special delivery.

Jennifer unfolds it. She skips the other grades, the other girls, and goes straight for the seniors.

Margo Gable, prettiest.

Jennifer wishes Margo didn't deserve it, but she does.

And right above her name, ugliest, for an unprecedented fourth year in a row.

Jennifer pretends to be surprised.

Someone claps. Someone actually claps.

Drumroll, please.

Jennifer shrugs off her book bag. It hits the floor with a thud, amplified by the vacuum of noise. She paddles her hands against her locker door rapid-fire until they burn. The sound smacks off everyone watching her, shocking them like those heart-attack paddles.

Jennifer spins around to face her crowd. She explodes into a jumping jack, legs spread, hands shooting straight up, holding the list for everyone to see, as if she were one of the cheerleaders brandishing a FIGHT, MOUNTAINEERS, FIGHT! sign. She shouts the best "Wooooooo!" she can and pumps the list up and down in celebration.

A few kids grin. More clap, and when Jennifer curtsies, enough hands join in to make it full-fledged applause.

Jennifer skips down the length of the senior hallway, keeping her hands raised for anyone who might give her a high five. Many reach out for her.

At the end of the day, there is this fact: Jennifer has accomplished a feat no other girl at Mount Washington has, endured something no one else can touch. She can't help but feel special. It's how that old saying goes. *If life gives you lemons, make lemonade.* She pulls her smile as wide as it can go, so no one will think for a second that she might not be enjoying this, fully embracing this gift.

She wants everyone to know. She's come a long, long way.

CHAPTER EIGHT

Margo Gable is walking with her best friends, Rachel Potchak and Dana Hassan, three wide in a crowded hallway that always leaves room for them. The girls' heads are pitched forward in a secret-sharing way, their hair falling collectively to make a privacy curtain. They are not talking about the list, as an outsider might assume. They are giggling about Mrs. Worth's toes.

The toes, gnarled and stuffed into a pair of orthopedic sandals, had mesmerized Margo during fourth period, and she ignored the lecture on the algebraic equation of a Möbius strip in favor of mentally unlocking the twisted, overlapping joints.

"Why would a person with such hideous feet ever think to buy a pair of sandals?" Rachel asks.

"No clue," Dana says. "Also, hello! It's almost October. Why is she wearing sandals in the first place?"

Margo pulls her brown hair up in a sloppy bun at the very top of her head, secures it with a pencil, and thinks hard for an answer. Perhaps it's a medical condition?

This is why she doesn't notice Principal Colby lurking by the staircase until the principal's hand is on her arm, pulling her to an abrupt stop.

Principal Colby is new and, so far as Margo can tell, the youngest faculty member at Mount Washington High School. She's dressed in a red pencil skirt and a cream silk blouse with tiny yellow beads for buttons. Her dark hair is gathered in a low ponytail, except for her bangs, which Margo notices are kept long and shaggy in the way that is featured in lots of magazines right now.

Some in her group have said that Principal Colby could be Margo's older sister. But now, up close, Margo thinks Maureen, her *actual* older sister, is prettier.

"Margo. I'd like to talk to you about this list. Do you have a minute?"

Margo expects this to be a quick conversation, if that is even the right word for it. She tongues her watermelon gum down in her cheek and tells Principal Colby that she doesn't know anything about it.

Principal Colby narrows her eyes. "Well, Margo . . . you know that you're *on* the list, right?"

The suspicion in Principal Colby's voice catches Margo off guard, and it suddenly feels funny to be smiling. Like it gives the wrong impression of her. She threads some of her soft hair behind her ear. "Yes," she admits. "Someone mentioned it in homeroom."

Actually, Jonathan Polk, who had been cast as the lead in *Pennies from Heaven*, drowned out the morning announcements by performing the list as a monologue. Afterward, he tried unsuccessfully to coax Margo into taking a bow. It *is* nice, being on the list again. She'd been on it freshman year, Dana sophomore year, and Rachel last year, when they were juniors. That's when her sister, Maureen, had also been on the list, and then, five days later, was picked as homecoming queen, which was the way things usually went.

Margo had thought about texting Maureen at college with the good news, but decided against it.

It has been weeks since they've spoken.

Principal Colby produces a copy of the list from a small pocket at her hip. It has been folded several times to fit, like a piece of origami. "Since I'm new here, I was hoping you could shed some light on what this is, exactly. Fill me in."

Margo gives a light shrug. "I don't know. It's just a weird school tradition, I guess." It feels strange to be talking openly about the list with school faculty. Margo is almost positive the teachers at Mount Washington know about it. How could they not? The ones who've grown up here, like Mrs. Worth, could have even been on it back in the day! But they tolerate it in the name of tradition, like Margo said. Or maybe, she realizes, they just don't care.

"And you have no idea who is behind it?"

Dana and Rachel are lurking a few steps away, trying to eavesdrop. Margo says, "No," as confidently as she can.

Principal Colby regards her skeptically. "Do you know any of the other girls on the list?" She offers her copy of the list to Margo, but Margo keeps her hands clasped behind her back.

"A couple, I guess."

"Would you agree with the ones who were picked? Or would you have picked different girls?"

"Principal Colby, I haven't even seen the actual paper before right now. I don't know anything else. Really."

Instead of believing her, Principal Colby waves off Rachel and Dana, who have inched a little too close. "Go on, ladies. You don't want to be late."

As her friends disappear down the stairs, Margo is guided over to the wall. She recognizes Principal Colby's perfume as one of the bottles on her dresser, but decides not to comment on it. "Am I in trouble?" she asks.

"No," Principal Colby says. Which, to Margo, should be the end of it, but she goes on. "I'm wondering how you plan to respond."

"Respond?"

"You seem like the kind of girl who has influence around here, Margo, and how you choose to deal with the list will have an effect on your peers." Principal Colby pushes up her sleeves and folds her arms. "This is a sick tradition, don't you think? And I plan on getting to the bottom of who's behind it. So if you know something, I would suggest you let me know right now."

Margo stares blankly. What does Principal Colby expect her to do? Confess? Rat someone out? Um, please. "I didn't make up the list, Principal Colby. And I don't know who did."

Principal Colby lets out a long sigh. "Think of the girls who are on the ugly side of things. Think of Jennifer, and how she must have felt this morning, seeing her name on the list for the fourth year in a row."

I heard Jennifer was pretty psyched is what Margo wants to say. That's what she'd been told, anyhow. But Margo doesn't want to think of Jennifer. Not at all. If there was one sucky thing about this morning, it was finding out that Jennifer was on the list, too. It made Margo feel like she was living the drama of freshman year all over again.

Margo starts backing up. "I'll think about it. I promise."

She makes it halfway down the stairs before she has to stop and catch her breath. Principal Colby was so suspicious. It was as if she'd heard something.

Margo arrives at the cafeteria with cheeks brighter than the heat lamps burning red over the casserole special. Feeling slightly dizzy, she grabs a bottle of water and, aware that her hands are shaking, attempts to tide the miniature waves breaking against her lips with careful, measured sips. Margo pays for her lunch and then walks to where Rachel and Dana are sitting with Matthew, Ted, and Justin. On the way over, she passes a few tables of underclassmen. She senses them looking at her and quickly puts on a smile.

"What was that about?" Dana asks.

Margo falls into her seat. "I don't know. Principal Colby's all worked up over the list." She fights the urge to look at Matthew to see if he's heard.

Of course he has.

Rachel cups her hands and whispers, "Does she think you wrote it?" in a hissy voice that everyone can hear.

"God, no." Margo quickly follows this statement with a breezy laugh. Underneath the table, she wipes her sweaty palms on her skirt, smoothing down the pleats. "Definitely not."

"I'd put Principal Colby on the list," Justin says, and licks his lips before taking a bite of hoagie.

Dana throws a napkin at him. "Ew."

Ted leans back in his chair and puts his hands behind his head. He's got on a plaid button-down, collar popped, sleeves rolled up to the elbows. He says, "Why's it such a big deal? I mean, the list doesn't say anything that everyone isn't already thinking. We all have eyes. We know who's hot and who's not."

Rachel taps a finger on her temple. "That's funny. I seem to remember you were sweating that freshman Monique Jones pretty hard after she got on the list last year."

"Busted," Justin says and gives Rachel a high five.

The tips of Ted's ears turn bright red. "The list had nothing to do with that," he argues, louder than he needs to. "I always thought Monique was hot. She freaking modeled, dudes. The list just gave me a reason to go and introduce myself."

Matthew pulls his sweatshirt hood up over his buzzed head. "Who wants to play me in Ping-Pong?"

He'd worn his blond hair long and floppy throughout high school, but decided to cut it short late this summer. None of the other girls liked it, but it reminded Margo of fourth grade, when Matthew first moved to Mount Washington. They'd been assigned desks next to each other, and Matthew appeared intrigued with her collection of tiny rubber erasers, which she kept in a pencil box. He'd always sit on his feet when she'd bring out the pencil box, trying to look inside as she picked which one she wanted to use. Around Christmas, she bought him a football eraser and slipped it secretly into his desk. Margo never saw him use it. She likes to imagine that maybe he still has it.

Dana shakes her head, confounded. "Principal Colby needs to relax. Next thing you know, she's going to institute a 'No Freak Dancing' rule for homecoming dance." She takes a sip of her iced tea and then adds, "Hey, speaking of freaks, did any of you guys see Sarah Singer parading down the hall with *UGLY* written on her forehead?"

"What a rebel," Rachel says, rolling her eyes.

Matthew pushes away from the table. "Come on, Ted, play me. I want a rematch."

"One ass beating, coming right up." As Ted collects his garbage on his tray, he leans down over Margo's shoulder and says, "I think you're going to make a beautiful homecoming queen, Margo. And if I'm lucky enough to be your king, you should know right now that I'm not letting go of you the entire night."

Matthew groans. "Come on! Lunch is almost over."

Margo answers, "Um, thanks, Ted," and tries not to appear disappointed at Matthew's non-reaction. Maybe he hasn't heard that she's on the list?

Ted perches himself on the corner of the table. "I mean, don't you think it's funny that we've never hooked up? Homecoming might be fate bringing us together. I mean, I've always thought you and I would make a good —"

"Dude!" Matthew calls out, cupping his hands. "Let's go!"

Ted shakes his head. "Whatever. I'll talk to you later, Margo."

Rachel stares at Ted as he walks away and whispers, "Ted is such a list fucker! I mean, could he *be* any more transparent?"

Margo watches Matthew reach for the Ping-Pong paddles, which are kept on top of the soda machine. The two of them have never been single at the same time before. She tended to date older guys, guys who could get her friends beer and who had cars. Matthew dated younger girls, the sweet girls who did well at school and were friendly to everyone. Girls from his church. Margo didn't go to church.

"Anyway . . . as I was saying, the only one I feel bad for is Jennifer." Dana spins in her seat and scans the tables behind her. "Look at her. Even the chorus girls have abandoned her."

Though she doesn't want to, Margo looks. Jennifer is across the room, sitting at a table full of other kids, but she isn't with anyone.

"Do you buy her whole happiness act?" Dana asks.

"No way." Rachel bites into a fry. "It has to be a cover. I mean, four years of being the ugliest in your class? How do you not kill yourself?"

"I give her credit. If I were Jennifer, there's no way I could walk into school like she did and hold my head high," Dana says. And then she whispers, "Remember at the junior picnic, when someone whipped that hot dog at Jennifer's head? And Jennifer was laughing, like it was funny? Ted never copped to it, but I know he did it. I saw him. A-hole."

Rachel shakes her head in disgust. "She probably deals with that kind of crap every day."

The girls watch Jennifer pick at her sandwich. Two younger boys, obviously freshmen, pass behind her as they carry their trays to the wash line. As they do, they point Jennifer out to friends across the cafeteria and make gagging faces. Jennifer is oblivious to it.

Rachel throws down her fry. "That's it. I'm going to ask Jennifer if she wants to sit with us today."

Margo reaches out to stop Rachel from getting up. "Come on. No."

Rachel stares down the two freshmen boys as they walk back to their table. "I don't like those little turds thinking they can make fun of Jennifer because she's on the list. Don't they have any respect for the fact that she's a senior? If she's with us, they wouldn't dare say anything."

Margo sighs. "No one cares about hanging out with us that much." But she knows that isn't true. Especially when it comes to Jennifer.

"Huh. Easy for the prettiest senior girl to say."

"Shut up, Rachel. You've been on the list, too. Both of you. It's not a big deal."

Dana cocks her head. "Yeah, but *you're* the one who'll get to be homecoming queen."

"That's not a guarantee," Margo says, even though it basically is. "And anyway, I don't care about being homecoming queen." Sure, it will be nice. But if Margo hadn't made the list this morning, if it had been Rachel or Dana instead, she'd have been fine with it.

Rachel pats Margo on the back. "Inviting Jennifer to hang out for half a lunch period isn't going to kill you."

Margo pretends to concentrate on picking the lettuce out from her chicken wrap. It doesn't surprise her how quickly the legs of Jennifer's chair squeak against the floor.

"Hey, Jennifer," Dana says, sliding over so Jennifer can sit.

"Hi," Jennifer says. "I like your shirt, Dana. It's so cute."

Dana grins down at her front. "Oh, thanks."

It's quiet for a second. Margo glances over and sees Jennifer staring at her. "Hi, Margo," Jennifer says, all bright and cheerful. "Congratulations on . . . you know."

"Thanks."

Rachel drums her nails against the table. "So, Jennifer. We wanted to tell you that we're sorry that you're on the list again this year."

Jennifer shakes her head, like it's nothing. "Honestly, I'm used to it by now."

"Yeah, but you shouldn't *have* to get used to something like that," Dana says, pursing her lips. "Whoever made the list this year is a total sadist."

Margo thinks back to when senior year had just started. Dana got assigned a seat behind Jennifer in French II, and she complained every day for a week about the fat rolls on the back of Jennifer's neck. Whenever Jennifer looked down at her textbook, the folds of skin would smooth out, and when she'd look up, they'd squeeze together, like a disgusting human accordion.

It annoys her how easily Dana can forget the past.

But it also makes Margo jealous. Because she can't.

CHAPTER NINE

At three o'clock, Danielle shuffles from her last class of the day to her locker. She collects her textbooks and her swim bag as slowly as possible, in no rush to get where she needs to be. Well, that's not true. Danielle should be at swim practice with Hope. But she'd been instructed not to go to the pool.

Everyone in English had looked up when Principal Colby knocked on the door. Danielle's teacher welcomed her. Principal Colby didn't say anything to him, she just looked around the room. When her eyes landed on Danielle, she walked over and said simply, "I'll see you later." This left the bulk of the explaining to the note card she placed on Danielle's desk.

TO THE GIRLS ON THE LIST:
PLEASE REPORT TO MY OFFICE IMMEDIATELY AFTER SCHOOL.
THIS IS A <u>MANDATORY</u> MEETING.
PRINCIPAL COLBY

Danielle bit the end of her pencil. What could Principal Colby want with all the girls on the list? Were they in trouble? Had Principal Colby figured out who had written it?

Though her questions baited juicy answers, Danielle hardly cared to know them. Instead, she became aware of the boy sitting to her left, craning his neck as he tried to read the note. She quickly slid the card into her book and succumbed to humiliation for the second time that day.

Her cheeks are still hot from it.

Just then, Sarah Singer, the ugliest junior, passes by. Principal Colby is right behind Sarah, her hand pressing into Sarah's back, forcing her forward. Sarah's steps are comically laborious — flat-footed trudges, punctuated by tortured sighs, the toes of her sneakers dragging across the linoleum floor.

Danielle had heard about this girl and the word she'd scrawled on her forehead, but this is the first time she sees it for herself. Part of her is impressed by Sarah's toughness — a different Game Face than the one she'd worn today, when she pretended there was no list, that she hadn't been on it. But the rest of her is humiliated knowing she is the same as Sarah. That all of Mount Washington will look at her and see the same word, whether or not it's written on Danielle's face.

Danielle closes her locker and leans against it. It is the kind of hurt that feels permanent, more like a scar than a scab. Something she'll always carry with her.

"I was already off school grounds!" Sarah complains. "You can't force me back inside once the day is over!"

Either Principal Colby doesn't hear Sarah or she doesn't care to respond. Instead, she locks eyes with Danielle as she passes her and says, "Come on. You, too."

The other six girls are already in the principal's office. The room is too small for there to be any order to where people sit, no division of space with the pretty girls in the chairs and the ugly girls against the wall, that sort of thing. It is crowded, uncomfortable for everyone.

Abby is in one of the two chairs in front of Principal Colby's desk. She scoots over, allowing a small patch where Danielle can squeeze in next to her. Danielle smiles faintly at the offer, but instead perches on the armrest.

Candace is in the other chair, inched forward to the very edge of the seat, her weight tipping forward. She's pulled herself up close to Principal Colby's desk.

Lauren sits on the radiator, her knees drawn to her chest, staring out the window.

Bridget is on the couch.

Margo sits next to her, hands folded in her lap.

Jennifer slumps against a tall, black filing cabinet.

Sarah won't enter the office farther than the doorway, her arms crossed and defiant. She barely moves as Principal Colby squeezes past her.

Once she settles behind her desk, the principal says, "I'm sure you've probably figured out why I've called you here."

If anyone knows Principal Colby's intentions, no one says so. Margo wraps a strand of her hair around her finger. Bridget cracks her knuckles, tiny little pops. Jennifer scratches something stuck to her shirt.

Principal Colby sighs. "Okay," she continues. "I'll spell it out." She leans forward dramatically. "A terrible thing has happened to you girls today. And I think it would help if we talked about it as a group."

Candace snorts bitterly. Her legs are crossed, one shearling boot kicking the air rapid-fire. "Don't you mean to *four* of us?" she quips. "I bet the prettiest girls had a great day."

Principal Colby shakes her head. "I meant exactly what I said, Candace. Something terrible happened to *all* of you girls. Someone took it upon himself or herself to single you out, give you a label, and present you as nothing more than the most superficial, subjective version of yourselves. And there are emotional consequences to that, regardless of which side of the coin you are on."

Candace turns in her chair and looks behind her at Margo and Bridget on the couch. "Consequences? You mean like Margo having a lock on homecoming queen?"

Margo continues to examine her hair for split ends. "I get that you're mad, Candace, but please leave me out of it."

"Of course I'm mad, Margo," Candace says to her, and then her eyes dart around to the other girls' faces. "Wouldn't you be if you were called ugliest when you are clearly *not*?" Her voice rolls, unsteady.

The other ugly girls look at each other sheepishly. Except for Sarah, who stares Candace down.

Principal Colby holds up her hands. "Girls, please. Don't fight with each other. No one here is the enemy. You're all victims."

Margo raises her hand. "Principal Colby, I know you're new at Mount Washington, but seriously, this is not a big deal."

"Easy for you to say," Danielle mumbles, surprised that she's spoken up at all.

Jennifer steps forward. "I agree with Margo. I mean, if anyone here has a right to complain, it's me. And I don't care. It doesn't bother me."

Principal Colby locks eyes with Jennifer before she says, "I can't believe you don't care, Jennifer. You should care most of all."

Jennifer's cheeks turn pink.

Sarah groans. "What exactly are you trying to do here, Principal Colby? Force us into some kind of group therapy session?"

Principal Colby shakes her head. "Sarah . . . girls . . . look, I'll concede that maybe it's a bit too soon for you to be able to process what's happened today. I've reached out to a few of you already, but I want you to know that I am here if you want to talk. And if you *do* have an idea of who might have made the list this year, I hope you will trust me enough to share that information. It's time for this hazing to end, and I'd like for whoever is responsible for the list to be held accountable."

Danielle looks around the room. Though she respects Principal Colby's attempt at a locker-room pep talk, the reality of the situation doesn't give her much hope. Although each of their names had appeared on the list, none of them seem to be playing for the same team.

Not even close.

Her Game Face would have to stay put. It is every girl for herself.

TUESDAY

CHAPTER TEN

Bridget wakes up bright and early. She showers, does her hair and makeup, and picks out an oxford shirt to wear with leggings and a long drapey cardigan. Once she hears Lisa turn on the shower for herself, Bridget hops down the stairs two by two, excited to get to the kitchen. Really, honestly excited for breakfast. Not faking her way through it, like she's been doing.

Mrs. Honeycutt set out the cereal boxes, two bowls, and two spoons on the breakfast bar for her daughters, as she does every morning before leaving for work. Bridget takes her clean bowl and her spoon and puts them both into the dishwasher with the dirty plates from last night's dinner. She ate the chicken breast and a couple baby carrots. No rice.

Not bad.

She takes a piece of paper from her front shirt pocket and flattens it out on the counter. Then she opens the cabinets and goes digging for the ingredients.

Maple syrup. Cayenne pepper. A lemon from the fruit bowl.

She found the recipe on the Internet last night. A cleanse. All the movie stars cleanse before big events, to make sure they look their very best. It's not a diet, it's a way to rid your body of toxins, of all the things that pollute your insides.

Most importantly, a cleanse is different from simply not eating. Not eating is not good for you. Bridget knows this. She knew it all summer. She didn't go about losing weight the way she should have. She was too gung ho, got a little too carried away. She didn't want to be the kind of girl who thought the things she did, who restricted herself.

But Bridget also knows that she was put on the list because she lost weight. It said as much, right there on the paper. How she'd spent her summer did make a difference.

Except you've gained almost all of the weight back, Bridget.

Bridget doesn't want to let anyone down. She wants to be better, smarter this time. With the homecoming dance just five days away, this cleanse is the answer. All she has to do is follow the directions.

If you were sick, you'd just stop eating again.

But you're not sick.

You're healthy.

Bridget carefully measures out the ingredients according to the recipe. She tips the measuring spoon over the lip of her plastic water bottle, sending a tiny pile of red dust to the bottom. Next, she slices a lemon and squeezes it into her hand. Her fingers trap the seeds, and the juice stings where she's bitten the skin around her fingernails. The maple syrup is the last part. The glass jar is sticky, the cap fused shut with sugar crystals that break apart and powder her hands. She sends a thick chestnut stream into the well of her tablespoon. Bridget wishes there wasn't so much syrup involved. Two tablespoons seem like a lot. She checks the calorie count on the syrup bottle, frowns, and makes the executive decision to cut the amount in half.

She uses the water filter on the refrigerator door and fills her bottle up to the tippy-top. If she takes small sips, she should have enough of the cleanse mixture to last her through the school day. She shakes the bottle, then removes the cap. Tiny specks of cayenne pepper float on the top of the frothy tea-colored water. Bridget holds it under her nose. It smells like lemonade on fire.

Lisa comes downstairs and sits at the breakfast bar. She's got on a corduroy jumper that Bridget had picked out during their back-to-school outlet excursion. Bridget gets the milk out for her. "You look cute, Lisa."

"Bridge, can we please go shopping for homecoming dresses after school? I feel like I've been looking at pictures online for weeks, but I want to try things on."

"I don't think I can today." Bridget wants to give the cleanse time to work. The paper says she can lose up to ten pounds in a week. Only she doesn't have a week. Just five days. "Maybe Thursday."

Lisa's mouth gapes. "Thursday? But the dance is on Saturday! What if we can't find anything?"

"It'll be fine." Bridget senses the disappointment in Lisa, and quickly adds, "You can ask Abby to come with us, if you want. And I already talked to Mom about the makeup thing. I think she's going to be cool with it, so long as it's a light touch." The last part is a lie, but Bridget will ask her mother for Lisa tonight.

"What are you making over there?"

Bridget quickly crumples up the paper and throws it in the trash with the squeezed lemon half. She puts the rest of the ingredients away. "It's this health food thing that's supposed to boost your immune system." When she turns back to face Lisa, she puts a hand to her throat. "I feel like I might be getting sick. And I don't want to miss the dance."

"Can I try it?"

Bridget shrugs and hands it over. A guinea pig for the first sip.

Lisa puts her lips to the bottle. Almost immediately, Lisa puckers and gags. She pushes past Bridget and spits the liquid into the sink. "Ew, Bridge! This stuff is nasty!"

"It's not that bad." It can't be. She's not allowed to eat or drink anything else all week.

Lisa grabs a paper towel and starts wiping down her tongue.

Bridget groans. "Don't be so dramatic." And then she takes her first tentative sip of the cleanse. It burns the back of her throat, burns all the way down.

You know, it might be easier not to eat anything.

Bridget takes another swig. A big, bold, defiant gulp to drown her brain. She can do this. And then, after homecoming, the pressure will be off.

Lisa frowns and climbs back onto her stool. She pours herself cereal, her favorite kind, with marshmallows in it. Bridget likes that kind, too. The way the little bits crunch and dissolve, how they turn the milk sweet and a little bit pink. Bridget sips from her water bottle again.

"I can still taste that crap," Lisa complains, and a dribble of milk rolls down her chin.

Bridget turns her back to Lisa and says, "Well, make sure you take care of yourself and stay healthy, so you won't ever have to drink this. And quit slurping like a little kid."

CHAPTER ELEVEN

It's the homecoming dance, and Abby is pressed against a boy, her cheek snuggled on his brushed flannel shirt. They shuffle to a song she doesn't recognize, the music fuzzy and deep and far away, like when you hold your fingers in your ears next to the DJ speakers. Abby is in her perfect dress, the black one with the white ribbon sash, and the layer of tulle under the skirt rustles against her legs. A disco ball spins overhead, flashing tiny patches of light over the gymnasium floor. As Abby twirls, the light falls on the faces of the couples dancing around her. Everyone smiles in her direction. The whole thing is warm and soft, the way the best dreams are.

But then it falls away.

Abby loses the dream to the whip of fabric, the slap of morning cold.

She opens her eyes and sees Fern standing over her. Fern lets Abby's quilt fall on the bedroom floor.

"What's going on?" Abby mumbles, still half-asleep and suddenly freezing. She pulls her sheet up around her.

"Our alarm didn't go off." Abby hears the accusation in her sister's voice, as if Abby had been the one to screw it up. "I've totally missed academic decathlon practice." Fern clicks on their bedroom light. "Hurry up and get dressed. We're leaving in five minutes."

Abby sits up and shields her eyes from the brightness. Fern is already dressed, her bed made. She tosses her textbooks into her bag. "Five minutes? But I need to shower!"

"There's no time," Fern says, and walks out of their room.

Abby stands so fast she gets woozy, but manages to make it to the bathroom without falling. Five minutes tick down to four.

Her hair is unwashed and dented from having been slept on, so she twists it into a little knot at the nape of her neck, and then braids the front section so it runs across the edge of her forehead and down behind one ear. She washes her face, brushes her teeth, puts on a touch of blush. Because there is no time left to actually plan an outfit, Abby throws on a navy wool A-line dress with cream kneesocks and her new brown loafers, and wraps a striped scarf around her neck. She loves the fresh-faced schoolgirl look, even if her grades don't match up to her studious image.

Abby stops at the foyer mirror on her way out the front door. She looks fine. Better than fine, considering the five minutes she had, but it disappoints her that she won't be looking her absolute best this morning. She hopes her classmates won't take one look at her and think her inclusion on the list was a mistake. Already the list has made her a person to notice. She's never had so many people smile at her before. Strangers, girls and guys from every single grade, acknowledging who she is, congratulating her for being prettiest. She spent four weeks as an anonymous freshman to most, and as Fern's stupid little sister to her teachers, but now Abby is somebody in her own right.

Only one person didn't mention the list yesterday. Fern. Maybe she is hurt about the genetics comment. Or maybe the only list Fern cares about is honor roll.

Abby runs out of the front door, closing it so hard, the knocker taps a couple of times. Her family is already in the car, waiting. She hears the monotone voices of news radio through the closed windows.

Fern coughs as Abby slides into the backseat. "God, Abby. How much perfume did you put on?"

Abby pulls her arms inside her dress sleeves. "I only used two squirts." And anyway, it's her cupcake perfume. Who doesn't like the smell of freshly baked cupcakes?

Fern inches away until she's pressed against the passenger-side door and then opens the window, even though it's cold outside. "I feel like I'm going to throw up a pile of icing."

Abby leans forward to the front seat. "Hey, Dad? Can I get ten dollars for my homecoming dance ticket?"

"Sure," Mr. Warner says. He pulls out his wallet.

"Fern?" Mrs. Warner asks, eyeing her older daughter in the rearview mirror. "Do you want money for a ticket, too?"

"I'm not going," Fern says in a way that implies they should have already known that.

Abby watches her mother share a look with her father. "Oh? Why not?"

"Because the *Blix Effect* movie is opening this weekend and all my friends are going to see it."

"Why don't you see the movie on Friday?" Abby asks. "Then you can go to the dance on Saturday." Not that she cares if Fern goes to the homecoming dance or not. She's just saying. It *is* possible.

Fern doesn't look at Abby while she answers. Instead she speaks to their parents, as if they were the ones who'd posed the question. "Because we're going to see the movie on both nights, two different theaters. Once in 3-D and once in regular."

Abby stares at Fern, utterly perplexed. She knows the Blix Effect novels are super popular, but who wants to see the same movie twice, back-to-back? The homecoming dance is so much more exciting, more special. It's a once-a-year thing, and the only dance at Mount Washington High that every grade is allowed to attend.

Her sister must see her staring, because Fern suddenly pulls her hair out from behind her ear and lets it cover her face. The morning sun lights up Fern's split ends. Fern's hair is the flattest shade of brown, without any of the reddish highlights Abby had gotten when she was at the beach.

Abby scoots across the backseat and takes Fern's hair in her hands. "Do you want me to twist up your hair for you, Fern? I could do it like mine, so it's up off your face."

"No thanks," Fern says, jerking her head so her hair pulls out of Abby's grasp.

"Come on, Fern. It's all ratty in the back. Trust me. It'll look so much better this way." Abby doesn't know why she's being so nice, seeing that Fern is giving her major attitude. But it feels mean to know Fern looks like crap and not do anything to help her, especially after the list had compared them.

Fern whips around. Her eyes are big and angry, but she sighs and pulls an elastic off her wrist. "If you want to do two French braids for me, fine. But I'm not walking around school looking like I'm your twin."

It is the last thing Fern says to her. Abby does the French braids, and the rest of the car ride is silent.

When they pull up to Mount Washington, Fern bolts past Freshman Island and goes straight into school.

Lisa sits, leaning against the base of the ginkgo tree, doing homework. "Morning, Abby!" she calls as Abby walks over.

"Hey," Abby says and kneels down next to her. The ground is cold and hard, and not all that comfortable in a dress, but she doesn't feel like standing. She doesn't feel like doing much of anything, to be perfectly honest.

"What's wrong? You look upset."

"Nothing." What was there to say, after all? She and Fern hadn't fought, exactly.

"Well, I've got some news that might cheer you up. Bridget said she'd take me shopping for homecoming dresses on Thursday. I know it's kind of late in the week, but she hasn't been feeling well. Anyway, do you want to come with us? She said it's totally cool if you do."

Abby picks at some dead grass and wishes that she could have the kind of relationship with Fern that Lisa does with Bridget. But Lisa has so much in common with Bridget. Abby and Fern are as different as could be. Abby wonders if she and Fern would even like each other at all if not for the fact that they were related.

Probably not.

"That would be awesome, Lisa. Thanks. And tell Bridget I said thank you, too."

Lisa doesn't say anything for a few seconds, so Abby looks up from the ground. Lisa is staring off into the distance.

"Oh my god, Abby!"

"What?"

"Act natural," Lisa whispers tersely, "but practically every sophomore boy on the varsity football team is coming over here right freaking now."

"Seriously?"

Lisa pushes her black hair behind her ear. "Like this?" Then she shakes it out. "Or like this?"

Abby threads the hair back for her friend. "Like this," she says. "What about me? Do I look okay? I had, like, zero time to get ready this morning."

Lisa pouts. "Are you kidding? You always look beautiful."

It is a little compliment, and not even one that Abby is inclined to believe. But it still is nice to hear.

About six sophomore boys walk casually across the lawn toward Freshman Island. It is unheard of, really, for any non-freshmen to be seen around the ginkgo tree.

"Hey, Abby," the biggest boy says. His name is Chuck. Abby knows this because Chuck is the biggest sophomore boy in the school, and he usually smells like musk. "Nice job on the list yesterday."

"Thanks," Abby says, quickly looking over the rest of them. A few of the boys are definitely cute. Chuck, not so much. But he is the only one making eye contact with her. So that's where Abby focuses.

"I wanted to let you know that a bunch of us are going to be hanging out at Andrew's house after the homecoming dance." Abby doesn't know who Andrew is, but she assumes it's the skinny boy who Chuck punches on the arm. "His parents are going out of town, and we're going to get some beers. If you two want to stop by, you can."

Abby looks at Lisa, who is grinning a smile of metal. She can tell Lisa is excited, and Abby herself is excited, too. But she tries to play it cool. "Thanks for the invite, but I'm not sure what we're doing yet."

"We're probably not doing anything," Lisa quickly adds.

Chuck laughs. "Well, don't spread the word, okay? We don't want every freshman thinking they can come over. It's just you two who are invited. And maybe a couple of your other friends, if you want. But no guys."

"It might not even happen," Andrew says. "My parents might come home early. Who knows?" From the grimace on Andrew's face, Abby can't tell whether he's upset or relived that his party might be canceled.

Chuck gives Andrew a hard elbow. "Excuse my buddy, here. He's having a bad week. Look, ladies, unless you hear otherwise from me, the party is *on*," Chuck says, and then starts to walk backward, away from Abby and Lisa. His friends follow.

When the boys are out of earshot, Lisa grabs Abby's arm tight. "Um, did that actually happen?"

Abby laughs. "I think it did!"

Lisa looks like she might explode. "I can't wait to tell Bridget! She is going to freak! She never got invited to a single nonfreshman party when she was my age." Lisa rolls her eyes. "She says it was because she was pudgy back then."

Abby shakes her head in disbelief. "I don't remember Bridget ever being pudgy."

"Exactly." Lisa twirls her finger around in a tiny circle next to her head. "She's totally crazy. I bet boys were too nervous to talk to her. But seriously, this is so exciting." She takes a deep breath. "I mean, they only asked us because you are on the list. Abby, you have no idea how lucky I feel to be your best friend."

"Thanks, Lisa. That means a lot."

The first bell rings, and the two friends hurry inside. Abby is glad to see a few copies of the list still hanging up, despite Principal Colby asking the janitors to take them down.

It was a relief that no one volunteered any information about who might have made the list during yesterday's meeting. Abby didn't want the person who had rewarded her to get in trouble, even if other people were mad about it.

Abby sees Fern standing near the water fountain with her friends and suddenly gets the urge to tell her about the party and invite her along. Chuck did say she could bring whomever she wanted. It might be a way to smooth things over from their kind-of fight this morning.

Abby walks over and waits for Fern to notice her.

It takes a while.

Finally, Fern turns her head. "Yeah?"

"Guess what."

"What?" Fern asks.

"I got invited to a party after the homecoming dance."

"Oh," Fern says flatly. "Congratulations."

Abby watches Fern turn her attention back to her friends. She can sense it's her cue to leave, but she keeps talking. "And the guys told me I could bring whoever I wanted with me. I know you're planning to go to the movie, but maybe you'd want to stop by afterward. I could find out from Chuck where Andrew lives and give —"

Fern finally looks back at her. "Wait. Whose party are you talking about?"

"Chuck and some other sophomores. It's going to be at this guy Andrew's house. His parents are away." Abby considers telling Fern about the beer they'd have there, but decides against it. It wouldn't be a selling point for Fern.

Fern laughs haughtily. "I'm a junior, Abby. Why would I want to go to a sophomore party?" Fern makes a funny face at her friends, and they all laugh, too.

Abby feels suddenly hot. She unwinds her scarf from her neck. "Okay. Whatever. I thought I'd ask to be nice."

As she walks away, Abby bites her lip and holds in what she really wants to say — that Fern and her friends would *never* get invited to a junior party, never mind a sophomore party. Instead, she just pulls up her kneesocks as they slide down her legs.

CHAPTER TWELVE

It takes Sarah a while to find her old bike. It's deep in the back of the garage, covered by a dirty flowered sheet her dad uses when he rakes up the leaves. A playing card is folded into the spokes, and seeing it makes Sarah remember the last time she rode the bike — away from the group of girls she'd hung around freshman year, fighting back tears for the millionth time about some innocuous thing she was supposed to know and didn't.

"Why is it so hard for you to be normal?" these "friends" wondered aloud in uniform bafflement after she'd shown up for a boy/girl party sticky and sweaty on her bike. Like they hadn't ridden bikes together all summer long! It wasn't the first time the girls she hung around with had said something like that. Sarah had heard it constantly since middle school had started. How everything she did was wrong.

She leaves the playing card there, liking the flutter it makes as she coasts down her driveway and past her bus stop, where kids wait in clusters to be picked up. Sarah rocks her weight from side to side, pushing the gears in a lumbering circle. The metal teeth edging the pedals poke through the soles of her fraying canvas sneakers. The seams of her black jeans burn strips of fire up the insides of her thighs, rubbing the skin raw with each pump of her legs. Sarah coughs up a ball of phlegm and spits it on the road.

Damn cigarettes.

Her old bike is in even worse shape. The frame's too small and her knees knock the handlebars, where brittle plastic streamers hang like uncooked linguini. The chain needs grease, the back tire sags, the brakes are dangerously unresponsive.

But she will not ride the school bus to Mount Washington High for the rest of the week. She's come up with a plan, a brilliantly diabolical plan. Clearly, the geniuses at Mount Washington have realized that she isn't trying to be their kind of pretty. But what will happen if she tries to be ugly, like the list said? The ugliest she can possibly be, an ugly they can't look away from?

She has Principal Colby to thank for the idea.

When Sarah was stopped in the hallway by Principal Colby and given the note about the after-school meeting, she'd forgotten about the word written on her forehead. Principal Colby noticed it right away and actually reached out to push Sarah's hair off her face, but then thought better of it and pulled both her hands behind her back.

"Who wrote that on your forehead, Sarah?" Her voice was concerned, worried, sad.

Sarah scrunched up her face. Did Principal Colby seriously think that someone had pinned her arms and legs down and done it without her permission? Hello?

"I did," she said proudly.

Principal Colby gave a stiff, incomprehensible smile, as if Sarah wasn't speaking English. "This isn't the way people see you."

Sarah read the meeting note Principal Colby handed to her. "Maybe you haven't noticed, but everyone shares the same brain around here. It's like a mass cult. They've all drunk the Kool-Aid."

Principal Colby sighed deeply. "Please wash that word off your forehead before our meeting."

"It's permanent marker," Sarah said. "And I'm not going."

"The meeting is mandatory, Sarah. And your forehead is a distraction. Also, I don't agree with what it says about you."

Sarah narrowed her eyes. Principal Colby was trying way too hard. Like she'd read too many How-to-Be-an-Effective-Principal books over the summer. Sarah almost preferred Principal Weyland, who had retired at the end of last year. Weyland was a billion years old and ran the school like a dictator. He was clueless, but he never tried to be anyone's friend. It seemed crazy that Principal Colby would be picked as his replacement. Maybe she got the job because she gave Weyland a boner. Principal Colby was pretty in the generic, boring way that all the girls at Mount Washington aspired to be. Sarah was positive that Principal Colby was completely full of shit and didn't find Sarah's necklaces, her nose ring, her weird haircut, attractive at all.

Sarah raked her hair down in front of her face. "There. No distraction."

Principal Colby dropped her head to the side and tried again. "I know you're upset, Sarah, and that's perfectly —"

"I am *not* upset."

Principal Colby was getting flustered. Sarah could see her cheeks blush, even under all her makeup. "Okay. Well . . . it's clear that you have strong feelings about the list. And I appreciate you trying to make a statement. It's shocking to me that Principal Weyland let this go on for so long under his watch." This last bit took Sarah by surprise. Principals never talked shit about other principals, as far as she knew. "And I would love it if you could help motivate the others into taking a stand, so this same sad event won't happen next year to more girls."

Sarah tried not to laugh. Principal Colby was delusional if she thought she could put a stop to the list. Or that Sarah would have any interest in helping her try. "I don't care about any of the other girls on the list. I don't care if it goes on forever. In fact, I hope it does! The fact that people put so much stock in this is insane. It serves them right for buying into it."

Principal Colby frowned. "Please go wash your forehead now, Sarah. I'm not going to ask you again."

Sarah stormed to the bathroom, grabbed a paper towel, and held it under the faucet. Was this lady for real? What was so different between the list and homecoming? Both were stupid beauty contests, except one was school-sanctioned.

She wiped the wad over her forehead. Of course, it barely lightened the black ink. The cheap-ass soap in the dispensers didn't help, but the suds dripped into her eyes and stung them. Great. Just great. She sank to the floor and tried rubbing away the burn. If anyone saw her, they'd think she'd been crying.

She'd have to wait until she got home to wash it off. Wash it off so she could come back to school tomorrow and pretend like none of this had happened.

That's when Sarah had the idea. How to take her rebellion to the next level. How to show everyone at school what she really thought of their opinions, their rules. She'd been too silent, too complacent, letting them get away with murder. And the beautiful thing was, if it went off the way she thought it could, she'd ruin homecoming, too, courtesy of one giant act of badassery.

Sarah takes a left and skids to a stop at the base of a hill that she doesn't remember being there. Or maybe it never seemed this enormous when riding the bus. She can't see Mount

Washington High School at the crest, just an endless stretch of tar paved to the sky.

She pedals hard, rocking her weight from side to side to get some speed going. At the halfway mark, she clocks barely enough to remain upright. Her wobbling bike drifts into the middle of the street. Cars and school buses begin backing up behind her, and a few hop the curb in order to pass her by.

But Sarah is determined. The autumn air bites the edges of her ears. Dead leaves explode underneath her tires. She stands and pumps harder, sweat bleeding into her T-shirt.

Milo's T-shirt.

Whatever. The same shirt she wore to school yesterday.

Milo has beaten her to their bench. "Hey!" he calls out, surprised. "Nice bike." His eyes move up to her forehead. "I, um, guess they call it permanent marker for a reason, huh?"

"I guess so." Sarah can barely speak, she's panting so hard. She picks up the hem of her T-shirt and dabs lightly at the sweat on her forehead, careful not to disturb the word. It is still scrawled there, a little lighter than it had been yesterday.

"Is that my shirt? Again?"

"Who are you? The fashion police?" She feels for her cigarettes, but then thinks better of it. Smoke will camouflage her smell. She will quit smoking this week. "Yes, it's your shirt." She sits down at the end of the bench and pulls her legs close to her chest. They are already sore, cramped from the ride.

A curious look crosses Milo's face. It makes his eyes go squinty behind his glasses. "Why are you wearing it, when you've been acting like you can't stand me?" He digs in his school bag and hands her a folded square of black fabric. "Here's yours back, by the way. I washed it."

It's funny how direct Milo can be about stuff sometimes. It's like his awkwardness trumps the shyness.

Sarah has not yet said anything to Milo about ending things between them. It's been too crazy, with yesterday's events. And seriously, why should she? Why should she have to do the dirty work when she's not the one who did anything wrong? Why should she give Milo the easy way out?

She lifts her chin a few degrees. "I've decided not to take a shower for a whole week."

"For real?"

"Yup," she says, making the *p* pop. "I'm not showering, I'm not brushing my teeth, putting on deodorant, anything. I'm wearing these same clothes, not just the shirt, but the jeans, the socks, the underwear, the bra. My last shower was on Sunday night, before I went over to your house." She folds her arms. "I won't participate in any kind of hygiene until Saturday night." It feels good to say her plan out loud. Now there can be no backing out.

"What's on Saturday night?"

"The homecoming dance." It sounds so utterly ridiculous, but she keeps a straight face. "I'm going as smelly and disgusting as I can possibly make myself, dressed in these clothes."

Milo laughs and laughs, but when Sarah doesn't join, he stops. "Wait. You're not serious."

"I am."

"Why are you letting that stupid list get to you? You hate the girls at this school, obviously for good reason. And now you want to show up at their dumb dance? This isn't like you at all."

Sarah runs her fingers through the brittle streamers on her old bike, trying to detangle them. This last bit is proof. Proof that Milo doesn't really get her. He never did. And she doesn't feel like explaining everything to someone who's not going to understand it. "Look, can you not make a big deal about this? I've made up my mind. It's happening."

He shrugs his shoulders. "Can I go with you?"

She turns her head fast and looks Milo over. "Shut up."

Milo grins. "It could be funny. I'll wear a tie. I'll get you a corsage."

Sarah stops herself from being surprised that Milo would want to go to the homecoming dance. It actually makes perfect sense, considering what she knows about him now.

"So it's a date?"

Sarah shakes her head, baffled. "If by *date* you mean that you and I will show up at the same place at the same time, then yeah, I guess it's a date. But don't you dare get me a corsage."

The bell rings. It's funny how absolutely insane this is. Sarah never in a million years thought she'd ever go to the Mount Washington homecoming dance. With a boy. And though she'd never admit it, there is a tiny glimmer deep down inside that is excited in a disgustingly typical way.

On the way into school, Sarah watches the faces that pass her by. No one seems to notice that she's in the same clothes as yesterday. Sucks.

And then, out of freaking nowhere, Milo takes her hand. Easily, as if they hold hands all the time. Which they don't.

Sarah doesn't pull away, even though she wants to, and even though she knows she'll regret it later on. It is a glimmer of the Milo she thought she'd met. And it feels nice for one brief, too-fast moment.

CHAPTER THIRTEEN

"I wonder if Mr. Farber will call today," Mrs. Finn says, as she turns to check her blind spot. "I hope he's decent enough to tell me if I don't get the job. Some people don't give you that courtesy. That's cruel, don't you think?"

"Yeah."

The word comes out a little too slow, a little too dragged out, because Lauren's not really listening. She's looking at the back side of the list, tucked between pages of World History notes.

Yesterday had been full of introductions. A few girls took a formal approach, telling Lauren their first and last names. Others simply threw an arm over Lauren's shoulder as she walked down the hall and struck up the kind of conversations that seemed reserved for old friends — complaints about period cramps, tidbits of gossip about people she'd yet to meet, confessions of crushes.

Lauren tried to keep track of everyone she met. She wrote everything down on the back side of the list — a five-petal flower as a bullet point, followed by a name and a brief physical description. Initially, Lauren liked watching the page blossom like a springtime garden, but toward the end of the day, it grew into a tangled jungle, and it seemed impossible to distinguish one person from another. She worries about this now, as Mount Washington High appears before the windshield.

"Do you have a history test today?" Mrs. Finn asks, and

tries to get a look. "You didn't mention it last night. We could have studied together."

Lauren flips her notebook over and curls her fingers around the spine. "No. I just have this feeling we might get a pop quiz."

Lauren hadn't told her mother about the list. Obviously.

First off, Lauren knew she would not approve. It was exactly the kind of thing that Mrs. Finn had wanted to shield Lauren from with homeschooling.

But also, they'd spent the night going over every single moment of her mother's job interview. Mrs. Finn seemed sure she hadn't gotten the job. Lauren assured her mother that she'd done fine, but worried what might happen if she hadn't.

It's hard sometimes, she thinks, having a mother for a best friend.

Her mother manages a weak smile. "I wish you didn't have to go to school today. I'll be at home alone, driving myself crazy. Hey! I've got an idea! Do you want to go grab pancakes? There's a little diner your grandfather took me to every Sunday and they make the best ones. I could write you a note. I'll say you had a doctor's appointment."

Though the pancakes are tempting, Lauren is actually kind of excited to go to school this morning. It's the first time this has happened. "I can't, Mommy. Sorry. That pop quiz would be first period."

"Right. Okay."

"If you're bored, you can always unpack." Though they moved to Mount Washington almost two months ago, most of their things are still in boxes.

"I want to know we're staying first. You never know. If I don't get this job, we might have to sell the house."

"You'll get the job, Mommy. I know it." Lauren says this expecting her mother to smile. But Mrs. Finn doesn't. Instead, she looks at Lauren as if she's said the wrong thing entirely.

As the sedan pulls up to school, Lauren notices other students noticing her. In a way, the list was like a birth certificate; it officially marked the beginning of her existence at Mount Washington High School. Lauren turns, hoping to see that her mother isn't noticing, and she's not. She's glancing out her side-view mirror, looking backward.

Lauren gets to homeroom. She takes a seat and again reviews the notes on the back of the list, trying to focus only on the girls in the tight circle who'd seemed the most interested in her.

One by one, these girls arrive to find Lauren. They pull their seats close to hers. Others stand to get a better view, and they all beam down at Lauren as if she's a baby in a nursery they've collectively adopted.

They appear charmed by her innocence, sharing pleased little looks as they point out Lauren's social transgressions to each other — her lack of makeup, that she's covered her textbooks in brown paper, the barrette she uses to keep her hair pinned off her face.

Blood rushes to Lauren's head and makes her woozy and warm.

And then, the questions begin.

"So, have you lived in Mount Washington your whole life?"

"No," Lauren answers, once she's picked out the girl who'd asked from the crowd. "I used to live out west with my mom. We moved here when my grandfather died."

"Are your parents still together?"

Lauren turns her head toward a girl perched on the desk to her right. "No. It's just the two of us."

"Where's your dad?" a girl leaning against the bulletin board asks.

"He died, too. When I was a baby."

"Wow. That's so sad," comes a voice from behind her. The girls nod in solemn agreement.

"He was a lot older."

Lauren senses their urgency to get to know her, and she tries her best to keep pace, answering their questions as quickly as they're asked. It is clear from the unspoken ways they communicate — head nods, glances, smiles — that most of these girls have known each other for practically forever. Lauren herself has watched them from afar the last few weeks walking through the halls with their arms linked, hugging in between classes. She wants to be a part of what they have. There seems to be so much time to make up for.

Lauren wishes it wasn't so one-sided. She wants to ask them things, too. But their questions keep coming.

"What kind of stuff do you like to do?"

"Um, I don't know. Read? I like reading."

"Do you have a boyfriend?"

"A couple of the guys told us to ask you that," a girl says slyly, and the others laugh.

Lauren shakes her head. "I've never had a boyfriend. I've . . . I've never even been kissed." As soon as she admits this, it hits her that she isn't just talking to these girls. Her answers will be reported back to more people she doesn't know.

"Never?!" they all squeal with shocked delight. A few inch closer to her desk, as if to protect her. She can't remember any of their names.

"Well, that's about to change," a girl says. She is speaking to the others in the group but keeping her eyes on Lauren. "I bet Lauren gets a boyfriend by the homecoming dance."

Lauren feels herself blush. It seems impossible. "I don't know about that."

"Have you bought your ticket to the dance yet?"

"No."

"But you're coming, right?"

Lauren nods. "I think so," she says, even though she hadn't considered it before now. Even though she'll have to ask her mother.

"Good. And you should totally help us work on our Spirit Caravan for the homecoming parade. Everyone in school decorates their cars and drives around town, like a parade before the game starts. People come out on their lawns to watch. It's seriously so fun."

"I'd love to help." The idea of riding in a car with these new girls, who are maybe becoming her actual friends, is extremely exciting. Suddenly the reality of high school is matching up with how she dreamed it might be, and not at all what she'd been told.

One girl cocks her head to the side and says wistfully, "I bet this is kinda crazy for you. Like, one minute, you're invisible. And then the next, everyone knows who you are."

"I thought you looked friendly," another girl admits. "I don't know why I never said hi or anything."

"Me, too," says another.

Lauren shakes her head. "It's partly my fault. It's not like I was talking to you guys, either. I'm really shy." She spreads her eyes on all the girls. And as she does, she sees Candace walk by the homeroom, alone. Candace, the former leader of this group.

Lauren sees Candace's eyes flit sideways into the classroom, looking but not looking. The other girls don't notice. They're too busy staring at Lauren.

"I feel bad for Candace," Lauren says in a low voice. "She seemed upset yesterday." More upset than anyone else in Principal Colby's office.

One of the girls moans. "Ugh. Don't."

"Why not?"

"Because she's evil!" another cries.

Lauren watches the girls nod solemnly. "Wait. Aren't you all friends with her?"

"We *are* friends with her," someone says. "We're *still* friends with her."

"But . . . Candace had this coming, you know?"

"She gets away with a lot of stuff, because she's . . . you know . . . so pretty. And that's not right."

"She's said a lot of bad things about a lot of people." It seems like the girl who says this wants something to register on Lauren's face, and when whatever it is doesn't, she adds, "Including you."

Lauren cycles back through the last four weeks of school. She'd tried hard to blend in, but even still, there'd been mistakes. The waterproof hiking boots she'd worn on the first rainy day had gotten her a few weird looks. Her clothes were plain and sensible, not stylish. Her hair was longer than anyone else's by several inches, and no one wore the side pinned back with a tarnished old barrette.

She lifts up her hand and quietly removes her barrette. She knows there's so much still to learn. Things her mother doesn't know, or never taught her.

When homeroom ends, Lauren still feels like she should say something to Candace. Making new friends is great, and so exciting, but she doesn't want them at the expense of an enemy.

She sees Candace duck into the girls' bathroom. Lauren follows her.

"Hi," Lauren says. "I'm Lauren."

"I know who you are." Candace walks into a stall and closes the door.

Lauren wrings her hands. "I . . . wanted to say that I'm sorry about everything that happened yesterday. You don't deserve to be called ugly. By anyone."

After a second, the toilet flushes, though Lauren doesn't recall hearing Candace pee or anything. The door opens and Candace walks over to the sink to wash her hands. She never looks at Lauren. But she does say, "I know I don't."

Candace is obviously upset. Lauren can't blame her for that. Maybe talking to Candace is a mistake, but she still feels relieved to say her piece. "And, I'm sorry your friends aren't talking to you right now. But I'm sure that will blow over." Candace laughs, and it sends a shiver over Lauren. Because really, what does Lauren know about all this? She doesn't know these girls. She doesn't understand how things go in high school. "Okay. Right. Well, I just wanted to tell you that."

She is nearly at the door when Candace calls after her, "You know that the only reason people are suddenly being nice to you is because of the list, right?"

This time, it's Lauren who doesn't answer. Because she does know that. And because she doesn't care. The point is that they are being nice to her. And she plans to enjoy every minute.

CHAPTER FOURTEEN

Danielle reaches for the tile marking the end of her swim lane. Then she twists around, presses her feet against the wall, and blasts the last lap of her heat.

Her mind is usually blank when she swims, clear and chlorinated like the pool water. But not today. Today her thoughts are murky and dark, like the water had been during the summer at Clover Lake.

The camp was nearly a hundred miles north of Mount Washington. Neither Danielle nor Andrew had been there before, but each had a relative who'd been a camper back in the day and who pulled strings to get them the extremely well-paying summer jobs.

The rest of the teen counselors were veteran campers, a tight clique who'd gone to Clover Lake as kids and knew all the campfire songs and the indigenous trees and probably didn't care if they got paid anything, so long as they could spend another summer at the lake. Danielle and Andrew were the outsiders, and sometimes they'd share an eye roll when the other counselors critiqued the stability of their pinecone birdhouses or corrected their pronunciations of the Native American tribes who'd once inhabited the area. But it wasn't like they were friends or anything.

The kids loved Danielle. The other counselors barely paid any attention to their campers, but Danielle included herself in their activities, mainly so she'd have people to talk to. The girls in her bunk wove her a special lanyard for her lifeguard whistle. The boys constantly challenged her to impromptu races across the lawn or to swim to the buoys and back. At first, they seemed frustrated to lose, and lose badly, to a girl, but after a while, those disappointed feelings evolved into something closer to respect.

It was around that time that Andrew began to make himself more visible. She'd see him walking the edge of the lake while she sat in her lifeguard chair. She'd feel him standing close behind her in the food line. She'd catch him watching her through the flickering orange flames of the nightly bonfire.

It was the first time a boy had paid her attention.

She'd been writing old-fashioned pen pal letters to Hope for fun. But the topic of Andrew required more immediate communication. So she took to sneaking phone calls to give Hope a daily report on the comings and goings of Andrew.

"I feel like he wants to talk to me," Danielle whispered to Hope one night, once her campers were asleep. She leaned against the cedar-shingled bunk and watched the stars in the sky, waiting for one to fall.

"So go talk to him first."

"Are you kidding?"

"Danielle! Don't be dumb. You talk to boys all the time. And we're gonna be freshmen!"

"Never boys that may possibly like me," Danielle clarified.

Hope said, "He's probably nervous. You're kind of . . . intimidating."

Danielle closed her eyes and breathed the thick, humid air. She was nervous, too, which would hopefully level the playing field.

The next day, Andrew made his move.

Danielle was in the lake, up to her waist, leading a swim relay for the eleven-year-olds. She saw Andrew sitting on the dock, his legs dangling in the water. Maybe that was as far as he could go. She decided to swim over.

"Hey," Andrew said when she reached the dock. "I came to warn you."

"Warn me about what?" Danielle pulled herself out of the lake and sat next to him, far enough so that the water dripping off her wouldn't get him wet.

Andrew kept his eyes on the lake. "Every boy in my bunk has a crush on you."

Danielle wondered if Andrew counted himself among those boys in his bunk. She dropped her head to the left so the sun was not in her eyes and took Andrew in. He was tan with tufts of sandy hair. The sleeves of his navy camp polo were rolled up to his shoulders, exposing his lean, muscular arms.

"They were talking about you last night," he continued. "Danny Fannelli said he was going to pretend to drown so you'd rescue him and give him mouth-to-mouth."

Danielle burst out laughing. "Wow. Well, thanks for the tip."

He waited a second, and then asked, "You're going to Mount Washington next year, right? I think I heard someone say that."

"Yup. Why, do you go there?"

"Yeah." He scratched his head and squinted into the sun.

With that, the potential for a little summer fling, a chance to try out love with a boy for a few weeks, turned into a bigger, more exciting possibility. She struggled for something witty and funny to say back. Luckily, Danny Fannelli was near the shore, flailing and splashing dramatically in water that maybe came up to Danielle's knees.

"See what I mean?" Andrew grinned. "I told Danny that you probably have a boyfriend, so he shouldn't even bother trying."

"I don't have a boyfriend," Danielle said with a laugh. She stood up and let her toes hang over the dock edge.

"Good to know." He got up, too. "I'll see you around, Danielle."

"See you," she said, before diving back into the water. Clover Lake had never felt so warm.

Danielle pops to the surface and pulls off her goggles to get a look at the timing clock. Seconds later, the girls in the lanes on either side of her splash up.

Mount Washington's varsity swim coach stands over Danielle's lane with her clipboard and whistle. Coach Tracy is tall and thin, and she wears her blond hair cut close, like a boy in the army, except for a few long pieces in the front that curl behind her ears. She'd swum through college on a full scholarship before tearing both rotator cuffs during a butterfly sprint for Olympic trials.

Coach Tracy has sat in a few other freshman practices before, watching from the bleachers, but this is the first time she actually participates, relegating their freshman coach to the lifeguard chair. Danielle heard a few of her teammates whisper in the locker room that Coach Tracy wants fresh meat to round out the varsity relay teams.

"Nice one, Dan," Coach Tracy tells her. "But you're losing at least a second on your flip turns. You need to be tighter."

Danielle doesn't hear the compliment. Or the critique.

As Coach Tracy steps over to address another swimmer, a bubble rises up in her throat. "It's Danielle, actually," she finds herself calling out.

Coach Tracy turns and raises her eyebrow. "What was that?"

"I'm sorry," Danielle stammers, this time a little quieter. "I would rather you call me Danielle. That's . . . my name."

The freshman coach shouts from his perch. "Did you hear what Coach Tracy told you?"

"Yes. Got it. I was only —"

A shrill whistle silences her. Coach Tracy spits it out and calls, "Alright. Girls out, boys in. Let's hustle."

Danielle paddles over to the ladder. She tells herself not to feel bad about correcting Coach Tracy. After all, her name *is* Danielle.

But the nickname given to her by the list has taken on a life of its own. Despite the fact that she's wearing makeup today, and flatironed her hair, people she doesn't know have been calling out to *Dan the Man* in the hallway, offering fake hellos, mimicking what they assume to be her husky voice. Except Danielle doesn't have a husky voice. They'd know that if they bothered to talk to her. Each time, it's been a fight not to spin around and scream *My name is Danielle!* at the very top of her lungs.

But she hasn't. And what she said to Coach Tracy is as close as she's come to defending herself. But even this little stand makes her feel guilty, especially after the things that Andrew said. Plus, she wants to impress Coach Tracy. And yet, for some reason, Coach Tracy is the only person she feels okay correcting.

Hope grabs Danielle's foot and pulls her backward through the water. "Way to kick ass," she says, and splashes Danielle as she makes it to the ladder first.

"I blew my chance," Danielle responds, following Hope out of the water.

"Please. It's obvious that Coach Tracy came down just to see you swim." Hope takes a sports bottle from the bleachers and shoots a stream down her throat. "I'm almost positive you're getting called up to varsity. I'm thinking about lodging an anonymous complaint and getting your DNA tested. I swear, the way you swim, you must be part mermaid."

Danielle smiles meekly as she runs her hands fast over her flat stomach, flicking the water off her bathing suit. When she looks up, she sees Andrew lurking near the door in his practice jersey and football pads. And her heart, which had started to slow down from the sprints, revs right back up.

She spent an entire summer wearing her bathing suit around him without a second thought. But before walking over, she stops to grab her towel from the bleachers and wraps it tight around herself.

"Nice job out there," Andrew says, folding his arms. "You're as fast as a fish!"

A fish is different from a mermaid, but Danielle doesn't let it bother her. She's glad he's seen her this way. At her best.

"Thanks," she says. "Aren't you supposed to be at practice, too?"

"I pretended that I had to use the bathroom so I could see you." His eyes go to the concrete floor. "We didn't get much of a chance to talk in school today. Sorry about that."

Danielle says, "It's fine," though she'd been hurt about it for most of the morning, after looking unsuccessfully for Andrew in all the usual places. By lunch, Danielle had accepted that Andrew was probably avoiding her. Strangely enough, this made her feel relieved. It was hard for her to pretend that she didn't care about the list around Andrew, and especially around Andrew's friends, who'd tease her worst of all. So in a way, it was good that Andrew was lying low. It made things easier on her. And on him, too.

Andrew pats her on the back, and then wipes his hand on her towel. "Well, I'd better go before Coach sends the guys to find me. I'll call you later."

"I'm supposed to go shopping with my mom for homecoming dresses. Hey . . . do you guys have a plan yet for Saturday night?" She isn't sure how the dance thing works in high school. If people who are dating go together, like junior formal or prom.

Andrew shakes his head and starts to walk backward for the door. "I'm not sure what's going on. Chuck has his ideas . . . We'll probably hang out, but I'm not sure where yet. Everyone's pretty focused on Saturday's game right now. I mean, we have to win this one, or else we'll be the laughingstock of the whole division. But I'll let you know when things firm up."

Danielle feels better as she walks away from Andrew. She can keep up the tough act a little longer, till this whole list thing blows over. Tonight, she'll get something beautiful to wear to the dance. And then there won't be a doubt in anyone's mind, least of all Andrew's, that she's a girl.

CHAPTER FIFTEEN

Cheer practice is much more fun than it was a few weeks ago. This is what Margo thinks as she gets dressed in the locker room. She changes into her workout gear — leggings, a tank top, tennis shoes, and a sweatshirt for the warm-up run outside. Dana and Rachel wear essentially the same thing. Tri-captains. They like putting on a united front.

Today the dance coach, Sami, is coming to do the final run-through of the halftime routine. The squad already has the moves down. This practice will be about fine-tuning. Making sure things look perfect.

Margo says, "Maybe one of us should sit out each time we run through the routine, to make sure everyone's looking sharp."

"Yeah," Rachel says. "Sami can't watch everyone."

"Good call," Dana adds. And then she laughs. "Anyway, when Sami dances along with us, she's only looking at herself in the mirror."

There are only a few more practices before the homecoming game. It will be the biggest game of the season. Students who graduated will come back for it. Last year's cheering captains will be there, too, and they'll expect the squad to look great. All except Maureen, who won't be coming home. She might not even make Thanksgiving, depending on midterms. But it is still a lot of pressure.

Most of the cheer squad is already outside, waiting on the bleachers.

The younger girls start clapping for Margo when she gets close. It's awkward, especially because Sami is there. Also because they'd done it the day before, too.

"What's this about?" Sami asks.

The girls tell Sami about the list, which they shouldn't. The list isn't a thing to talk about in front of teachers, and Margo is paranoid about her encounters with Principal Colby. But it ends up being okay. Sami gets bashful and admits to the squad that she'd made the list once herself. Nine years ago, when she was a junior. Then the whole squad applauds Sami, and Margo is happy to have the attention off her for a moment.

But then Sami says, "As a prize, Margo gets to sit out the laps and hang with me. Alright, ladies, let's hustle up!"

Margo thinks she sees Dana and Rachel roll their eyes at each other.

"I bet your friends are jealous of you," Sami says when the squad takes off running.

"Nah. They're not like that."

Sami laughs drily. "Your sister, Maureen, had a lot of trouble with that last year. I don't think people understand how hard it can be on us pretty girls."

Margo watches as the squad reaches the other side of the field. She pushes herself up off the grass. "I'll be back," she tells Sami. And then she runs the laps anyway. It feels weird not to.

After cheer practice, Margo stops at her locker to trade her pom-poms for her books. Then she walks to the parking lot to meet Rachel and Dana at her car. The plan is to shop for homecoming dresses and grab dinner in the mall's food court. Her mom has given her a charge card to use. Margo never abuses the privilege. She always hits the sale racks first. But tonight, she won't hesitate to buy herself the perfect dress. Not when it's the very last homecoming of her life. A year from now, she'll be away at college, the dance just a memory. She wants it to be a good one.

She pulls up the hood of her cheering sweatshirt against the breeze. Maybe she'll go someplace warm for college. Of course, that is months away. She hasn't even filled out one application yet, or given her personal essays any thought. But the inevitable future looms over her, clouding everything with a sad nostalgia. She wonders where Dana and Rachel will end up. If they will still talk. She hopes so. They're good friends. She loves them both.

Margo's mind wanders back to her first homecoming dance three years ago. How she'd almost burned herself with the curling iron while fighting with Maureen for space at the bathroom mirror. How amazing it felt to be dancing next to Dana and Rachel in dresses, drinking sodas and hoping older boys would talk to them.

She'd been on the list that year, too. Bry Tate had made homecoming court for the senior boys, and he gave her his rose when the DJ put on a slow song. He was no Matthew Goulding, but more than a fine second choice. Bry had worn his football jersey to the dance and Margo remembers it smelling of grass when they did the slow dance shuffle underneath the disco ball. The rest of the football team had worn their jerseys, too, because they'd won the homecoming game, beaten rival Chesterfield Valley to a bloody pulp. Later that night, Margo kissed Bry in his car, while Dana and Rachel kissed other boys in other cars. When she got home, she pressed his rose inside her diary. She still had the petals.

Everyone was so happy. Everyone had a great time.

Jennifer had been on that list, too, and she'd skipped the dance for obvious reasons. Still, Margo had kept an eye out for her. And though Margo didn't want to admit it, Jennifer's absence from the dance was a big part of why she was able to enjoy herself. Hopefully, Jennifer won't show this year, either. There are only so many good times left.

Rachel and Dana sit on the trunk of her car. Margo waves.

And then, from the corner of her eye, Margo sees a round shape make a beeline for her. It's Jennifer, waving, too.

Why is she still at school?

Margo strolls over, trying to appear unnerved. "What's up?"

Rachel hops off the trunk. "We invited Jennifer to come shopping with us. She doesn't have a homecoming dress yet."

"I wasn't even planning to go," Jennifer says quietly.

Dana pushes her books into Jennifer's arms, freeing her hands to tie her shoelace. "You're *going* to the dance, Jennifer. You are definitely going. This is your senior year!"

"Maybe, if I can find a dress," Jennifer says, hugging the books that aren't hers.

Dana stands back up and pats Jennifer's back. "We *will* find you a dress."

The girls turn to Margo, waiting for her to unlock her car. Margo squeezes the keys tight in her hand. "I'm so sorry, you guys, but I have to bail."

"What do you mean?" Rachel whines. "It was your idea to go shopping today in the first place!"

"I know." Margo sighs, giving herself a second to think up an excuse. "But my mom just texted me. She wants me to come straight home. We're meeting my dad for dinner near his office. She's upset about how we never spend time together as a family now that Maureen's in college. I think she's having empty nest syndrome, you know, because I'll be leaving next year."

Too many details, Margo thinks to herself. Rachel and Dana eye her, visibly annoyed. But Margo is annoyed with them, too. Why didn't they mention that they'd invited Jennifer along? Did they want to blindside her? Didn't it occur to them how uncomfortable this might be for her? Of course, Margo couldn't get into any of that now. Especially not with Jennifer right next to her.

Dana takes her books back from Jennifer. "I thought the plan was to buy our dresses together to make sure we didn't clash. So we'll all look good standing together in the pictures." There is a definite edge to Dana's voice, hung entirely on the word *all*. And she doesn't even register how screwed up it is to say that in front of Jennifer. Who wouldn't be going with them to homecoming. Who wouldn't be in any of their pictures.

Margo is about to suggest they go shopping tomorrow instead, even with the risk that Jennifer will elbow her way into that outing, too, but Jennifer turns away from Margo and speaks only to Rachel and Dana before she has the chance.

"If you guys still want to go shopping . . . I could drive us. My car's parked right over there."

Margo sits behind the wheel, thinking for a long time.

She should have gone with them. She could have played along, helped Jennifer find a dress, pretended that everything was fine. Like they had no history. Like they were never best friends.

It had been the last day of school, minutes into no longer being an eighth grader but a high school girl, and to Margo, everything felt different. All that had happened earlier — the gym class water-balloon fight, the good-bye pizza party with soda served in little paper cups — were memories written in a kid's diary. She'd suddenly grown out of her life, even though she could still see the rounded tip of her middle school's flag-pole from where she stood, like a doorknob for the sky.

She and Jennifer stood at the end of Margo's street. Jennifer was finishing up a story about Matthew, how she'd heard him admitting to the other boys that, once he got to high school, he would only date girls who had at least a B cup. Otherwise, what was the point?

It didn't sound like something Matthew would say, but when guys talked with other guys, all bets were off. Margo glanced down at her chest, barely an A.

Almost immediately after Margo called out "See you later" to Jennifer, her lips still warm from the words, from finalizing the sleepover plans Jennifer had made for them weeks ago, it occurred to Margo that she did not want to go.

Not only that, but she did not want to be friends with Jennifer anymore.

It wasn't something Jennifer had done.

Not exactly.

But once the thought was there — or rather, once Margo finally accepted the feelings that she'd tried for months to talk herself out of — she couldn't ignore it for one minute longer.

Instead of walking home to pack her sleeping bag and pajamas, Margo edged the toes of her Keds until they were cantilevered over the curb and watched Jennifer lumber up the hill with a lumpy backpack filled with relics of the past year: old binders, stale gym clothes, notes they'd passed, book reports from the first marking period. Margo herself had stopped carrying a backpack months ago, and everything that had been in her locker, she'd pitched into a trash can.

This image, juxtaposed with the lightness Margo suddenly felt, seemed to encapsulate everything, their entire friendship, the whole history, and why she wanted to let it go.

But letting go, she knew, would not be easy.

When Margo got home, she went to her sister's room. Margo entered quietly, sat on the corner of Maureen's bed, and waited for her to get off the phone. Maureen usually screamed at her to get out, but Margo supposed she looked upset, because her sister let her stay.

After Maureen hung up, she reached for her comb and began brushing her hair. "What's up, Margo?"

"It's Jennifer. I . . . I just . . ." She struggled to put today's revelation into words.

"You don't want to be friends with her anymore." Maureen said it plainly, matter-of-factly.

It was a relief.

Margo had brought her diary with her, tucked into the waistband of her shorts, so she'd be ready to explain herself. If pushed for reasons, she could recall specific moments when Jennifer had been annoying, made her feel bad or guilty, acted weird around her other friends. It comforted Margo to have this proof pressed against her. It helped her feel like what she wanted to do was right.

It wouldn't be necessary. Maureen didn't need any convincing. If anything, Maureen looked relieved that she'd made this decision.

"Just prepare yourself, because Jennifer's going to freak out. I mean, the girl is obsessed with you."

"She's not obsessed with me," Margo said, even though it had felt that way lately.

"Please. She gets so jealous when you're with your other friends. You try to include her, but she ends up holding it against you."

Their friendship hadn't always been like that. They'd had years of fun, years of good, easy times with each other. Margo resisted the urge to say as much, because it would just complicate things. She leaned back into the bed's pillows. They puffed up around her.

"If I were you, I'd do it as soon as possible," Maureen went on. "I mean, you're about to be in high school. You can't have Jennifer holding you back, making you feel guilty about meeting new friends and being invited places where she isn't."

That very thing had happened that afternoon.

A couple of girls invited Margo out for the night to celebrate the end of school. They were going to walk to the ice cream shop, see who was hanging out, and probably go night swimming in someone's pool.

Dana and Rachel had waited to mention it until Jennifer left class to use the bathroom. All their invitations were like that. Secretive. Exclusive.

Margo was glad for their discretion. Because if Jennifer knew that Margo had been invited, she'd absolutely expect to come along. Jennifer seemed to think that, because they were best friends, they could never do anything apart. And maybe that was true. Maybe that was how best friendships were supposed to work. But to Margo, it just felt suffocating. It was another reason to want out.

"I'm supposed to sleep over at Jennifer's house tonight. I guess I could do it then," Margo said, even though the idea of a face-to-face confrontation with Jennifer made her incredibly anxious. What was she supposed to say? List off all the reasons she didn't want to be friends? What if Jennifer put up a fight? Argued with her? That definitely felt like a possibility. She would certainly cry. Margo, too, because it was sad. And after they'd had it out, would Margo still be expected to spend the night? For old times' sake? She couldn't imagine anything more uncomfortable.

Maureen cleaned the hair out of her comb and dropped it into the wastebasket. "If you don't want to go, don't go. Pretend you're sick or something."

"But she'll know I'm lying. I told her ten minutes ago that I'd be there. Her mom's coming to pick me up in an hour."

Maureen nodded enthusiastically. "Perfect!"

"Huh?"

"You're overthinking things, Margo. It's not up to you to spell out for Jennifer why you don't want to be her friend. She'll figure it out. And if she doesn't, well . . . that's not your problem."

A while later, Margo heard a car horn outside. She tiptoed to her bedroom window, made a tiny gap in her blinds, and watched her mom jog out to deliver the news. Jennifer and Mrs. Briggis both looked concerned. Mrs. Briggis acted like any mother would toward a sick child. Worried, sympathetic.

Jennifer was different. Her face turned as pale as the sidewalk, and she stared through the windshield up to Margo's bedroom window, her mouth a straight, flat line.

A shock of anxiety hit Margo. Did Jennifer know? Even though Margo had been careful, had she seen this coming? And if she had, would it make things easier?

Margo fought the urge to step away from her window. She raised her blinds all the way up, to make sure Jennifer saw her. She felt brave and cowardly.

Mrs. Gable waved good-bye as Jennifer and Mrs. Briggis drove off. She walked back up to the front door, yanking out a dandelion on her way and flinging it into a bed of ivy that separated their property from the neighbors'.

Later, when Margo asked to be dropped off at the ice cream shop, where she knew Rachel and Dana would be, Mrs. Gable refused. If Margo was sick, then she was sick. Margo looked at Maureen, silently begging her to help, but Maureen stuck out her tongue and slipped out the door.

The next morning, Margo didn't reschedule the sleepover plans with Jennifer. She didn't pick up the phone when Jennifer called, nor did she call her back, even when her mom would leave Jennifer's messages taped to her bedroom door. It took a few weeks of this before Jennifer stopped calling.

Without Jennifer, Margo had a great summer. There were pool parties and barbecues and late-night chats on the roof of her garage with her new friends. Dana invited her to ride on a fire truck for the town's Independence Day parade. She and Rachel spent weekends selling antique Coke bottles at an outdoor flea market, but mostly getting tan in lawn chairs. She didn't miss Jennifer at all, and no one ever wondered why Margo never brought her around anymore.

Only one person wouldn't let Margo move on.

Looking back, it had been a mistake. She should have never involved her mom. Throughout high school, Mrs. Gable was a huge source of guilt, always asking about Jennifer, always wanting to know if she was good, how Mr. and Mrs. Briggis were, if Jennifer had a boyfriend. She asked the questions even though she knew Margo had no clue. To prove a point, Margo guessed. What a mean girl her daughter was. Not that Margo could blame her. She knew what it looked like from the surface. The pretty girl leaves her ugly friend behind. It's what everyone probably thought.

Jennifer, too.

Margo didn't care to set the record straight.

She'd gotten what she wanted, and that was the end of that.

A knock at Margo's car window jolts her back to reality. It's Matthew in his football practice gear.

She unrolls her window and forces down a dry swallow. "Hi."

"Is something wrong with your car?"

"It's fine. I'm fine. Thanks. I guess I zoned out."

"Oh. Alright then. I'll see you tomo —"

"How was practice?" she asks to keep the conversation going.

Matthew sighs. He seems tired. "Intense. We haven't beaten Chesterfield since we were freshmen. Plus our team is way overdue for a W."

She pulls her hair into a fresh ponytail, smiles a very pretty smile. "Oh!" Margo says. "I've got some news about my party on Friday. My parents decided they want to stay at home. I guess Maureen's friends went a little crazy last year, and someone went in my mom's closet and stole her robe. We can still drink and everything. And they promised they wouldn't leave their room."

Matthew nods, but then takes a step back from the window and regards her skeptically. "You sure you're okay? You look, I don't know, worried."

Her overstretched smile makes her cheeks ache. "I'm sure." Even though she's not. And she doesn't like that Matthew sees it.

She rolls her window back up and thinks about Jennifer and Rachel and Dana. Margo's sure she'll come up in conversation, if she hasn't already. What will Jennifer say about her?

Nothing good, that's for sure.

CHAPTER SIXTEEN

Jennifer walks as quickly as she can away from Margo's car, surprised by the footsteps crunching leaves behind her.

Maybe she shouldn't have offered to drive to the mall. Margo will surely be mad at her for that. She isn't blind. She'd noticed the dirty looks Margo shot her. As if every time Jennifer came around, she was trespassing on Margo's private property.

But what did Margo expect her to do when Rachel and Dana invited her to the mall? They were going out of their way to be nice to her, and Jennifer certainly wasn't about to refuse their kindness. Anyway, she really did want to go dress shopping, now that they'd convinced her to go to the homecoming dance. And Rachel and Dana could have said no. They could have made up an excuse and waited for Margo.

But they hadn't. They'd said yes.

Rachel calls shotgun as they approach Jennifer's car, then searches the radio stations for a song they can sing along to. Dana turns in the backseat to check Jennifer's blind spot for her as she merges onto the highway. These small things warm Jennifer. They make up for the fact that, for most of the ride, her two passengers talk exclusively to each other. Jennifer chimes in when she feels she can add something to their conversation, to remind them every so often that she is there. Otherwise she keeps her attention focused on the road, like a good and responsible driver, and tries not to take it personally. Things are good. Great, even. And the fact that yesterday she'd been crowned Mount Washington

High's ugly queen and now she's riding with the cheerleaders to the mall to buy homecoming dresses is still unbelievable.

But it is also a glimpse into the life she could have had if Margo hadn't ditched her back before high school started. And look, was she such a drag? Would it have been that hard to fit Jennifer in? Jennifer knows she could have done it. She could have made it work. Margo could have been honest with her. Did she need new clothes? A new haircut? To lose a few pounds? Whatever it was, Jennifer would have tried. Only Margo never gave her a chance.

But now that Jennifer's gotten one, she plans to prove herself worthy.

As they near the mall, discussion turns to strategy: which shops in what order. Rachel turns in her seat to face her. "So, what kind of dress do you think you want, Jennifer?"

Jennifer shrugs. "I haven't given it much thought. I still can't believe I'm going."

"I bet you'd look great in bright yellow," Dana says.

"Yellow?" Jennifer asks, eyeing Dana in her rearview mirror. She doesn't own anything yellow. And she typically shies away from anything bright. "Are you sure?"

Dana laughs. "Yellow is, like, *the* color right now."

Rachel slips off her sneakers, takes off her ankle socks, and puts her bare feet up on the glove box. They are a little stinky from cheer practice, but it hardly matters, because Rachel's toes cascade like a staircase, in even steps from big toe to pinky, and the nails are polished a perfect cherry red. Jennifer keeps looking at them out of the corner of her eye. They are so perfect, Rachel could be a foot model. *If I had feet like that,* Jennifer thinks to herself, *I'd never wear any shoes but flip-flops.*

"Don't worry, Jennifer," Rachel says. "Just leave everything to us. Dana and I will find you the most beautiful dress in the history of homecoming dresses. Promise."

Jennifer suddenly feels the urge to cry, but she won't allow herself to do it for fear of looking lame. Instead she turns into the mall parking lot and finds a spot right up front, near the glass doors. "That's a good shopping omen," she tells the girls.

They nod like it's true, even though Jennifer just made it up.

The department store dressing room is empty except for the three girls. Rachel and Dana share the large one designated for handicapped people. Jennifer is across from them, and listens to their voices through the slats in her door.

"Ew," Rachel says. "Ew. Ew. Ew. Ew. Ew."

Dana's groans are muffled by the rustling of material. "Yellow never works for me."

Jennifer stands in her underwear, her back to the mirror, and stares at the last dress hanging from the door. She only brought in two others, which now lie discarded on the carpeted floor.

The first, a lavender sheath with a sweetheart neckline, had looked so pretty on the hanger. But it didn't sit right, the seams shifting right and left like a winding country road to accommodate her, as if every part of her body was where it shouldn't be.

The second was a black lace tea-length dress with shimmery peach lining that peeked through. Jennifer felt it was a little old-fashioned, but Rachel and Dana explained that faux vintage was super hot and that Jennifer could definitely pull it off.

It wasn't true. Jennifer couldn't even get the thing on.

She'd known it would be too tight, but Rachel had insisted that she try it anyway, after a salesperson informed them that the sizes on the floor were the only ones in stock. As Dana and

Rachel ricocheted off the round racks like two pinballs selecting dresses for her to try, their criteria shifted from what was cute to what was actually offered in her size. This is why Dana got to try a yellow dress, and Jennifer did not.

Jennifer tried hard to stay positive. Especially because the girls were picking out lots of other things for her, too — new bras that would be more supportive, a pair of zebra-print flats that would go with everything. The mission was no longer about just a homecoming dress. It was a full-on wardrobe intervention.

She said yes to practically everything they threw at her.

But the shopping spree, now in its third hour, is wearing on her. And it annoys her, the lack of sympathy from the girls. They don't understand that it's hard to be her, to be shopping with them.

Like when Dana had pointed out a pair of jeans that Jennifer *had* to try, before darting into another section. Skinny girls can walk by a table full of pants, piled in high stacks, and peel a pair off the top. Easy. Effortless. But not girls like Jennifer. She had to dig to the very bottom of the pile, upending the neat stacks to search for the large sizes. Even then, sometimes they weren't on the table, but hidden in cubbyholes underneath the display. Jennifer got down on her knees, her purse slipping off her shoulder, and rummaged like a pig in a trough for them while Dana called out, "Jennifer! Hurry! You need one of these, too!"

But Jennifer is trying to be a good sport. Even though there is no perfect dress, as they'd promised. And as critical as Rachel and Dana are being about their dresses from their fitting room, Jennifer knows everything looks great on them. They could wear any one of those dresses and be gorgeous. The flaws that they see, no one else would. It is as if Dana and Rachel are inventing them on her behalf, to make her feel better. Except it doesn't. It makes her feel worse. On top of everything, Jennifer is hungry. It is time to go home.

"How are you doing, Jennifer?" Rachel calls out.

"Um, I think I'm done." She doesn't even want to try on the last dress. It seems like too much effort.

"Really?" Dana asks, and Jennifer can't tell if she's genuinely surprised or sympathetic.

"Come on," Rachel says. "You have to show us at least *one* dress."

Jennifer sighs and pulls the last dress off the hanger, probably harder than she should, considering the price. It is cornflower blue cotton taffeta, strapless, with an empire waist that blossoms into a wide skirt. She slips it on over her head and then holds her breath for the zipper at the side. It takes a bit of a fight to get it to the top, but after some pulling, it closes.

The corners of Jennifer's mouth lift. She does a little spin.

"This one's actually not bad," she announces, no one more surprised than herself.

She opens the door. Rachel and Dana sit on two overstuffed chairs beside the three-way mirror. Each has a lap full of discarded dresses. "Did you guys not find anything?"

"Forget us! Look at you!" Rachel says.

"Wait a sec." Dana springs up and tucks the hanger straps down into Jennifer's bodice. "Okay. Now, let us see."

Jennifer steps onto a platform in front of the three large mirrors. "I think I love it," Jennifer says, pulling up her hair in an impromptu twist. She does love it, but she wants the girls to love it, too.

"I think it's perfect," Rachel announces.

Dana nods. "A perfect homecoming dress! And with red shoes, don't you think, Rachel?"

"Yeah! Red heels would be so cute."

Jennifer pops up and down on her toes. She imagines herself in the gymnasium, with her makeup and hair all fixed, dancing with Rachel and Dana and Margo in a circle. Hopefully, someone will take a picture for the yearbook.

At that moment, a salesgirl enters the dressing room to check on them. She's dressed in black from head to toe, her hair in a tight ponytail. She looks at Jennifer and bites her lip. She wants to offer an opinion, Jennifer can tell.

Against her better judgment, Jennifer asks, "What do you think?"

The salesgirl pouts and shakes her head. "I don't like it." She steps forward and gestures with a manicured hand. "See how it cuts your middle here? The bodice is pinching you. And that makes the skirt fall funny on your hips. It should be a straight, smooth line, not jutting out like that."

Jennifer stands motionless as the salesgirl points out her flaws in the three-way mirror, the imperfections duplicated again and again and again to infinity. Her lip begins to quiver, her chin wrinkles and dimples and prunes.

The salesgirl, noticing this, steps back apologetically. "You might have better luck in The Salon on the third floor."

The Salon is where Jennifer's mother shops. The Salon is for fat old ladies. They don't have clothes for teens there. They don't have televisions playing music videos, or bins of bright-colored nail polish at the register. They wouldn't have anything for homecoming.

Rachel gets up from the armchair and pushes all the dresses

she'd been holding into the salesgirl's hands. "Thanks for your help. I'm done with these," she says curtly.

"I — I'm sorry, but she asked —"

"I said, thanks for your help. We're all good in here. So why don't you go and . . . I don't know . . . fold something."

The salesgirl turns and walks out. Jennifer feels the tears coming, and this time she can't stop them. She sits down on the little platform in front of the mirror and cries.

"Jennifer!" Dana says quietly, rushing over. "If you feel good in it, who cares what that dumb salesgirl says?"

"Seriously. People who work retail are, like, the lowest of the low. She hates her life. Clearly."

But Jennifer keeps crying. And through her tears, she watches Dana and Rachel share sad, pitiful looks. They finally get it. They finally understand. One of them rubs her back.

But even worse is the feeling that Margo had been right. She doesn't fit in this life, in this world. She doesn't belong with these girls. She's failed. Forget the dance. Forget everything.

"You seriously look great in the dress, Jennifer," Rachel says. She pulls her hand inside her sweatshirt sleeve and gently dabs Jennifer's tears away.

"Homecoming is going to be amazing," Dana says, kneeling down in front of her. "We're going to have so much fun together."

The *we're* and the *together* is like music. It is an invitation. They want Jennifer to go to the dance with them. *With* them. Like real friends.

She wonders what Margo will say.

After she changes and wipes her face, Jennifer walks up to the register and buys the dress from the bitchy salesgirl. And it feels like a victory. Or at least like something she deserves.

CHAPTER SEVENTEEN

A little before midnight, Candace stands at the lip of her backyard swimming pool. A silvery tarp stretches across the rectangle, pulled taught like the skin of a trampoline. Dead leaves, dropped acorns, and dirt marinate in shallow puddles, the remains of a recent rainstorm.

Her mom's boyfriend, Bill, closed the pool weeks ago, at the end of August, despite Candace's pouting that there were plenty of hot days still to come. She hadn't wanted summer to end. Summer had been entirely too much fun. Her friends had come over nearly every day, depending on whom Candace had been in the mood to invite. There were only four patio chairs to lie out on, and that had been her excuse for being selective. Really, though, Candace liked the power of this musical chairs game, with her stopping the music and her friends scrambling for an open seat. All her friends wanted to be invited, and even if one girl was mad to have been skipped over on a particular day for whatever reason struck Candace, she'd be so happy to be asked the next that she'd forget about the hard feelings. They listened to the radio, shared bottles of coconut oil, passed magazines, rotated themselves in tandem with the sun.

Candace's tanning drove her mom crazy, and it was probably why she'd been so insistent that Bill close it up. Ms. Kincaid would regularly emerge from the patio door veiled by a straw hat with a ridiculously large brim to lecture the girls on the dangers of the sun, show them department store receipts of how much a good wrinkle cream went for these days, warn them that they'd never look as beautiful as they did right now.

Candace would roll her eyes behind her sunglasses and recall how her mom had looked when she was a teenager spending the summers at Whipple Beach, with tan lines that rivaled the swirls of vanilla ice cream in a caramel sundae. If Candace's bikini wasn't wet, she'd even bring out some pictures from the mantel to prove her point.

And then Ms. Kincaid would soften and lower herself to a seat on the edge of Candace's lounge chair. She'd share a couple stories about the boys who'd tried to get their Frisbees to land on her towel, how Candace's grandfather had taken to sleeping on the porch swing to make sure no boys came to steal his daughter away, the catalog work she'd done for a now-defunct department store. Then she'd kiss Candace's forehead and offer vague life advice to the girls, such as "Live like there's no tomorrow."

When Ms. Kincaid would leave, the girls would tell Candace how beautiful her mom had been, and how Candace looked just like her. Candace knew her mom listened from behind the venetian blinds.

This performance occurred every few weeks. Each seeking compliments over applause.

Now Candace peels back a corner of the pool cover. She is pleased to find the water underneath still turquoise and beautiful. But despite her being careful, a bit of the slippery muck slides into the pool and clouds it.

Last year, Candace began to wonder if maybe she'd be tapped to make the list before she graduated. She imagined herself getting mailed an envelope with an anonymous note and the embossing stamp, or perhaps an invitation to join a secret society of girls at the fifty-yard line of the football field at midnight or something dramatic like that. She'd do a great job making the list, because she has the confidence to tell it like it is, to be completely objective evaluating other girls. Not like whoever had made the list this year. Putting her as the ugliest sophomore is clearly a cheap shot from someone jealous of her.

She gingerly dips her toe and the chill bolts through her, shaking her as if she'd been dreaming. She takes a small step back, the sight of her bare legs and torso catching her off guard. Looking back toward the house, she sees her pajamas discarded in a pile next to the patio chair. On the cushion, the pages of her open notebook flutter in the breeze. In the sliding glass door, there's her ghostly reflection, wearing only her bra and underwear, surrounded by the raw colors of autumn and a smoky night sky.

A lump fills her throat.

She'd been online for hours after school. And not one chat window had opened.

No one had said they were sorry that Candace had been on the list.

No one had said it was wrong.

No one had even talked to her at school today.

No one but Horse Hair.

Candace takes a deep breath and leaps toward the water. She jumps too far and her feet hit the pool cover, ripping it free from its tethers and sinking it down with her. When she hits the bottom, a twig pierces the sole of her left foot, and pain momentarily overtakes the squeeze of the bitterly cold water.

She pops back up, breaking the surface with a yelp, and swims for the edge.

The patio door slides open and her mom darts out, all perfect hair and makeup and perfume and clothes. "Candace! Candace!" Halfway to the pool, Ms. Kincaid clips an ottoman and upends it. She stops to check her stockings for a rip.

Candace pulls herself up and sits on the edge, the cement prickling her underwear, the water streaming off of her. She pulls her foot into her lap and squeezes where it's bleeding, hoping to push out whatever punctured her. "Get me a towel, okay?"

Ms. Kincaid stands over her in disbelief. She raises her hands, then lets them drop to her sides. Her silver bracelets jangle. "You've ruined the pool cover! I'm going to have to beg Bill to come and fix this. He'll probably have to drain the water, with the crap you've spilled in. What in god's name were you thinking, Candace?"

Candace looks up at her mom. She wants to tell her about the list, about everything. But it's too embarrassing to try to explain what had happened. Her mom would probably get so worked up over it, she'd go into school and raise hell with Principal Colby. And Candace has already caused enough trouble on that front. She knows the way she acted in Principal Colby's office only made things worse for her, made her look even more pathetic.

So instead Candace snaps, "Are you going to get me a towel or what?"

Ms. Kincaid walks away and picks up Candace's notebook instead. "Are you running Spirit Caravan again this year?"

"Yeah."

"And these are all the girls who want to ride with you?"

Candace knows what her mom is looking at — a column of names stretching down the page. A list of her friends. Girls she thought had cared about her, girls who now celebrated her misfortune.

A list of suspects.

"Who's Horse Hair?"

"Some new girl."

"Sounds . . . cute," Ms. Kincaid says with a chortle.

Candace shakes her head, grabs her things, and says sharply, "Actually, she is."

Horse Hair, who's been transformed overnight into a symbol of beauty and niceness. It had been completely embarrassing how earnest Horse Hair had acted when she'd tried to talk to Candace in the bathroom. Like she was so pious and above it. Like she didn't care about being on the list one bit.

Who knows? Candace thinks. *Maybe she didn't. Maybe she is that weird.*

Candace walks inside the house, dripping water onto the carpet. She heads for the first-floor bathroom, the one adjacent to her mother's bedroom. Candace grabs a towel hanging next to the sink. She is about to dry her face but stops. The towel is smeared and stained like a painter's rag, a rainbow of colored blotches. "Ew, Mom."

Ms. Kincaid huffs and pulls another towel out from under the sink. "Here. This one's clean," she says. It is also stained, but at least it smells like fabric softener.

Candace wipes herself down, careful not to knock anything over. Every inch of the counter is covered by glass bottles and tubes and pots and brushes and sponges.

Her mom doesn't need it. She is a beautiful lady. But she's

hardly ever without it. Candace hates seeing her in bright light. Painted women have a different look to their skin. Fuzzy. The little invisible hairs thickened with powder.

"I brought you this from the studio." Ms. Kincaid digs in one of the tackle boxes full of makeup and produces a tiny palette of gold eye shadow. "Won't this go nicely with your homecoming dress? Oh, Candace. Will you pleeeease let me do your makeup for the dance? You know I can do younger looks, too." Ms. Kincaid works as a makeup artist for the local news, camouflaging high-definition wrinkles.

"Maybe," Candace says. Though at this point, she wonders if she'll go to the dance at all.

Her mom is always pushing a weird green eyeliner, a matte coral lipstick, or fox-fur eyelashes on her. She didn't seem to get that kids in high school didn't go for the overly dramatic, editorial look. For prom, maybe. But certainly not every day. Still, it is great to have someone who can expertly mix Candace's exact shade of foundation for her occasional pimple.

"Why don't you invite the girls over to take pictures before the dance?"

Candace thinks about it. A pre-party. It might help to smooth things over. "Can you get us alcohol?"

"Candace . . ." Ms. Kincaid groans. She'd hooked Candace up a few times for parties over the summer, but had said that was over now that school had started back up.

"Two bottles of rum," Candace pleads. And then, to sweeten the deal, she adds, "I'll let you do my makeup."

"Really?"

"Yup. You can do whatever you want to me. Gold eye shadow, black lipstick —"

"Come on," her mom says. "I would never put black lipstick on you."

"I'm just saying, Mom. You can go wild."

"I don't need to *go wild*," Ms. Kincaid corrects. "A makeup artist's job is to accentuate and highlight your natural beauty. Which you, my darling, have oodles of."

Candace leans forward to hug her, even though she's still all wet. As she does, a bottle of foundation falls into the sink and breaks, sending glugs of thick orange down the drain.

WEDNESDAY

CHAPTER EIGHTEEN

After smacking her alarm, Sarah rolls over in her bed and sniffs her armpit.

She frowns. It's been three days without a shower, and she is not nearly as stinky as she wants to be. Barely smelly, in fact. Which completely blows.

Then again, when her grandma started to have bladder problems, she had absolutely no idea her whole house reeked of piss.

Sarah gets up and checks herself in the mirror. At least she looks disgusting.

The *UGLY* on her forehead is still surprisingly intact, but she doubts it will last until Saturday. Maybe on the night of the dance, she'll retrace it for effect.

The front pieces of her hair are greasy from the roots down to the tips, and no matter how many times she brushes them, they don't fall like normal hair. Instead, they stay separated with grease, like they don't want to touch each other. The back of her hair, where it had been buzzed, is terribly itchy and dry, and though she's never had a problem with dandruff before, white flakes float down and land on her shoulders when she rakes her fingers over her scalp.

Sarah has good skin without even trying, except for the occasional pimple before she gets her period. But today she finds tiny clogged pores dotting her cheeks, hard zits that don't have heads but make her face look pebbled.

The moons of her fingernails are rimmed in black.

The insides of her ears itch.

She gets dressed as quickly as possible. It is definitely a test of will to put these dirty clothes on her dirty body. The neck of Milo's T-shirt is stretched out, the collar sagging precariously low on her chest, like a shirt one size too large for her. The armpits are rimmed in white from the salt residue of dried sweat. Her jeans are no longer tight, but baggy in the ass and the knees, and have a dusty feeling. Her underwear is just straight-up gross, her socks, too — fibers stiff and crusty.

At least it's Wednesday, she tells herself. It's already half over. By the dance, she'd hopefully be as ripe as a homeless person.

On her ride to school, it occurs to Sarah that most of the kids in Mount Washington have probably never even seen a homeless person before. Sheltered little babies.

Milo is at the bench. His sketchbook is open in his lap, and he's hunched over, drawing. Sarah climbs off her bike and walks slowly, quietly over.

She remembers Sunday.

She'd been on his floor, flipping through that sketchbook, checking out his drawings. Milo was an excellent artist, and she really wanted to work with him, maybe on a comic, or just get him to illustrate some of her poems. Milo didn't even know she wrote poems, because her poems were mostly crap that she would die if anyone saw, but there were a few that Sarah might share with him. Maybe.

Most of Milo's sketches were of manga girls. Schoolgirl fantasy types with big chests ready to burst from their uniforms, long shiny hair, puckered lips. Always so vulnerable and demure, so primed to be taken advantage of. It made her uncomfortable, which she knew was ridiculous. It wasn't jealously, exactly. After all, they were cartoons. And it wasn't like she and Milo were girlfriend/boyfriend or anything.

Sarah flipped a page and saw a drawing of a girl. A very real Asian girl. A school picture was taped in the corner of the page for reference. It was the first time Sarah thought that one of Milo's drawings wasn't awesome. It didn't even come close to capturing how pretty this girl was. She wore a pink blouse, her hair falling over one shoulder, a perfect smile, sparkling eyes, a tiny gold *A* pendant draped over her collarbone. She looked like an Asian angel.

"Who's this?"

Milo was sitting on his bed, watching her. "That's Annie."

She'd known Milo had an ex-girlfriend back in West Metro. They'd broken up before he'd moved to Mount Washington, but they were still friends. Every so often, Sarah would see Annie's name on his phone or in his e-mail. He'd talk about her, too. Now, thinking back, it seemed to Sarah like he brought up Annie a lot. Sarah had never seen Annie's picture.

She'd always assumed they looked relatively the same.

Something stormy and panicked grew inside her. It was the feeling of having caught Milo in a lie, or in a disguise that she now saw through. All the times he'd talked about Annie, he never once mentioned that she was beautiful. It made her question everything about Milo, that he'd picked this girl to be with. Maybe, if she hadn't invited him to come and sit on her bench, he would have waited to get adopted by the people she hated, and he would have dated someone like Bridget Honeycutt.

A shadow crossed the page as Milo crawled down from the

bed, leaned forward, and kissed her on the lips. Sarah pulled away, shocked . . . and saw Milo's extremely pleased look. He was happy he'd thrown her for a loop. There was no trace of the shy, timid boy she'd met. No trace of him at all.

Sarah quickly got her bearings. She closed the sketchbook, rocked forward to her knees and kissed Milo hard on the mouth, hoping it might wipe the image of Annie out of her mind.

It didn't.

After that, it was a game of chicken, raising the stakes until there was nowhere else to go. Sarah never backed down. Ever. Milo probably knew as much. Maybe he even used that against her. Maybe he'd known that she'd wanted this to happen all summer long.

But the whole time, she couldn't make sense of how Milo could want to be with her when he'd had a girl like that. It wasn't even hurtful so much as common sense. These opposites didn't attract. That and the embarrassing fact that she'd had her first kiss, her first everything, all in one night, with a boy she suddenly hardly knew.

As she chains up her bike, Milo says, "So Annie says I have to get you a corsage for the homecoming dance."

Sarah lets her bike crash on the ground, and she doesn't bother picking it up. "What did you tell her?" For the first time, she is embarrassed about what she's decided to do. And she feels dirtier than she has all morning.

In a low voice, he says, "I didn't tell her about, you know, the not-showering thing. Only that we were going to the dance together."

148

Sarah shakes her head. She's not sure if that's better or worse. "Milo, I told you I don't want a corsage."

"I know, but Annie said you probably want me to buy you one, even if you tell me you don't."

Sarah is shaking. "Annie doesn't know me. And apparently, neither do you."

"Sarah, I only thought —"

"I don't want a fucking corsage!" she screams at the top of her lungs. Everyone at Freshman Island turns to look.

"Okay! Okay! No corsage!" Milo closes his sketchbook. He takes a deep breath, so deep his shoulders nearly touch his ears. His face is bright red. "Sarah, I need to ask you something. Did I suck? You know . . . in bed?"

Sarah winces. "Oh my god, what?"

"I'm serious. You've barely wanted to look at me for the last few days. I keep thinking it's because I . . . I was disappointing."

Couldn't Milo tell that she'd liked it? Or was he holding her up to someone like Annie? She takes a seat at the other end of the bench, making sure there's some distance between them. "First of all, *ew*, Milo. I am not going to comment on that at all. Ever. Secondly, I've had other things on my mind besides you."

"Then can we talk about that? I mean, am I such a dick that you can't talk to me about what you're feeling? Like I can't understand how hurtful it is to have people call you ugly?"

Sarah laughs. What she wants to say is, *Oh! Why? Did Annie have that problem?* She doesn't say it. She laughs and tries to make Milo feel stupid so he'll stop talking.

"You know I like you. Right, Sarah?"

The words are nice to hear, of course. But there's too much going on for Sarah to feel the warmth. It's already so cold out.

If she and Milo were together, she'd always be wondering. She'd compare herself to Annie, and worry that he'd leave her for someone better if he got the chance. "Don't. Just don't."

"So you regret . . . *you know* . . . with me?" He looks physically pained.

"I regret this whole conversation, Milo. I mean, I'm not looking to have a big talk-show moment with you on our couch."

"I'm trying to be there for you."

"What do you want me to do? Cry in your arms?"

"I want you to talk to me like we're friends."

Sarah lets her head drop into her hands. "So now we're friends? Okay. Then I don't have to worry about you trying to hold my hand anymore?"

Milo's mouth gets thin and tight. "No."

"Look, don't get all crybaby about it. I'm going to buy my homecoming ticket. If you still want to come with me, you can. If not, whatever. That's fine, too. Do what you want."

Milo fishes in his pocket. "I'm going with you. I haven't changed my mind." He hands her his money.

Sarah feels something tucked into the folded bill. A small rectangle.

A piece of gum.

Milo drops his head. "Don't be pissed. Your breath kind of stinks, Sarah. And I don't want anyone to say something that might hurt your feelings."

Sarah takes the gum and throws it back at him. "Gee, thanks, Milo."

It would be so much easier, she thinks, if she had never become friends with him at all.

She marches into school. Near the main office, there's a

table manned by two senior girls selling dance tickets. They both have little stickers on their chests that say VOTE QUEEN JENNIFER.

Jennifer Briggis. For homecoming queen? Are they fucking serious?

If anything, this makes Sarah even more determined to see her anarchy through to the end. Jennifer is proof positive that this sick tradition of the list needs to be subverted and fucked up from the inside out. Jennifer is like a prisoner of war, passed out from having been beaten down so terribly after all these years. Sarah would be the smelling salts.

She wants to puke all over the girls at the table. Instead she says, "Gee. That's one hell of an apology."

One girl, the one making up the stickers, looks up, confused. "What do you mean?"

"I mean the whole 'Vote Queen Jennifer' thing! It's nice. You know, after calling her an ugly piece of shit for four years." She holds out her money. "Two tickets."

The girls share unsure looks with each other. Neither one takes Sarah's money.

Sarah leans forward, opens the cash box, and shoves her money inside. Then she grabs two tickets. "See you both on the dance floor!"

As she walks away, she hears one of the girls hiss, "God, she smells disgusting!"

Sarah smiles as she walks away, the first time today. She'll smell up the entire gym on Saturday night. She'll shake her stench all over the place. The pretty girls in their pretty dresses will have to sit on the bleachers, pinching their noses. She'll make sure she's the only one having a great time.

CHAPTER NINETEEN

argo arrives at school with ten dollars for her dance ticket and a picture of the homecoming dress she ordered last night on the Internet. She hopes Rachel and Dana like it. She hopes that it doesn't clash too badly with whatever dresses they bought.

It is emerald green, short, sleeveless, and fitted, with a trail of little fabric-covered buttons running from the collar down to the small of her back. It is maybe a bit sophisticated for homecoming, but Margo, who bought it while balancing a dinner plate of spaghetti on her lap at the computer desk, figured that was probably a good thing. She was a senior now, a month away from turning eighteen. Plus, she planned to wear the dress again, maybe to a sorority function if she decided to pledge next year. She paid a fortune for overnight shipping, almost as much as the dress itself, but it was more than worth it, as the dress was pretty enough to get her excited about going to the dance again. She'd wear her hair down, probably. And her black peep-toe heels, the velvet ones she found on sale after last Christmas. It would be the first chance she'd had to wear them.

She felt back to her old self, for a while anyway.

When she didn't hear from Dana or Rachel after their trip to the mall, Margo called Vines on Vine florist shop and ordered three wrist corsages, clusters of baby red roses with lemon leaves. Maureen had done the same thing for her friends last year. The flowers would be an apology to her friends for acting weird about Jennifer ever since the list came out.

She is still a little paranoid about what Jennifer may have said about her during the shopping trip, but Margo tells herself not to be. What happened that summer was old news, and in all likelihood, Jennifer wouldn't want to bring it up. It wouldn't make either of them look good.

Dana and Rachel sit at a desk near the main office, selling homecoming dance tickets out of a metal cash box. There's already a line of people waiting, and Margo takes her place at the end of it. A few people promise Margo that they'll be voting for her for homecoming queen. They show her that they've already written her name on the ballot, which is printed on the back of the ticket stub. Margo politely thanks them. She makes sure the people who should know about her party on Friday night do.

"One ticket, please," Margo says with her best smile when she reaches the front of the line. When she hands over her money, she notices that both Dana and Rachel are wearing HELLO MY NAME IS labels. In the white space they've written *Vote Queen Jennifer.* There's a stack of them on the desk, and Dana's making up more with a pink marker.

"'Queen Jennifer'?" Margo asks, her voice dripping with disbelief.

Dana looks down and starts working on another sticker. Rachel sighs and says, "Don't take this personally, Margo."

"My two best friends are campaigning against me. And campaigning for a girl they know I don't like. I'd say that's about as personal as it gets."

"Look, if you had come shopping with us last night, you'd understand."

"It was horrible," Dana says solemnly, while dotting the *i* in *Jennifer* with a star. "Like, beyond horrible. It makes me want to cry just thinking about it."

"I mean, she wasn't even going to come to homecoming!" Rachel adds. "Four years, and the girl has never been to one single school dance. Jennifer needs this, Margo." Rachel hands her a ticket and a VOTE QUEEN JENNIFER sticker. "Way more than you do."

Margo slides the homecoming ticket in the back pocket of her jeans along with the picture of her homecoming dress. The sticker she holds in her hand.

It's obvious to Margo what she should do. Slap the thing on her chest and be a good sport. That would certainly put an end to the tension between her and her friends. People would think she was a good person. No one could think badly of her, not even Jennifer.

But instead, she sets the sticker back onto Dana's pile. Her palm sweat has smeared the ink.

"I can't," she says.

Rachel leans back in her chair. "You're not serious."

"Margo, come on," Dana says. "Why are you acting like this?"

An itch crawls through Margo. The students waiting behind her impatiently shift their weight, and the whole hallway comes suddenly off balance. "I'm not sure it's a good idea. You know, people could think you're making fun —"

"Fine," Rachel says and waves Margo away with a flick of her hand. "Whatever you want."

"Rachel, let me just —"

"No, really. I guess I figured you'd want to clear your

conscience more than anyone. But maybe you don't feel you have anything to be sorry for."

It wasn't like that. Margo knows there are things she should feel sorry for. But severing ties with Jennifer had been difficult enough the first time around. She was not ready to open up that door again, even a crack. And she definitely didn't feel the need to concede the homecoming crown as penance. After all, Margo wasn't the only one to blame. Jennifer was as much a part of the friendship ending as she'd been.

Margo wants to defend herself. She wants to explain. But the sharp stares from her friends make her realize that anything she might say about Jennifer would be taken the wrong way. It wouldn't be a defense; it would be Margo kicking the ugly girl while she's down. So she backs away from the table and walks away without saying another word.

It seems like everyone she passes has on a VOTE QUEEN JENNIFER sticker. Those kids check her chest, expecting to see one, too. And when they don't find it, their expressions quickly change. They duck their heads and whisper to each other. About Margo, obviously.

Margo had wondered about this last year, but now she knows for sure. Being the prettiest senior on the list isn't always a blessing. Sometimes it's a curse.

By the time Maureen graduated, things had definitely gotten weird. There'd been so many fights with her longtime friends, too many to count. Maureen bailed on the senior trip to Whipple Beach, even though their parents had already paid for her hotel room. She'd dumped her boyfriend, Wayne, right before prom for no good reason — Wayne who was hot and whom she'd dated for two years and lost her virginity to (according to a love letter Margo had found in Maureen's underwear drawer). None of Maureen's friends showed up to her graduation party. Maureen got drunk and passed out in a pool chair in front of their grandparents, waking up every so often to burp.

It felt reckless to Margo, as she watched her sister systematically dismantle everything she cared about. The end of high school was about holding on, but Maureen wanted to let it go.

Maureen ended up selecting a college that was far away from Mount Washington. Margo had wanted to help her sister pack, but by then the two sisters were not getting along so well, so she just tried to stay out of Maureen's way. There was always tension between them, tension Margo could only interpret as hatred. At Maureen's good-bye dinner, before her mother flew with Maureen out to her college on the other side of the country, Maureen didn't look at Margo once.

It was almost a relief to see her go.

After Maureen left, Margo went into her sister's room. The pictures of Maureen's friends, the ones that had once covered an entire wall, had been stuffed in the wastebasket.

Margo sat on the floor, carefully unsticking the tape and flattening the ones that'd been bent. Some were of homecoming — Maureen, her tiara holding back waves of her brown hair, dancing with Wayne.

It was hard to tell, because of how badly the picture had been crumpled. One fold went straight down Maureen's face. But from what Margo could see, her sister had never looked so happy.

◎ ◎ ◎

On her way to homeroom, Margo spots Principal Colby. She's watching the students pass though the hallway, her eyes darting about.

What will Principal Colby think of this "Vote Queen Jennifer" charade? Either Margo participates, and she can be looked down upon. Or Margo doesn't, and she'll be viewed as even more suspicious.

She doubles back the way she's just come, avoiding Principal Colby altogether.

CHAPTER TWENTY

The cramps are worse than the ones that come with her period.

Bridget presses her lips together and concentrates on the jagged graffiti scratched into the almond paint on the bathroom door. She's in the girls' gym locker room on the toilet. Her body is pitched forward, her elbows pressing into her bare thighs, her chin in her hands. A half-empty water bottle stands on the floor between her sneakers, the liquid inside oily and separated.

It is not a cleanse. It is a magic potion.

The need to go has hit at various times all morning, growing more and more pressing. This is the third time during gym class alone, and the urge was so intense that Bridget had to sprint off the volleyball court in the middle of a play, leaving her side down a setter. The cramps made it hard to walk, so she hobbled, her fingers pressing into her sides. She barely got her shorts down in time.

If only she were home, able to go in private. Maybe with a magazine or book to take her mind off the pain. Oh, god. What if one of her teachers decided not to give her the bathroom pass? She worries about the cramping, too. It doesn't feel right. Like appendicitis or something.

No. It is nothing to worry about. The cleanse instructions had mentioned severe cramping as a possible side effect. It also said that she'd be crazy for food. Yesterday, it was madness how badly she wanted to eat. Not a craving for anything specific, just food in general. Way worse than the normal days. But the instructions promised that, if she could stick with it, if she could stand up to that voice inside her telling her to eat, she'd plateau and the hunger would disappear. And it has, pretty much.

She needs to trust the process.

Another flash of lightning strikes her abdomen. Splashing sounds bounce off the porcelain bowl. Each time, Bridget is sure that there can't be anything left inside her. But she is always wrong.

A distant whistle trills through the cinder-block walls. A few seconds later, the locker-room door swings open and the girls dash in to get changed before next period. Bridget quickly stands and looks down at the muddy water. As disgusting as the aftermath is, a strange sense of pride comes as she flushes away what had been clogging her, watching the toilet refresh itself with clear, cold water. She feels lighter, almost buoyant, despite her stomach being an overfilled water balloon.

Isn't it nice, never feeling hungry?

It is. Honestly.

After washing her hands, Bridget heads to her locker to change. Most of her friends are already back in their school clothes and have lined up along the rectangular mirror that runs the length of the locker room. They talk straight into the mirror, their confessions bouncing cruelly back in their faces.

One girl groans. "I swear, I have the most disgusting skin in the whole school."

Another girl pushes the first girl playfully. "Are you kidding? Your skin is beautiful! You don't have any blackheads." This girl leans in close, like she's about to sniff the mirror. "My entire nose is covered in blackheads."

"Shut up! Your nose is perfect. I'm begging my parents for a nose job for Christmas. Seriously. I don't even want a car."

"If you went in for a nose job, the plastic surgeon would laugh you out of his office. But he'd probably write an academic paper on me. I mean, do you know of any other junior in the universe who has wrinkles this bad?" The girl takes her hair and yanks it up toward the ceiling, pulling the skin on her face tight. Bridget can see the ridges of her skull and blue veins.

The last girl snarls at the mirror, peeling her lips back as far as they can go, baring wet flesh the color of chewed cinnamon gum. "I'd rather have your invisible wrinkles than my crooked teeth. I don't think I'll ever forgive my parents for not getting me braces. It's, like, child abuse."

Bridget pulls her white sweater over her head. She does it slowly, hiding in the woolly softness for a few seconds. Her friends always one-up each other with invented flaws, seeing who can top the next with phony self-hatred.

But she can top them all.

She grabs her brush and heads to the mirror. "You guys are *all* crazy," she says, locking eyes with herself. "I'm the ugliest one here by far."

She'd said this sort of thing before, of course. It was her go-to put-down, because it didn't leave out any of her flaws. It covered absolutely everything. And she means it. Bridget has known these girls since kindergarten. She's grown up with them. Watched them trade boyfriends, try new hairstyles, attempt smoking, get drunk on whatever liquor they could get their hands on, choreograph dances to stupid pop songs. They're practically women now. She thinks they're all beautiful. She's the one who doesn't fit.

Bridget lets her hair down from a ponytail and runs her comb through. Static sparkles like glitter in the black strands. She notices that the locker room has gone quiet. She turns and sees her friends staring at her.

"Oh, shut up, Bridget," one of the girls says with a heavy sigh.

"Seriously," someone else snarks.

"What?" Bridget says, a nervous buzz in her chest.

A collective eye roll spins in her direction.

"Right. You're the ugliest."

"Do you honestly expect us to believe you?"

Bridget is suddenly unsteady. This is a play that they've acted in a hundred times before, and now she suddenly can't remember the words to her part.

"I . . . I . . ." Bridget trails off. She has thought about telling her friends. Sharing with them the strange things that had happened to her this summer. She didn't because she didn't want them to worry. To think she was broken inside. She didn't want them to panic. It was why she had chosen not to invite any of them down for the summer. There would have been too much explaining to do. And anyway, she had been doing better.

"Everyone's happy you made the list, but —"

"We'd all *kill* to be you, Bridget."

"It's kind of rude. You know. Because we've actually got things to complain about. You, well . . . everyone knows you're pretty. It's been, like, certified."

Another cramp swings through Bridget as the bell rings. Her friends walk out together to lunch, and Bridget ducks back to the bathroom stall.

She's about to undo her jeans when she notices that this urge is different. It is another sort of squeeze.

The cleanse rises up in her throat.

The sensation shocks her. Bridget has never, ever vomited. Counted calories, counted bites, counted swallows. But that's it. And yet, the urge is twisting in on her. She feels the toxins bubbling up inside. Like it isn't even her choice anymore.

She backs out of the stall. She reaches for her water bottle, but thinks better of it and cups faucet water to her lips instead. It is not cold. Just lukewarm and tasting the tiniest bit like rust.

Next period is lunch.

Bridget goes to the library. On the way, she dumps the cleanse out in the water fountain. The bottle stinks, and Bridget can't imagine the smell ever washing out, so she tosses that, too. She is not drinking it anymore. If there's nothing inside her, she won't throw up. And though her logic is terribly blurry, she knows that's a line she doesn't want to cross.

CHAPTER TWENTY-ONE

At lunch, Lauren and her new friends sit at the sunniest lunch table in the cafeteria and make their own plans for the Spirit Caravan.

The first half of the period is spent excitedly debating how to diplomatically proceed with the sharing of decorating ideas. They choose going in a circle over hand raising so everyone will be given the chance to pitch an idea without anyone having the responsibility to choose who gets to speak in what order. Someone makes the point that no ideas should be shot down in this initial brainstorming, that everyone's input is welcome and valued. No suggestions would be called stupid or dumb or retarded.

Nothing would be like it had been when Candace was around.

For the first time, Lauren wonders if Candace might be as terrible as the girls had said. They all seem to be blossoming now that they're out of Candace's shadow. It is a feeling Lauren completely understands. The liberation. The autonomy. She used to feel guilty about coming to school, being away from her mother, wanting her own life. But no longer. These girls, her new friends, inspire her.

And it is just so exciting to witness this new burgeoning utopia being forged. Someone produces Candace's plans for the Spirit Caravan, and when she tears it up, all the girls cheer. It reminds her of the early revolutionaries who banded together to end Britain's tyrannical rule.

"I can be the secretary. I'll write down everything in my notebook," Lauren happily volunteers. "That way, we won't lose anyone's good ideas."

She has already made the decision that she will not participate in the brainstorming. It feels too early to start throwing out her opinions and thoughts about things she doesn't really know, experiences she's never had. She's just so glad to be here, to be welcome at this table.

Lauren readies her pencil on a fresh page.

And waits.

But though there was so much to discuss about how things should go, the actual ideas of what to do for Spirit Caravan don't flow nearly as freely.

After a few quiet seconds, one girl sighs and says, "I seriously don't care what we do, so long as our idea is better than what Candace wanted us to do."

Lauren doesn't want the girls to get discouraged. On the back of her fresh page, the grooves of her pen marks push up, like little ridges. She flips back to what she'd written last period.

"Um, I made a few sketches during English, since I've read *Ethan Frome* like fifteen times." The girls curl around her. Lauren's sketch isn't too detailed, so she explains it. "Mount Washington's mascot is the Mountaineer, right? So what if we made cardboard mountains along the sides of the car? Like we're mountain climbers?"

"Oh my god, I love it," someone says.

"We can use my dad's pickup truck," another volunteers. "That way we can all fit!"

Lauren adds, "And we can wear flannel shirts and have walking sticks and rope and stuff."

"Lauren! These are great ideas!"

"I can't believe we were just going to use shaving cream and streamers. This is . . . a concept!"

"Hey, Lauren. You have to come with us after school and help us buy supplies."

Lauren smiles until she remembers. "I get picked up right after school. But I can help you make up a list of —"

"Call your mom and tell her you need to stay late," one girl says. "Here. Use my cell." She glances over both her shoulders for the cafeteria monitors. "Just, like, don't be obvious about it."

Lauren dials the house. Luckily, she gets voice mail. "Hi, Mommy. It's me. Don't worry about picking me up today. I've got a school project I need to stay late for. I'll walk home when I'm done. Okay? Thanks, Mommy. See you later. Love you."

Lauren hangs up the cell phone and hands it back to its owner. That wasn't so hard.

And then, the cell phone buzzes to life. The girl checks the screen. "Lauren, I think it's your *mommy*." A couple of the other girls snicker.

Lauren wrings her hands. "Um. Let her leave a message."

"Okay."

It is maybe a minute later that the phone buzzes again.

"I'm so sorry," Lauren says. "She's a little crazy since I started school."

Someone looks up and says, "Shhh. Here comes Candace."

Lauren watches Candace walk up to the table. None of the girls make room for her. This makes Lauren feel uncomfortable, as if Lauren is in Candace's seat. Lauren is about to get up, but one of the girls puts a hand on her lap underneath the table, silently telling her to stay put. Candace drops into a seat on the periphery.

"You guys working on the Spirit Caravan?"

"Yup."

"How's it going?"

None of the girls answer her, so Lauren turns her notebook around so Candace can see it. "Good. Do you want to see the plans?"

"No," Candace says flatly before flipping her hair off her shoulder, but Lauren sees her eyes linger a bit on the notebook. "I can't make the Spirit Caravan this year. I'm going to be busy setting up . . . which is actually why I came by." Candace sighs a breezy, apathetic sigh. "I'm throwing a party on Saturday night, before the dance. Everyone can come over to my house and take pictures together. My mom's getting me a couple bottles of rum, and there'll be food and stuff."

Lauren perks up at this, but the other girls don't seem impressed.

"Cool," one of them says, and pushes her food around with her fork.

"Yeah, maybe," another girl says.

The corners of Candace's smile sink. "Um, alright," she says, backing up slowly. "Well, I hope you guys can make it."

As soon as Candace is out of sight, the girls at the table bow their heads and begin a whispered conference.

"What does Candace think? That a party is going to make us like her again?"

"Please. We're already going to Andrew's house after the dance. It's not like we need her to get us booze like last summer."

"Maybe now Candace will realize that you can't treat people like crap. There are consequences."

"Candace has been a bitch for practically her whole life. She's never going to change. She's always going to think she's better than us."

Lauren goes back to her notebook. It is clear to her that Candace's invitation was a peace offering to try to smooth things over. But the hurt Candace caused these girls obviously runs deep. Deeper, apparently, than a party can fix.

One of the girls presses her lips together, deep in thought. And then she says, "But . . . it *could* be cool to have a buzz at the dance. It might make it more fun."

"Hey! We could go to Candace's house for the rum, but, like, not have any fun."

"That's true," another girl says, nodding.

Lauren bites her lip. She doesn't like the idea of going to Candace's party just for the free alcohol. But then again, maybe the girls are starting to see that Candace is sorry. Maybe they need to be in a room together to hash things out. Maybe at her party, Candace will offer up a better, more heartfelt apology.

One of the girls folds her arms decidedly. "Well, if Lauren's not going to Candace's party, I'm not going."

"Me, either," another girl chimes in. The rest nod their heads.

It amazes Lauren to see the girls, her new friends, rally around her. Candace was wrong. This isn't only about Lauren being pretty. They like her. Really.

The girl who lent Lauren her cell phone dips her head below the cafeteria table and checks her voice mail. "Um, Lauren?" she says. "Your mom said to tell you she got the job."

Lauren brightens. "Yay! Do you know what this means? We're staying in Mount Washington!" She squeaks with excitement. The girls smile politely, though they seem maybe a bit embarrassed. Lauren claps her hand over her mouth. "Sorry. I'm just so happy," she says with a nervous laugh.

The girl holding her phone looks a bit confused. "Oh. Okay," she says. "That's good. 'Cause your mom sounded kinda bummed."

CHAPTER TWENTY-TWO

The sixth-period bell rings. Abby waves good-bye as Lisa bolts from their lab desk and disappears into the hallway. Lisa's next class is on the opposite side of the school, and she has to sprint out of Earth Science to make it on time. Their arrangement is that Lisa does most of the actual lab experiments and calculations, and Abby records the results and takes care of cleaning up the work space. It's an excellent deal, in Abby's opinion. Abby's next class is gym, so she takes her time rolling up their relief map and returning the rock samples to the cabinet, because she hates gym almost as much as Earth Science.

She is on her way out the classroom door when her teacher, Mr. Timmet, raises his pencil in the air.

"Abby?"

She stops just past the doorway and turns to face his desk, careful to keep her body in the hallway. "Yeah, Mr. Timmet?"

"I'm afraid we have a small problem." After beckoning her closer, he shuffles papers around his desk and avoids eye contact. "Between your first two quiz grades and Monday's incomplete worksheet, you're not doing very well in my class."

Crap. Monday's worksheet. With all the excitement of being named on the list, Abby had forgotten to copy the answers down from Lisa.

"Abby, I know it seems like we've only just started back in school, but the marking period's nearly half over," he continues, producing a rectangle of light blue card stock. A progress report. "Please have one of your parents sign this before the end of the week."

Abby shoves her hands in the pockets of her jeans, down to the linty seams. "But I'm trying, Mr. Timmet. I am." She tries to sound sweetly desperate and vulnerable. Teachers like Mr. Timmet, who think they're still young, who think that their students might find them cute, respond to that sort of thing. "And I'm sorry about Monday's worksheet. Something exciting happened that morning and I . . ." Abby pauses, hopeful that a glimmer of knowing about the list would register on Mr. Timmet's face. Or, at the very least, sympathy. "Anyway, I seriously *meant* to do it. Really."

Mr. Timmet sets his glasses on top of his head and rubs at his eyes. "Like I said, Abby, this is about more than Monday's worksheet. I'm glad you're trying, and I want you to know that it's not too late to turn your grade around. Remember, we've got a big test next week, and a good score could bring your average back up to passing. But I still have to let your parents know that you're currently failing my class."

Abby's bones go soft. Failing? Already?

She'd started with such high hopes. That high school would be different from eighth grade, when she'd scrambled and pleaded and made all sorts of deals with her teachers to do extra credit and make-up exams to keep her from getting left back.

This year, Abby actually tried to pay attention from the very start. She took notes, even on the first day. She wrote down everything Mr. Timmet said in her notebook as neatly as she could.

And for a while, Abby did feel like she was getting it. Understanding the concepts of natural disasters and the craziness going on inside the Earth's core. But then, as the days passed, his lessons changed from learning the names of rocks to hieroglyphic equations. Now she had no idea what was going on.

"If my parents see this progress report, they're going to kill me. Please, please, pleeeease, can't we work something out? I'll make up any homework I've missed. And I'll come every day for detention until I bring my grade up."

Mr. Timmet sets the progress report on the very edge of his desk, just shy of teetering to the floor. "I'm obligated to do this, Abby. It's nothing personal."

Mr. Timmet was Fern's favorite teacher. Abby can imagine Fern staring at Mr. Timmet from her desk in the front row, counting the tiny pinstripes on his shirt. His watch is the kind you could wear underwater. Practical. His wire-rimmed glasses, unlike the other teachers who wear them, are never smudged or dirty. He made lots of corny science jokes in class, stuff that the smart kids laughed at. She could see why Fern liked him so much. But all those reasons annoyed her.

"Mr. Timmet, I'm begging you. Could you at least wait until after next week's test? The homecoming dance is Saturday night, and my parents will probably ground me, and . . ." Abby lets herself trail off as Mr. Timmet turns to his computer. Obviously he doesn't care about her or the homecoming dance. Abby has never had the kind of relationship Fern does with teachers. They love it when Fern stops back in their classrooms, talks to them about the things going on in her real life.

When he realizes that she's stopped pleading her case, Mr. Timmet looks back at her. Abby thinks he seems a little nervous. Or maybe just regretful that this is becoming so awkward.

"I'm afraid this is nonnegotiable," he says.

The weight of Abby's books increases tenfold. She squeezes them tight in her arms and her eyes fill with tears. "But I'll do better," she whispers. "I promise."

"I would like nothing more than to see that, Abby. You know, you should ask your sister to tutor you. Fern had no trouble with this stuff. She's a very smart girl."

Abby finally snatches the progress report off of Mr. Timmet's desk. She does it so fast, a bunch of his other papers flutter onto the floor. "Right," she mutters on her way out.

If there is one thing Abby *does* know, it's that.

All through the crab soccer game in gym, Abby thinks over her options. If she gives the progress report to her parents, she'll definitely be grounded, and there's an extremely good chance that they'd forbid her to go to the homecoming dance. If she doesn't get it signed by Friday, Mr. Timmet will probably call home, and then she'll also be forbidden to go to the dance. All the great attention she'd gotten from the list, the invite to Andrew's party, will be wasted.

It is pretty much a lose/lose situation.

Abby sits on her bed. She doesn't want to do her homework or watch the talk show flashing on the small television atop her cluttered dresser.

Across the room, Fern is hunched over her desk in the valley between mountains of books piled high on either side, the reading lamp picking up the dust in the air. Abby watches Fern's pencil fly so fast, so confidently across her notebook.

Because both her parents needed home offices for their work, Fern and Abby have to share a bedroom. It is set up to be a mirror image, the same furniture and accessories pinned to each wall. A bed, a desk, a dresser, a night table. But beyond the skeleton, that simple architecture and layout, each side is vastly different from the other.

The walls that cuddle Abby's bed are taped over with photos, glossy magazine shots of models and boy actors, and fun trinkets from different adventures she's had with her friends, like a strip of red paper tickets from the Skee-Ball machine at the pier arcade when she'd gone to visit Lisa at her family's beach house. The floor is covered with her dirty clothes.

Fern's side is the after shot of a cleaning demonstration. Everything is neat and arranged by right angles. Her clothes are hung up and put away. A tangle of academic ribbons hangs from the left bedpost. An inspirational poster of a beach at sunrise is taped to her ceiling. THERE IS NO SUBSTITUTE FOR HARD WORK, it says. There are only white pushpins stuck in her corkboard, pinning up a monthly calendar where assignments, tests, and debate competitions have been marked in perfect penmanship.

If Abby had a sister like Bridget, they'd be able to talk this over and figure out a plan. At the very least, Bridget would step in and try to get her parents not to make a huge deal about the progress report, find an angle to help convince their parents to let her go to the dance.

Fern would never help her that way. Never ever.

Abby feels around for her remote and inches her television volume up slowly, click by click, until the applause from the audience sounds like thunder.

Fern, scribbling away furiously, pauses a moment. "Why don't you go watch that in the den, Abby?" she asks, not politely.

"Oh, so you're talking to me now?" Abby mumbles.

"What?"

Abby mutes the television. "I know you're mad at me about the list." There. She's said it.

Fern lets go of her pencil and it falls onto her notebook. "I'm not mad at you for the list," she says slowly, as if Abby is an idiot. "But I don't know what you expect me to say about it."

"Um, I don't know. How about . . . *congratulations?*"

Fern spins around in her desk chair. "Are you serious?"

"Maybe," Abby mutters, suddenly wishing she hadn't said anything. "You shouldn't blame me. It just happened. It wasn't my fault."

"Of course it's not your fault. I know how the list works. But you don't have to parade around school acting so proud about it."

"You mean the way *you* act whenever you make honor roll?"

Fern snorts. "That's different, Abby."

"How? Even though I never get on honor roll, I'm still happy for you."

"Because getting on honor roll is an actual accomplishment. It's a direct reflection of the hard work and effort I've put in. You're not going to put the fact that you are the prettiest girl in your freshmen class on your applications for college, are you?"

Fern starts laughing at her joke, and Abby wants to crawl inside herself. "Whatever."

"Why don't you concentrate on doing your homework instead of watching television? Or spending all your free time looking at stupid dresses online," Fern says before spinning her desk chair back around to her homework. "Why don't you work on something that matters? Try to win a prize that can actually help you in life?"

"They aren't stupid dresses, Fern. And maybe you think being on the list is stupid, too, but it isn't. It's an honor."

Fern picks up her pencil. But instead of going back to her homework, she stares at the wall. "The list isn't changing your life, Abby. I'm not trying to be mean, but I'm also not going to fall at your feet over something so meaningless. Now, if you ever make honor roll, I'll be the first one to congratulate you. I'll tie balloons to your bed."

Abby doesn't want to cry, but she feels like it's inevitable. Luckily, her cell phone rings. Without saying another word to Fern, she grabs it and walks out of their bedroom. And she unmutes the television, just to be a snot.

"Hey, Lisa." Abby presses her back up against the wall, and the frames of family photos dig into her spine. She hears Fern let out a deep sigh as she rises up from her desk chair to shut off Abby's television.

"You sound upset," Lisa says. "What's wrong?"

Abby bites her lip. She wants to tell Lisa about the progress report and Mr. Timmet, but she's too embarrassed. So instead she says, "It's my sister," kind of loud, and peeks inside her room. Fern is back at work, leaning over her books, and Abby shoots daggers into her. "Honestly, she's been horrible to me ever since the list came out."

Lisa lowers her voice. "I don't want to start trouble or anything, but look . . . Fern is just jealous of you. You know that, right?"

Abby huffs. "No, she's not."

"Yes she is, dummy! Okay, sure. She gets better grades than you do. But guess what? I bet Fern would give up all her perfect report cards for your DNA. I mean, you're soooo much prettier than her."

A part of Abby thinks that herself, somewhere deep down inside. It was the last place her mind went when she fought with Fern. Abby always felt dirty about that, like it was a dark and terrible secret, and she was an awful person for ever thinking it.

Hearing Lisa say it makes her feel better.

Kind of.

CHAPTER TWENTY-THREE

After practice, Danielle steps out from the steamy pool showers and clicks open her gym locker. The inside of the cube is lit yellow-y green. She's received a text from Andrew.

Meet me @ the pool entrance after yr practice

Last night, after getting home from the mall, she'd called Andrew and they'd spent another night talking on the phone until dawn. She told him about her homecoming dress — a pale pink dress with sheer cap sleeves. It was nothing like what she'd ever worn before, but it was definitely girlie and looked good on her, despite the fact that the sleeves were a bit snug around her shoulder muscles. No one was more stunned by the choice than her mother, who claimed to the saleswoman that she hadn't seen Danielle that dressed up since her first Communion.

Though the list never came up once, a part of Danielle wondered what Andrew was feeling about it, what his friends were saying about her. She could have asked him, but she didn't want to risk ruining their good conversation.

But today is another story. Again Andrew avoided her during school, and Danielle is starting to feel paranoid. Is Andrew embarrassed to be seen with her? And his text seems a little curt. Is he planning to break up with her today?

Her hair drips water onto the phone screen. She wipes it with her towel and sees that she'd missed something.

:)

Danielle lets out a breath she didn't know she was holding. If Andrew wanted to break up with her, he wouldn't have put the smiley. All the doubts she'd been feeling drift away like a cloud passing the sun. She warms up. She can't wait to see her boyfriend.

Hope squeezes past Danielle to get to her locker. "Do you want to come over for dinner tonight? We're having tacos. And I want to show you my homecoming outfit. I know most girls are wearing dresses, but I was thinking I'd wear jeans and a cute shirt or something. I don't know. I never feel comfortable in dresses. I can't dance in a dress."

Danielle had felt the same way, but she'd bought a dress anyhow because she knew anything less would only invoke her new nickname. "I can't tonight," Danielle says. "I'm meeting Andrew."

"Oh." Hope sounds surprised. "Is everything okay with you guys?"

"Of course everything's okay," Danielle says. "Why wouldn't it be?" She can feel Hope watching her as she wrings the water out from her hair.

"Well . . . because you said Andrew's been acting kind of weird since the list came out. Distant."

Danielle had indeed confessed that feeling to Hope in a weak moment during study hall, but now she regrets having said anything. "It's not that he's acting weird," she tries to clarify. "We just haven't talked much about it, that's all."

"Do you think he'll ever want to? You know, talk about it?"

"I hope not." Danielle slides on her deodorant. It is vanilla-scented and will hopefully mask the smell of chlorine on her skin. No matter how hard she scrubs in the shower, it always lingers on her. "I don't want to have a big awkward conversation with him." She doesn't particularly want to have this conversation, either. So instead of running a comb through her hair and putting on a little makeup, Danielle shoves her stuff into her book bag in a hurry.

Hope sits down on the bench. "It wouldn't have to be a big awkward conversation, Danielle. But he should say *something*. Like . . . that it doesn't matter to him. That he thinks you are beautiful no matter what anyone else says."

"Can you please stop?" Danielle snaps. She hopes none of the other girls in the locker room have overheard these embarrassing attempts to pump her up. She turns her back to Hope and closes her eyes for a second, listening to the waves of murmured conversations, the white noise of hair dryers. Andrew hadn't said anything like that to her. Hearing those things would almost make it worse. As if she were a pathetic weakling who needed him to make her feel good about herself.

"Sorry," Hope says. "I just think you deserve the best."

"I know." And Danielle does know. But she doesn't stop packing up her things. "I'll call you later."

As Danielle heads out of the locker room, she makes a promise to herself, then and there, never to talk about what went on between her and Andrew again. Hope will only bring it up later, out of context, completely misinterpreted. And while Danielle doesn't want Hope thinking badly of her boyfriend, the truth is that Hope doesn't understand. She wasn't with them during the summer. She's never had a boyfriend. Andrew is simply a person who's come between her and her best friend.

Danielle enters the bathroom near her locker and fixes herself up there. As she descends the staircase, she sees Andrew with his friends out the window. She leans against the banister and watches the guys goof around for a minute. Andrew looks much younger from a distance, she thinks to herself, as he tries to fight his way out of Chuck's headlock. Andrew is the smallest of his friends.

Chuck gets picked up by his dad in a sports car. And then, a minute later, a minivan pulls up. The remaining boys pile in, while Andrew takes a seat on the curb, as if he's waiting for a ride himself. He waves as the minivan departs, and when it turns the corner, he stands up, grabs his book bag, and starts walking around toward the pool building.

Danielle turns and sprints. She wants to beat Andrew to their meeting spot. She wants to run away from the question of whether or not his friends know he's meeting her.

She catches her breath as Andrew turns the corner of the field. When he sees her, he has on a huge smile. He is happy to see her. And she is happy to see his happiness. It means more than any corny line or awkward apology for the list. It is completely genuine.

"Guess what," he says, slinging an arm around her shoulder. "My parents left town. Some last-minute project thing."

Danielle's eyes light up. "Oh, yeah?" Both her and Andrew's parents are strict. It feels like forever since they'd had a chance to hang out alone and unsupervised, the way they had at Clover Lake.

"We could order food and hang out for a while." He threads his hand through hers. "I've missed you."

"I've missed you, too."

Danielle calls her parents and tells them she'll be eating

tacos over at Hope's house. And then they take the path through the woods.

As soon as they are inside his house, Andrew presses her against the door and places his mouth over hers. They kiss hard. They sink down to the rug in the foyer, and then lie all over the mail that's been pushed through the slot in the front door. Danielle likes the intensity of Andrew's touch, gripping at her shirt, trying to hold on to her in ways he never has before.

She rolls on top of Andrew, trying to feel as sexy and powerful as the moment seems to call for. But something about this position intrudes on the moment. She feels so big on top of his body. She fears that she might be crushing him. Like she is the boy and he is the girl.

"Do you want to stop?" he asks her. His hands pull away from her in slow motion. "What's wrong?"

She doesn't want to say. But they haven't even talked about it, not since that first day. Danielle sighs. "This list thing is so stupid."

He runs his fingertips up and down her arms. "Don't think about it."

"How can I not think about it?" she asks, rolling off him. "How can *you* not?"

He sits up and drops his head in his hands. "Game Face, remember?"

Danielle doesn't like where this is going. "That's not what I mean. I can have the biggest, baddest, toughest Game Face in the whole world, but I still know people are talking about the list." Andrew doesn't say anything, so she goes on. "Are your friends still giving you crap because of me?"

"It's mostly Chuck. He gets everyone riled up. But that won't last forever. I can take it."

She hates to think of Andrew getting teased on her account. Maybe their strategy of ignoring it isn't helping. Maybe it is time they confronted the real problem. "You should punch Chuck the next time he talks about me." Though Danielle is being serious, she gives a little grin. "Or maybe I will."

Andrew groans. "Oh, yeah. Great idea, Danielle. That would only make everyone think of you even more as a dude. Do we have to talk about this?"

Danielle kisses him again. She tells herself that it doesn't matter what Andrew's friends think of her. All that matters is that she is a girl to him. His girl.

She nervously guides Andrew's hands back up to her shirt, curling his fingers around the hem and, with his help, she pulls it up over her head. She gives him a couple of seconds to go for her bra. When he doesn't, when he just sits there staring at her, she reaches around for the hooks herself. Her hands are shaking so badly, they keep slipping, but she manages to get it off.

Finally, Andrew starts to wake up. He reaches out and touches her where he never has before.

Danielle closes her eyes and concentrates on feeling Andrew's hands. She knows she is not a boy. But her boyfriend needs to be reminded.

THURSDAY

CHAPTER TWENTY-FOUR

Before Jennifer gets out of the car, Dana and Rachel are there, beaming two sunny, excited smiles.

"Oh, Jenn-i-fer!"

"We've got more good news!"

"Come on, you guys," Jennifer says. She grabs her books and locks up. "I don't think I can take much more." When she turns to face them, Jennifer sees they are still wearing the VOTE QUEEN JENNIFER stickers. She'd thought it was just an idea they had yesterday for fun. Apparently, it is a *thing*.

They walk toward school together. Rachel throws her arm around Jennifer and asks, "What are you doing tomorrow night?"

"I think you know the answer to that," Jennifer says. She keeps it light, coy. A joke that they all know the punch line to.

Dana jogs a few steps ahead and then spins around so she can look Jennifer in the face. "Do you want to come to a party on Friday? Everyone's going. The football guys, the —"

"Wait," Jennifer says. "I thought that the coach calls the varsity players on the night before a big game to make sure they're home and not out partying."

Rachel shakes her head. "Total bullshit to keep the younger players in check. Anyhow, everyone will be there, and *you're* going to be the guest of honor."

"Really?" A party. Such a little, inconsequential thing to probably everyone else at school. But it's something Jennifer has always dreamed about. Although never, not even in her craziest fantasy, would she have cast herself as the guest of honor. "You're not joking?" She's thought this to herself several times a day over the past week, wondering when the rug would get yanked out from under her, when all these good things would evaporate.

They reach the school steps. Dana pulls the door open and holds it for Jennifer. "We're making it a whole 'Vote Queen Jennifer' event," she says. "Like, we're not letting anyone into the party unless they show us their homecoming dance tickets with your name written on the back."

Rachel leans in and whispers, "I don't want to get your hopes up, Jennifer, but there's a chance, a *seriously good* chance, that you're going to be homecoming queen."

Jennifer gets goose bumps. How is it that so many of the people who'd been quick to put her down are now clamoring to hoist her up? It isn't everyone, obviously. Jennifer knows that for sure. There are plenty of guys who still look at her as if she has no right to exist, if they even look at all. And some of the girls, too, mostly the younger, pretty ones. It's as if Jennifer is threatening to ruin the sanctity of the homecoming institution by becoming queen. Like she's a narc who's going to bust up the party.

And then, of course, there's Margo.

"Thank you guys both so much. I'm . . . I'm totally in. Where is it?"

Dana says, "Margo's house."

Jennifer stops and shakes her head. "No. Margo wouldn't want that. She wouldn't."

"She does," Rachel says. "She told us so herself."

Dana says, "Margo suggested the idea! She's given her blessing to the whole Queen Jennifer thing."

"I mean, she's probably not going to be wearing a sticker," Rachel quickly adds, her eyes bouncing between Jennifer and Dana. "That would be weird. Since, you know, she's your competition."

Dana nods. "I know you two have had your issues in the past, but that's all water under the bridge."

Jennifer looks at the two girls so happy and excited, wanting her desperately to believe this lie.

Only Jennifer knows the truth. There's no way.

But Jennifer, much to her own relief and surprise, doesn't care.

"I'm so glad you're coming!" Dana goes in to hug her, and Jennifer feels something get pressed onto her chest. When they pull apart, Jennifer sees a VOTE QUEEN JENNIFER sticker on her shirt.

"Are you guys sure I should —"

Rachel is nodding before Jennifer even gets out the words. "It's good, I think, if people see that you're cool with this."

Jennifer blinks. "Why wouldn't I be?"

Dana pats her on the back. "Exactly. Alright, Jennifer. We'll see you later."

She has clearly died and gone to heaven. Jennifer gets her books, hangs up her jacket, and closes her locker.

But the voices in the hallway send her crashing back to earth.

"I heard that every time Sarah takes a shit, she saves it in a plastic bag and she's planning to throw it on the homecoming court."

"Oh my god. She'd get arrested for that, right? I mean, that's a crime, isn't it?"

"Maybe they'll cancel the dance. To keep us safe."

Sarah Singer.

Funny that her biggest obstacle to a fairytale homecoming wouldn't be Margo at all.

Instead of heading into homeroom, Jennifer walks back outside. It's cold there without her jacket. She hugs her books close to her chest to block the wind. It's easy to find Sarah. She's sitting on her bench. The boy who follows her around is next to her, his nose in a book. At first, Jennifer is nervous to interrupt them. But there's too much on the line to be shy. She marches over.

Sarah sneers up at her. "Why, hello, Jennifer."

"Can I ask you something?"

Sarah and her boyfriend share a look. As if Jennifer being polite was ridiculous. Sarah says, "It's a free country."

Jennifer takes a deep breath, which she instantly regrets. She doesn't know how Sarah's boyfriend can handle sitting that close to Sarah. In fact, Jennifer could smell Sarah from a few feet away. "I heard you bought tickets to the homecoming dance. Is that true?"

"Why? Are you asking me to be your date?"

Jennifer wants to tell Sarah to screw off, but she knows that's exactly the reaction Sarah is hoping for. The girl is all about trying to get reactions from people, and Jennifer won't let herself fall into that trap. "I want to know if you're planning a prank to ruin the dance."

"A prank? What kind of prank?"

Jennifer hates how Sarah is so proud of herself, so smug. "I . . . I don't know. Something to get even with everyone for putting you on the list? It's why you smell so bad, isn't it?"

Sarah raises a hand to her open mouth, feigning shock. "I don't know what you're talking about. I'm very excited for the homecoming dance. I already have my outfit picked out." Sarah's voice is proper and sweet, like a sitcom actress from an old television show. "And it's rude to tell other people they smell, Jennifer. I would think you'd know that better than anyone else."

Jennifer rolls her eyes. "Look. You're making a big mistake. Everyone's going to hate you if you ruin the dance."

Sarah scoots up to the edge of the bench and leans forward. "I don't care if everyone hates me. I hate them. I hate absolutely every single person in this school."

Jennifer takes a step back. This has been a mistake. There's no reasoning with someone so blinded by anger. If anyone should be upset about the list, it's Jennifer. Sarah has no right, being on the list for just one year. And if Sarah doesn't care, like she says, then why is she so hell-bent on ruining everyone's good time?

"Fine," Jennifer says. "But so you know, I'm telling Principal Colby about the things I've heard." Her eyes go up to Principal Colby's window. She hopes Principal Colby is in there right now, listening to this whole conversation.

"Why are you so desperate to protect the dance, Jennifer? I mean, you don't actually think you'll be voted homecoming queen, do you?"

Jennifer shifts her books from her left to her right, unintentionally revealing her VOTE QUEEN JENNIFER sticker.

"Oh my god," Sarah whispers, and pokes her boyfriend. "Look!" she says to him. "Look at her sticker! Oh, fuck, Jennifer, you really do! You've deluded yourself into thinking this is going to happen!"

"You're making a fool of yourself," the boyfriend says.

Jennifer stares Sarah down. "You're just jealous."

Sarah starts laughing obnoxiously. It definitely isn't a real laugh; Jennifer can tell. It's a put-on, for show. Like the dyed-black hair and all the necklaces, the word *UGLY*, nearly unreadable, blending in with the dirt on her forehead. "Jealous of what? That I'm not the popular group's ugly little mascot? It's a joke, Jennifer. At your expense! You should be telling these people to fuck off. They're using you. They're laughing at you behind your back! They've treated you like shit for four years, and you're basically giving them a free pass because they're dangling some pathetic, rotten carrot in front of your face. It doesn't matter if they give you a rhinestone crown or not. They all think you're ugly."

Jennifer yells back, louder than she wants to. "I know what I am, okay? I accept it. But I aspire to be better. You . . . you're mad because you wish you could be one of them but you're too scared to admit it."

Sarah stands up and jabs her finger at Jennifer. "You think those bitchy cheerleaders are your friends? They don't give a shit about you!"

"And what?" Jennifer laughs. "You do?"

"No." Sarah puts her hands on her hips. "I don't care about you, Jennifer. I just feel bad for you. For buying into this whole bullshit circus. I don't give a crap what you do. And I don't pretend otherwise. Now get the fuck away from my bench."

Jennifer is shivering as she walks away. She doesn't even begin to feel warm until she gets to Principal Colby's office. She walks right past the secretary, right in without knocking.

"Principal Colby? I need to talk to you."

"Come in, Jennifer. I hoped you would stop by to chat. I have to say, I've been seriously contemplating canceling the homecoming dance."

Jennifer is taken off guard. "Wait. What?"

Principal Colby lifts her eyebrows. "I'm sorry. I've seen those VOTE QUEEN JENNIFER stickers everywhere, and I figured —"

"That's not why I came by."

"So you're okay with everything?"

Jennifer smiles shyly and pushes her hair behind her shoulder so the sticker on her chest can be seen. "Yeah. I mean, I think it's nice. It's a nice thing for people to do for me. I've always been known as the ugly girl. It's kind of crazy to think that I could be known as homecoming queen." It really is. "So please don't cancel the dance on my account. People will hate me! They'll blame me!" She feels the tears come.

Principal Colby looks surprised. "Alright. Okay. I guess I had the situation wrong." She shakes her head. "So, what did you want to talk about, Jennifer?"

"Sarah Singer," Jennifer answers. She smooths her VOTE QUEEN JENNIFER sticker, paying extra attention to the corners that have pulled away from her sweater. "You have to stop her."

CHAPTER TWENTY-FIVE

Margo hovers over the lunch table, casting a shadow on her empty seat. She hates that it suddenly feels like she needs an invitation to sit with her friends. As if her chair is now reserved for Jennifer.

Rachel and Dana don't look up from their cups of yogurt. They just peel the lids back and quietly stir them, plastic spoons swirling in unison, the thick white cream slowing turning pink.

Margo sets her tray down and takes her seat. She thinks about giving her friends the silent treatment back. But she is too angry not to say something.

"Is Jennifer going to be joining us for lunch today?" she asks.

Dana says, "She's either in the library or still talking to Principal Colby."

"What about?"

"Why do you care?" Rachel asks, finally making eye contact with her. "Unless you're nervous."

The boys arrive. Matthew, Justin, and Ted. They slap down their trays.

Margo narrows her eyes and whispers, "Why would *I* be nervous?"

Dana leans over and whispers back, "People are starting to wonder if maybe you were the one to make the list. And now you're pissed off that it's backfiring. Because Jennifer might win homecoming queen instead of you."

"Are you guys serious?" Margo struggles to keep her voice low. She doesn't want the guys, Matthew mostly, to hear this conversation. "Is that what Jennifer is telling people? That *I* made the list?"

"No," Dana says. "It's only some people talking."

Some people. Margo wonders how many people equaled *some people.* Was Matthew one of them? She's never had to worry about the things other people said about her, because the things people said about her were nice things, were compliments.

"And just so you know, Jennifer hasn't said anything bad about you to us." Rachel shares a look with Dana before adding, "In fact, she thinks you're helping us with the whole 'Vote Queen Jennifer' idea. And . . . that you invited her to your party tomorrow."

Margo shakes her head. "No. No. No."

"I don't understand you, Margo," Rachel says. "I thought you didn't care about being homecoming queen. I thought you said it was no big deal."

"I *don't* care about being homecoming queen," Margo says. She says this part loud, so Matthew will hear. Even though a part of her still does care, despite everything, she feels compelled to hide it like a guilty secret. She can't let go of what she'd hoped would happen the minute she heard she'd made the list: that she'd be the homecoming queen, and Matthew would be homecoming king. They'd have their dance, and he'd finally see her the way she'd always hoped he would. As someone he wanted to be with.

Dana tilts her head to the side. "Then why are you trying to sabotage Jennifer's chance at winning?"

"I'm not trying to sabotage anything. I think it's embarrassing to basically beg people to vote for her. I wish you two would stop pretending that homecoming queen is a grand, benevolent prize that you guys are bestowing on Jennifer."

Rachel cuts her off. "First off, we're not begging. We're *campaigning* to make up for the fact that she's been told she's the ugliest girl in school for the last four years straight. Don't you think Jennifer deserves one night of feeling beautiful? After everything she's gone through?"

Margo chooses her words carefully. "I know that you guys think you're doing a nice thing, but let's be honest. There's not one person who'll be voting for Jennifer because they think she's pretty. It's either a big joke, to get the ugliest girl up on that stage, or people who want to give themselves a nice big pat on the back and feel better about treating Jennifer like crap all these years."

Dana laughs. "You mean like you have, Margo?"

Margo can't believe her friends are going to go there. "Are you saying I can't decide who I want to be friends with and who I don't?"

"Of course you can. But everyone knows why, Margo."

Margo takes a big sip of her milk. It is lukewarm and the cardboard container has a funny smell, but she keeps drinking it down. Once it is all gone, she says, "Okay. I'm not going to lie and say that how Jennifer looked didn't have something to do with it. It did." She lets this hang in the air for a few seconds, since some of the pressure to drop Jennifer had come directly from Rachel and Dana. Had they conveniently forgotten that part? Or maybe it was their own guilty consciences spurring their plan along. "But that wasn't the only reason."

Margo takes a deep breath and tries to clear her mind, which is suddenly all muddy with feelings and thoughts that she'd kept buried, that she didn't want to think about. "Jennifer . . . she used to make me feel bad about myself."

She steels herself for Rachel and Dana to react, because Margo knows it sounds crazy. How could Jennifer have any power over her? She was the one who left Jennifer. She chose to end the friendship. She walked away.

Dana gently pats her on the shoulder. "We know. And now this is your chance to make things right. To clear your conscience."

Margo wrinkles up.

Clearly, the girls have misheard her.

Or had she misspoken?

What she'd meant was that those bad feelings were there *before* she'd ended her friendship with Jennifer. Not something she'd felt after it was over. In fact, looking back, when Margo was friends with Jennifer, she felt like an entirely different person. Insecure. Awkward. Nervous. All those things went away after her friendship with Jennifer ended.

"What's going to happen after the dance, huh? Are you guys still going to be hanging out? Inviting her to my parties?" Margo already knows the answer, of course. They'd drop Jennifer. And honestly, she can't wait for it to happen. For the homecoming dance, for everything, to be over. "Maybe it was *you* guys who made the list. And now *you* feel guilty about it."

"Do you think we did?" Rachel asks, dead serious.

"Do you think *I* did?" Margo answers back, just as intensely.

Dana gets between them. "We know you're a good person, Margo. And that's why you need to listen to us."

"You're the only one who can come out looking really, really bad here. We're trying to protect you." Rachel nudges her chin down the table at Matthew. The boys, all of them, have their heads down. But Margo knows they are listening.

"Don't let your pride screw this up."

"Come on, Margo. Let Jennifer go to your party."

Margo wants to keep arguing, but she is tired. And anyway, it's not like she really has a choice. Barring canceling the party altogether, Jennifer will be there. Jennifer wouldn't pass this opportunity up.

CHAPTER TWENTY-SIX

Sarah lifts her arms and arches her back in a deep stretch. Not because she is sore, or tired, or anything like that. She fakes a yawn for the hell of it, mainly because Principal Colby's office is way too quiet. And also because her breath is just as bad as, if not worse than, her B.O.

She can almost see it, a smog floating out from the armpits of her filthy black shirt and her open mouth, skimming the top of Principal Colby's tidy desk. Principal Colby lifts her teacup to her mouth and breathes in the steam as she takes a small sip. Sarah bites her lip to keep from laughing. It's hilarious watching Principal Colby try to pretend like Sarah isn't as ripe as the Freshman Island ginkgo tree will be in the springtime. Principal Colby doesn't even set the teacup back down on her desk. She holds it under her nostrils and says, "There have been some complaints, Sarah."

Sarah is not surprised. She'd spent the day participating in her classes like never before. Volunteering to every question, her hand rocketing skyward again and again and again, unleashing her scent on the room. Teachers caught on quickly, and they tried their best to ignore her. But that didn't stop Sarah from raising her hand. In fact, it only encouraged her. She didn't give a shit if she got called on or not.

Sarah is quiet for a minute. She tries to appear contemplative, scratching her dirty fingernail across her cheek, filling the underside with a paste of dead skin. "I'm not sure I understand what you mean, Principal Colby." The smart-ass tone adds extra bite to her breath.

To think, she'd nearly given up this morning in a moment of weakness.

When Sarah sat down to cereal, her mom offered her a hundred dollars cash to shower, fifty dollars if she put on different clothes. Sarah's cover for her behavior was that this was an experiment for a school project, which wasn't even *that* much of a lie, and she stuck to her story. *Do you want me to fail, Mom?* Sarah laughed into her OJ and took a big sip.

It startled her that the juice had practically no taste. It could have been water, for all she could tell.

Sarah went up to the bathroom, opened her mouth, and stuck out her tongue. It was covered in a thick, fuzzy film. Like dense forest moss, the kind that covered the rocks of Mount Washington. Only this moss was the color of a dead body — pale and sickly gray.

Her toothbrush hung right there, over the sink. Right. There. It tempted her worse than cigarettes had so far this week. She closed her eyes, ran her tongue over her slimy teeth, and dreamed of how it would feel to foam everything up with some bright blue minty toothpaste. And mouthwash, too. It would probably burn like acid in the best way, sizzling the grit off her teeth and her gums. She'd spit it all into the bright white porcelain sink like wet sand. At least her insides could be a bright, healthy pink again.

She backed up from the mirror and turned out the bathroom light. She couldn't quit. Not now. Not when she was this close.

But before walking out, Sarah grabbed the dental floss from inside the medicine cabinet. She ripped a few inches of waxy white string and scraped it down the length of her tongue, raking the film up off the muscle like someone shoveling slushy snow off a sidewalk. The act didn't make her feel any better. If anything, it made things worse. She'd removed the barrier that kept her from knowing what the inside of her mouth tasted like.

Sarah wishes Principal Colby would get on with it. She wants to go back to class. She's missing a Bio II review. She's about to say as much when there's a knock at the office door.

Sarah twists in her seat. Milo stands nervously in the doorway. They lock eyes and she sees the disappointment drag on his face. Red hives have already begun to speckle his neck.

"You wanted to see me, Principal Colby?" he asks weakly.

"Take a seat, Milo," Principal Colby says.

Sarah knows her mouth is hanging open, and she doesn't care to shut it. Why has Milo been called down to the office, too? He's not involved with her plans. He isn't even her accomplice. This rebellion is *her* doing. And she'll be glad to take the credit for it, thank you very much.

Principal Colby clears her throat. "Sarah, I'm going to cut right to the chase here. Why are you doing this?"

Sarah cocks her head. "Doing what?"

"I'm concerned, Sarah. I'm concerned about you." Principal Colby gives her a pleading look. "This isn't healthy. You're leaving yourself open to infection, not to mention that you can't be comfortable in those clothes."

Sarah's not comfortable. But that hardly matters. She gives them both a phony smile.

"Milo, please. I know you care about Sarah. I see you together every day. You don't want to see her torture herself like this, do you?"

Milo looks at Sarah with sad eyes and his lips part, like he might say something. Like he might actually beg her to give this up. Sarah stares back hard. As hard as she can. A stare that says *Don't you fucking dare.*

Principal Colby leans back in her chair. She is not amused. "I'm going to ask you both one simple question." Her eyes dart from Sarah to Milo and back again. "Are you planning any sort of stunt for the homecoming dance? I know you have both bought tickets."

"No. I swear, I'm not," Milo says emphatically.

Sarah shakes her head as well. "Of course I'm not," she says, though she knows it doesn't sound all that believable.

"I hope you both are being honest with me right now. I want to make this perfectly clear: If you *do* cause any sort of disruption, there will be serious consequences. I will not hesitate to suspend both of you."

Milo looks like he's about to shit himself, but Sarah curls her upper lip. She finds it funny, in the unfunny way her sense of humor typically skews, that Principal Colby wants so desperately to protect the homecoming institution. There was none of this vigor, this effort, put behind finding who actually made the list. You know, cutting the thing off at the source, like Principal Colby had pledged to work tirelessly for during Monday's meeting. But all Sarah has to do is skip a shower or five and suddenly *she* might get suspended?

They get dismissed. Sarah follows Milo out into the hallway.

"She can't do that, you know. She can't suspend me for not taking a fucking shower." When she looks up, she sees that Milo is already halfway down the hall. "Milo! Wait up."

"I have to get to class," he says, and keeps walking.

"Why are you being so bitchy?" She grabs his arm, forces him to slow down.

"Because I just got called into the principal's office. I've never been called into the principal's office before."

She groans. "It's not a big deal."

"It is to me. And I'm not sure I want to go to the dance anymore."

Even though Sarah hadn't wanted Milo to come from the beginning, it pisses her off that he suddenly wants to bail on her. "Why? Because I'm not going to be in a pretty dress? Because you're embarrassed to be seen with me? Because I don't want a corsage like Annie would?"

He wraps his arms around himself, that defensive posture he had on his first day of school. "What does Annie have to do with anything?"

"I feel bad for you. You had this beautiful girlfriend in your old town, and now you're slumming it with me. I'd be depressed if I were you, too."

"I don't get why you're acting like this."

"Do you remember on Monday when you said *the so-called pretty girls are the ugly ones*? Well, you obviously don't believe that if you dated a girl like Annie."

"Yeah, Annie was pretty, but that's not the only reason why I liked her."

"Oh! You guys were soul mates, then?"

"Shut up, Sarah. She was nice, okay? Which is more than I can say for how you've been treating me lately. I'm not going to get suspended because you've got an ax to grind. I never wanted to go to the dance in the first place. I hate dances."

"*I* hate dances," Sarah says back, her voice rising.

"So why the fuck are we going?" It isn't a scream, but it definitely is the loudest Milo has ever spoken to her. His voice is stretched thin, frayed. He drops his head back as far as it will go. "I think this whole thing is a stupid idea."

"I don't care what you think."

"I know. That's sort of how we operate. You're the one who gets to call all the shots, have all the opinions. But I'm telling you anyway. This. Is. Stupid."

"You think I'm having fun, Milo?" She picks up some strands of her oily hair and lets them fall. They are heavy with grease. "You think this feels good?"

"Not really! Especially if your stank is any indication."

Sarah takes a step back. Her legs feel unsteady. In a way, she knows she's been testing him. Making sure, before she let herself completely fall for him. She realizes this now, as he fails. Fails miserably.

Sarah quickly puffs back up. "Screw you, Milo. You know what? Don't go to the dance with me. See if I give a shit!"

Sarah's not sure if Milo hears her. He's already stormed off. Down the hall, around the corner. Gone.

If she wants to do this, she'll need to not think about Milo, about Principal Colby, about anyone. She'll just need to push through. And that is something Sarah is good at.

CHAPTER TWENTY-SEVEN

As with everything difficult in her life, Abby avoids dealing with the reality of her unsigned Earth Science progress report until the last possible minute, which is why she finds herself sitting in the last stall of the girls' bathroom after school, waiting for the hallway noise to die down.

It is her own stupid fault. She should have shown her parents the progress report last night and begged for their mercy. Only, Fern was always within earshot, and it would have been too embarrassing for Abby to confess how much the homecoming dance meant to her, as well as admit that she was failing, in front of her sister. Knowing Fern, she'd probably burst in and tell her parents about the list, and then they could all lecture her on how dumb it was for her to feel good about being on it and how her priorities were completely screwed up.

But there was something else, too. Abby is scared. Scared to be in trouble, scared to be grounded, scared of the disappointed looks her parents were sure to give her.

And the disappointment is exactly why Abby is avoiding Lisa, too. The plan had been to meet at Bridget's car right after school and head to the mall to go homecoming dress shopping. Instead, Abby is hiding in the bathroom. She's hoping Bridget will run out of patience and force Lisa to leave without her. Lisa is going to be mad, but Abby just can't stomach buying her perfect homecoming dress until she knows that she can actually go to the dance. It would be too sad having it hang unworn in her closet or, worse, taking it back to the store. She'd rather not have the dress at all.

Abby hears the bathroom door open. She pulls her feet up.

Someone enters the stall next to her. After a few quiet seconds, Abby hears a couple dry choking coughs. And then a few retching gags. There's no vomit, and Abby wonders if maybe the person is choking.

"Hey," Abby says, climbing down off her toilet perch. "Are you okay?"

The gagging stops. "Abby?"

Abby steps out of her stall. The door to the other stall swings open. Bridget leans her head out. She looks pale.

"God," Bridget says lightly. "This is embarrassing!"

"Should I get the nurse?"

"I'm okay." Bridget pushes her hair off her face. "Something I ate at lunch didn't agree with me. Anyway, I'd go home and crash but Lisa's so excited to go dress shopping . . . and we're kind of out of time. I don't want to let her down."

Again Abby finds herself comparing Bridget to her sister, and Fern comes up way short.

Bridget hurries over to the sink and starts washing her hands. "You're still coming shopping with us, right? I hope I haven't scared you away. I swear it's nothing contagious. Please don't say anything to Lisa. I don't want her worrying. Please."

Something feels weird. Maybe it's how fast Bridget is talking. Or that Bridget wants her to keep a secret from Lisa. But she smiles back at Bridget. "No, of course. I won't say anything."

"Thanks," Bridget says. When Bridget reaches for a paper towel, Abby notices her hands trembling. "You're the best."

Abby walks outside and sees Lisa sitting on the trunk of Bridget's car.

"Hey! Where have you been?" Lisa asks.

"In the bathroom. I saw your sister . . . in the hallway." It doesn't feel good to lie to Lisa, but Abby did promise Bridget that she wouldn't tell. "She's going to be a few more minutes."

"Oh. Okay." Lisa offers a hand to Abby and pulls her up on the trunk. "Listen to this great idea I just had! I think we should both buy a dress for the homecoming dance *and* another cute outfit to change into for Andrew's party."

"Yeah."

"I mean, unless you want to stay in your dress all night. But I'm thinking we'll be more comfortable in jeans." Lisa bites her lip. "I hope Candace and those other sophomore girls don't go. I can see them being total bitches to us, because we're, like, moving in on their guys. Also, I hear Candace wants to kill every pretty girl on the list because she's so jealous."

"Oh."

Lisa snaps her fingers in front of Abby's face. "Hey, I was only kidding about Candace."

Abby takes a deep breath. "Look. I can't go shopping with you and Bridget."

"What? Why not?"

Abby fidgets with the zipper on her book bag.

"Come on. Tell me. I'm your best friend."

Abby opens her bag and hands Lisa the blue rectangle. Lisa doesn't recognize it right away, smiling as if it were one of the notes Abby wrote to her. It occurs to Abby that Lisa is confused because she has never gotten a progress report before. "I have to get this signed tonight," Abby explains. "And my parents are going to kill me."

Lisa gasps. "Crap. Okay. Well, you'll probably get in trouble. You might not be able to go to the football game or Andrew's party. But your parents *have* to let you go to the homecoming dance!"

"Except I know they won't. They don't care about dances. They care about this stuff. And they told me at the start of high school that I'm not allowed to get any more progress reports."

"Abby! I don't want to go to the dance without you!"

Abby doesn't want Lisa to go to the dance without her, either. Her mind spins. "I guess . . . I could sign it. You know, pretend to be my mom."

"Yes! That's a great idea! I mean, Mr. Timmet will never know. How would he know?"

He wouldn't. "And then I can try hard for the rest of the semester. I could even ask Fern to tutor me." Really, she would.

"I say go for it. What have you got to lose at this point?"

It is nice to have a friend who wants her to go to the dance almost as much as Abby herself wants to go. Lisa isn't at all jealous that she's the prettiest freshman. She sees it as a good thing, a thing to be proud of.

Abby takes one of Lisa's pens, because hers are all pink or purple. After practicing a signature that looks nothing like her own, she signs her mom's name with a little flourish on the dotted line. She says, "I feel better already!"

"Me, too," Lisa says, and rubs Abby's back. "Do you want to drop it off at Mr. Timmet's classroom now? I bet he's gone for the day. You can leave it on his desk and forget about it. And then we can go shopping!"

"Great idea."

The girls run into school together, their feet pounding on the floors, their laugher filling the otherwise empty halls. Abby feels a million times lighter, but she is resolved to do what she needs to do to pass Earth Science. This is her wake-up call.

The door to Mr. Timmet's classroom is open. The girls step inside, expecting the room to be empty, but it isn't. Mr. Timmet is still there, putting on his coat.

And sitting on a desk near the window, swinging her legs, is Fern.

Abby immediately notices that Fern has her hair done the same way Abby had worn hers earlier in the week, in a knot with a braid tracing along her hairline. Fern's is a poor attempt, lumpy and bumpy and uneven, but she has clearly tried to copy Abby.

"I . . . uh . . ." Abby mumbles.

Mr. Timmet waves her inside. "You almost missed me, Abby." He notices the blue card stock in her hand. "Is that your signed progress report, I hope?"

Abby forces down a swallow. She nods. Fern is staring at her.

"Wonderful. I didn't want to have to call home. And I hope that you aren't grounded the way you thought you'd be." He steps over and takes it out of Abby's hands, then turns back to Fern and says, "I should get home. I can't believe we've been talking for thirty minutes. But thanks for bringing me this article. I'm excited to read it." Abby watches Mr. Timmet slide her father's *Popular Science* magazine into his briefcase.

Fern gets up and heads to the door, nodding and smiling. "Oh, good. It's really . . . um, good."

Abby steps backward out into the hall. Lisa is there, pressed up against a locker, frozen. Abby quickly mouths to Lisa that she'll call her later. Lisa mouths *sorry* back, and then disappears into a stairwell.

Fern says her good-byes to Mr. Timmet and then joins her sister out in the hall. As she stalks past Abby, she says, "You're failing Earth Science, Abby? It's only the fourth week of school."

"Shut up, Fern." Abby trails a few steps behind.

"Who signed your progress report?"

"Mom," Abby says, trying to sound confident.

Fern laughs, and it cuts right through Abby. She pushes through the heavy double doors. "Oh, yeah? Let's go ask her."

Mrs. Warner's car is parked outside, and she waves to both her daughters. A few feet in the distance, Lisa and Bridget drive away together as Abby watches.

"Please don't tell on me," Abby pleads.

"Why shouldn't I?" Fern shakes her head.

"Because they won't let me go to the homecoming dance." Abby wipes away a tear with her sleeve. She knows Fern will hate her for crying over the dance. But Abby hopes she'll pity her, too.

"Of course I'm going to tell. They're going to find out anyway when you fail."

"Come on, Fern! Can't you do me this one favor? Please?" She is begging. Unabashedly begging for Fern's mercy. "Please. I never ask you for anything!"

"Why should I lie for you?"

"Because you're my sister." Abby can barely get the words out. Every part of her is shaking. "Sisters don't do this to each other."

Fern takes out the elastic from her hair. She shakes out the knot, yanks out the braid. "No one believes we're related. Especially not me."

CHAPTER TWENTY-EIGHT

During World History, Lauren's last period, a secretary knocks at the classroom door and hands a note to Lauren's teacher. The teacher reads the note, and then places it on Lauren's desk.

Principal Colby wants to see her immediately after school.

Lauren glances up at her teacher, silently hoping for more information, but he shrugs indifferently. This must be about the list. Her friends had said Principal Colby was on the warpath, trying to figure out who'd made it. Could she possibly think Lauren was to blame?

Lauren considers not going to the principal's office, pretending she never received the note. After all, her mother will be waiting to pick her up right when school ends. But she can't skip out on the principal. It would make her seem more guilty. Or maybe make Principal Colby call the house looking for her. She has no choice. So, after saying good-bye to her friends in the hallway, Lauren walks gloomily over to the main office.

Outside the office, she sees her mother sitting on a bench. Mrs. Finn is wearing the same cream blouse and wool skirt that she had worn for her interview on Monday.

"Mommy! What are you doing here? Shouldn't you be at work?" Lauren's heart is clogging up her throat. Would Principal Colby bring up the list in front of her mother? Lauren takes a seat next to her mother and quickly decides if that were to happen, she would play dumb. She'll pretend not to know anything about it.

But Mrs. Finn says, "I left early so you and I could meet with Principal Colby and discuss your English teacher." She looks down at her watch and frowns. "Since you haven't had the time to do it yourself."

From down the hall, Principal Colby's light voice cheerily says "See you tomorrow" to someone, probably another teacher.

"Is that her?" Mrs. Finn whispers. Lauren presses her lips together and nods. "She sounds . . . *young.*"

Principal Colby rounds the corner. She's wearing a black wool dress, black heels, and a long necklace of tiny pearls knotted halfway down. Her hair is in a low ponytail, a pair of tortoiseshell glasses holding back her bangs. Lauren feels Mrs. Finn stiffen next to her.

"Hello!" Principal Colby calls out, hustling to meet them. "You must be Lauren's mom. It's a pleasure to —"

"Good afternoon, Miss Colby," Mrs. Finn interrupts. She stands, but does not shake the hand extended toward her.

Principal Colby blushes, clearly caught off guard. "I'm sorry to have kept you both waiting. Today's been . . . well, quite a day." Her mother follows Principal Colby into her office, close on her heels. Lauren trails behind them, her mouth suddenly bone-dry.

Principal Colby takes a seat behind her desk and her gaze moves onto Lauren with concern. "Now, this is about Lauren's English class curriculum, right? Lauren, are you having trouble keeping up?"

Her mother's shoes. That's where Lauren sets her gaze. They are older than Lauren herself, and probably Principal Colby, too, though they do not appear to be at all broken in. Beige leather with a squat, square heel.

Mrs. Finn laughs drily. "Principal Colby, when it became clear that I could no longer be Lauren's primary educator, I met with her teachers and provided copies of my lesson plans to bring everyone up to speed on what we've already covered. I assume you've read them?"

"I . . . think I remember seeing them. Yes."

Mrs. Finn exhales a deep breath. "Then you must know that Lauren has already studied nearly every book on the sophomore AP English reading list. It's the fourth week of school, and her teacher has made no adjustments to accommodate her. I'm sure you can imagine how frustrating that is for me, knowing Lauren must sit in class, day after day, bored to tears."

Lauren cringes. She'd said those exact words yesterday afternoon, except they sound much worse now. She'd done it to smooth things over with her mother, because things had felt tense when she'd gotten home from working on the Spirit Caravan decorations. She'd had a great afternoon with the girls, painting snowcaps on their cardboard mountains, and had lost track of time. When she finally got home, her mother had already eaten her half of the stir-fry dinner she'd cooked for them. She sat with Lauren while she ate, but didn't say anything. Not until Lauren complained that her English teacher was horrible, especially compared to her mother. It had seemed a harmless compliment at the time.

Principal Colby shuffles some things around on her desk. Lauren has never seen her so flustered. "I don't know what to say, Mrs. Finn. I mean . . . I'm sure you'll understand that our teachers can't do away with the curriculum for the entire class on Lauren's behalf."

"Of course you can't," Mrs. Finn says with bitter validation, as if they both are agreeing this has been a huge waste of time.

"But," Principal Colby adds, "I will speak with her teacher about developing a secondary reading list Lauren can pursue on her own. I know Lauren is a brilliant girl, and it would go against every reason I became involved in education to let her languish unchallenged this year."

Lauren looks at her mother, hoping to see relief, but Mrs. Finn is barely pacified. "I guess that's the best I can hope for," she says.

Her mother stands. Principal Colby does, too, only with a bit more urgency, and says, "Actually, Mrs. Finn, I want to tell you that Lauren is making quite the impression around our school."

Lauren stares at Principal Colby harder than she's ever stared at anything in her whole life. *Please don't,* she shouts inside herself. *Please don't say anything about the list.*

Principal Colby seems to sense this, and mumbles her way out of things. "I . . . I always see her surrounded by a group of girls. She seems to have made lots of friends here."

Lauren sags. This is almost worse.

The business clothes had been stored in several zippered garment bags. Her mother tries everything on, emerging nervously in each outfit, rising up on her toes to see herself in the cracked mirror atop the oak bureau.

Lauren watches from her mother's bed. She is on her stomach, feet up behind her.

The suit separates are clean and well preserved, but tailored in old-fashioned silhouettes that show their age. There is no money for new work clothes, not yet anyway. And so Lauren feels it her duty to make her mother feel good no matter what. She offers only compliments. How the navy blazer brings out her mother's eyes. The timelessness of a herringbone skirt.

As Mrs. Finn changes outfits and regards herself in the mirror yet again, Lauren summons her courage and says, "There's a homecoming dance on Saturday night." Lauren pauses to see if her mother will say something, but she is too interested in picking some lint off a pair of slacks. "I'd like to go."

A good minute of silence goes by before her mother says into the mirror, "Money's tight right now, Lauren."

"The tickets are only ten dollars, and I've got that saved. And I wouldn't need a new dress or anything. I think most of the girls are wearing jeans." This is a lie, of course. Her friends have been talking nonstop about their dresses. Lauren knows she'll have to make do without, that jeans and a nice blouse will have to do. Or there's the black dress she wore to her grandfather's funeral. And there's always the chance that one of the girls will let her borrow something.

Mrs. Finn raises an eyebrow. "So you're planning to go with a group? The friends Principal Colby mentioned?"

"They're just girls from my grade. We're going to the football game together and then —"

"Football game?" Her mother shakes her head, like it's too much for her to process. "This is the first I'm hearing about this, Lauren."

Lauren takes a deep breath. She tries to stay patient, but what is her mother being so short with her about? It isn't like she's breaking any plans they'd had. "Yes. A football game, and then a dance. I'd like to go to both, please." Asking permission makes her feel like a little girl, though she had always felt like an adult with her mother. "Everyone's going to meet at one girl's house before the dance, and we'll walk over to the school in a big group."

Mrs. Finn sits down on the bed. "Don't you miss the old days? When it was just us, together?"

Lauren tenses up. Her mother is making it sound like she's doing something wrong. "Of course I do. But I've been trying to put myself out there."

"You need to be careful, Lauren. You don't know these girls that well."

"They're nice. They're my friends."

"This party? Who's it being thrown by?"

"Her name is Candace Kincaid."

"Why don't you invite Candace over for dinner tomorrow so I can meet her."

Of all the girls, her mother wants to meet Candace? That's not going to work. "Mommy! Please."

"So I should just let you call all the shots, now that you're a high school girl, huh?" She shakes her head. "I have a right to know whom you're spending time with."

Lauren uses the phone in the living room while Mrs. Finn takes a shower. She'd written the phone numbers of her friends down on the back of the list, and she calls one to get Candace's. The friend seems shocked and wants to know the details of what would necessitate this call, but Lauren manages to get the number without giving too much embarrassing information.

Lauren isn't sure she can get Candace to agree to come over. After all, Lauren was probably only invited to Candace's party because of the other girls, so Candace wouldn't look bad. And if Candace does say no, there's a good chance Lauren won't be able to go to the dance at all.

But then again, then none of the girls would go to Candace's party.

Candace sounds surprised to hear from her.

Lauren explains the situation. And she is surprised at how quickly Candace says yes to her dinner invitation.

Frankly, it scares her.

CHAPTER TWENTY-NINE

Danielle is about to jump into the pool with the other freshman swimmers when Coach Tracy beckons her over to her office.

"Do you have regular workout clothes with you today?"

"Yes."

Coach Tracy grabs some papers off her desk and says, "Go change out of your suit and head to the weight room."

"Okay," Danielle says, curious. "Sure."

The Mount Washington High weight room is directly across from the gym. At one time it had been two classrooms, but the adjoining wall had been torn down, the blackboards replaced with mirrors, and the room filled with free weights, benches, exercise bikes, and treadmills. An old radio stayed tuned to the classic rock station and provided a sound track of Led Zeppelin, Pink Floyd, and Steve Miller Band.

Danielle walks into the room in sweats, a plain white tank, and her favorite red sports bra. She is definitely nervous, in part because she's never done any weight training before, but more because most of the varsity swim team is already there, girls and boys, hanging around and talking with each other. There aren't many chances for the team to mingle this way, as everything in the sport is segregated by sex. But there's a clear unity to the swimmers. Everyone seems close. Like friends.

Danielle knows who some of them are, and a couple of people give her a little head nod, as if they know who she is, too.

The looks are different from the ones Danielle has been getting in the hallway since the list came out. These come with smiles. With recognition that she is a good swimmer.

"Alright," Coach Tracy says when she walks through the door with a stack of papers. "Today we're going to be concentrating on arms with the girls and legs with the boys. Break off into pairs and complete this weight circuit twice. And for those of you who don't already know, this is *Danielle*." Coach Tracy grins at Danielle, a nod to their private joke. "She'll be joining our four hundred freestyle relay team for Saturday's meet."

A rush of energy shoots through Danielle. She is officially a varsity swimmer! It is the first good thing that has happened to her this week, and she relishes it.

She thinks about asking to go to the bathroom. Not to pee, but so she can find Andrew to tell him the news. But before she can, she's paired up with a senior girl named Jane. Their first exercise is a bench press.

"Do you want to go first?" Jane asks her.

"No. I've . . . actually never done this before. So I think you'd better start."

Jane loads up the bar with two round weights, ten pounds on each side. Then she lies down on the bench. "Okay, Danielle. Stand behind me and keep your fingertips lightly under the bar. I don't want this thing falling and crushing me."

"Got it."

Jane lowers the bar until it is almost sitting on her chest, and then raises and lowers it eight times. As she works her way through the set, her limbs shake and her cheeks turn red. On

Jane's last rep, Danielle has to help lift the bar. Not much, but a little.

Jane sits up, a little winded. "Okay. Your turn."

Danielle lies down on the bench and takes a deep breath as she readies herself to lift the weight. Her heart is already pumping fast, mostly out of nerves. She pushes up and lifts the bar from the cradle. It is lighter than she expects. And, to her surprise, she pumps it up and down eight times without much trouble.

"Wait up!" Jane says, looking down at her in surprise. "That was way too easy for you." She slides another set of weights on the ends. "Now go."

Danielle does. It is slightly harder than the first time, but still totally doable.

"Coach Tracy!" Jane cries. "Come here a second. Danielle is rocking this bench!"

Coach Tracy approaches, and so do a few other girls on the team. Jane loads more weight on the bar. Danielle does eight more reps, and the girls whoop and holler.

When Danielle looks around, she sees that a couple of the boys have come over to watch, too. They peer down at her wearing looks of begrudging respect, like the boys had at Clover Lake.

More weight is added, and Danielle has to really work to lift the bar for the final set. Coach Tracy has taken over Jane's spotting duty, and the rest of the team gathers around the bench to cheer her on through the reps. When she lowers the bar and readies for the last press, Danielle's arms feel like overstretched rubber bands. But with her new teammates rooting for her, she finds some energy deep down and roars as she pushes with all her might to raise the bar back up. Her arms shake, and she drops the bar into the cradle with a huge crash. Everyone screams.

Danielle sits up, a little dizzy. Drops of sweat drip down the sides of her face. And as the crowd parts, she sees a couple of the football boys hanging around near the weight-room door.

One of them is Andrew.

Chuck laughs hysterically. "Dude. Does Dan the Man do that to you?" When Andrew doesn't say anything, Chuck turns to the rest of the guys and chides, "I bet that's their foreplay. She lifts Andrew up and benches him a few times."

Andrew stands terribly still, his forehead wrinkled and pinched. He looks pissed. But she can't tell whether he's upset at Chuck for saying those jerky things or at her for provoking them.

Chuck punches Andrew's arm. "Hey! Good thing Dan's not trying out for football. You'd be back down on JV. She'd definitely beat you out for tight end."

Danielle wants to stand up, to walk away from the door, but she can't move. She can't even wipe the drops of sweat rolling down the sides of her face, curling under her chin.

"Shut up," Andrew says. But his voice is drowned out by his friends' teasing.

"Move along, gentlemen," Coach Tracy says. "Stop distracting my swimmers." She closes the weight-room door on them.

Danielle, her chest still heaving, her muscles so sore, watches Andrew turn and leave.

CHAPTER THIRTY

"I should have gotten a salad," Lisa says, frowning down at her plate.

Bridget is sitting across from her sister at the pizza shop in the mall. She picked the table near the window, even though it was dirty and she had to clear someone else's plates away, so she could distract herself from the food by watching the shoppers avoid the man at the kiosk flying his rubber-band airplanes.

"Don't be stupid, Lisa. You love the pizza here. So . . . eat it and then let's go." Bridget stabs at a piece of wilted lettuce in the side salad she felt compelled to order so as not to be suspicious. As hungry as she is right now, it is wholly unappetizing.

Wasn't that the point? Really, she is angry for quitting the cleanse. If she hadn't quit the cleanse, she wouldn't have been starving, and if she hadn't been starving, she wouldn't have screwed up so badly today.

Lisa shakes her head. "I shouldn't eat like this. Especially because I'm not playing sports. I'm going to blow up."

Bridget sets down her plastic fork and eyes Lisa suspiciously. "Where's all this coming from?" She wonders if maybe Abby mentioned seeing her in the bathroom. She hadn't been able to throw up, though she'd wanted to. What luck, to have been caught in her weakest moment. Having dragged herself to the vending machines for some pretzels. Pretzels, for heaven's sake. Not nuts, not a pack of Life Savers.

Lisa shrugs. "I don't know. I'm not upset or anything that

Abby got prettiest. She totally deserves it. But it would be nice if maybe next year, I could get it."

"God, is that what you're worried about?" Bridget says. "You've got Dad's genes. He can't gain weight. I'm the one who has to worry, with Mom's side of the family. And anyway, one piece of pizza isn't going to make a difference."

"You never eat pizza anymore," Lisa accuses.

Bridget stabs her fork into the Styrofoam bowl. She doesn't even want to be in this pizza shop. But Lisa had insisted. And now she's going to complain?

"Here," Bridget snaps, and grabs Lisa's plate.

Take a bite.

Take a big bite.

That'll shut her up.

Instead, she reaches for napkins from the dispenser. "If you're that concerned about it, do this." Bridget lays a few napkins on the cheese, and taps them gently with her fingertips. They bloom bright orange. "This saves you, like, a hundred calories. I mean, you could peel the cheese off and just eat the bread." Bridget does exactly that, lifting the cheese off in one layer and dropping it on the side of the plate in a heap.

"But the cheese is the best part!" Lisa whines.

Bridget ignores her. She grabs another napkin and wipes off the sauce. "This is so bad for you, by the way. Full of sugar." Finally, Bridget tears off the crust. "And skip the crust. It'll just sit in your gut."

Lisa takes back her dissected slice — a pale piece of soggy bread — and frowns. "Gee, thanks."

Bridget can feel the oil on her fingertips. She wants to lick them, lick them clean. Instead, she takes another napkin and wipes them so vigorously, the paper tears. She feels guilty for bringing her sister into her shit, and for ruining a perfectly good piece of pizza. She can't wait until this stupid dance is over, until she can go back to being a normal person again. "I'll buy you another slice, okay? I just wanted to show you how stupid you're being."

"It's fine," Lisa says quietly. "I know you're only trying to help me." She eats the heap of cheese on the side of the plate and then says, "We can go now."

Bridget takes a deep breath, and then rustles her hand through Lisa's hair as they stand up. She would explain herself, but she just wants to get out of the pizza parlor.

Half an hour later, they are in the department store. Bridget sees the homecoming dress she wants right away. A little red strapless one. It's so pretty and feminine. As she circles the mannequin, she notices that the dress is folded and pinned in the back to make it even tighter. She starts thinking of those pretzels, imagines those pins popping out, ripping the fabric to make room for her.

"That is going to look SO good on you," Lisa says, and hugs her from behind.

"I don't know."

Lisa bounces off to another rack. "Try it on!"

Bridget pushes dresses along the rack. She picks her size, the same size as the summer bikini, and holds it up. It looks like so much fabric, so wide. A red circus tent. And she probably won't even fit into it.

In the dressing room, she frowns at the mirror. She is able to get the dress on and zipped up. She should be happy. She's lost the weight she'd put back on since leaving the beach. Plus, the red looks nice with her dark hair. But her hips jut out and ruin the silhouette. Her tummy, too. A little pouch in the very front of her, like a kangaroo. Even her knees are fat.

"I feel so bad for Abby," Lisa is saying from the next dressing room. "I mean, she's probably not going to be able to go to the dance now. All because of Fern."

"That sucks," Bridget says after a few seconds. She wants to cry, looking at herself in the dress.

If only you were a size smaller.

Bridget thinks about the bikini. How it was a goal. Because she'd bought it, she'd had to achieve it.

With two days to go until the dance, if she bought another size down, could she do it?

"Can I see?" Lisa asks.

"I'm already dressed. Just meet me at the register."

As Lisa gets her clothes back on, Bridget runs out to the floor and grabs the red dress in a smaller size. She'll test herself one more time.

FRIDAY

CHAPTER THIRTY-ONE

It is a sickness, one that's entirely infected her. There's no difference between the grime and Sarah's skin. It's fused together.

Her alarm goes off, but Sarah doesn't open her eyes because she doesn't want to feel the squeeze of dirt in the folds of her eyelids.

She slept naked last night. Really, she didn't sleep at all. Just lay there and itched.

Her clothes are in a damp pile on the floor. She cheats and puts her underwear on inside out. It barely helps. It takes everything tough inside her to put the rest of them on.

The whole bike ride to school, she imagines a conversation between Milo and Annie about the fight she'd had with him yesterday in the hall. Annie would tell Milo to stay away from Sarah. That she sounds deranged. Milo would tell Annie that he misses her. That he wishes he'd never had to move away.

As if to confirm her worst suspicions, Milo isn't waiting for her on the bench.

At least it's cold out. The chill makes her skin contract, tighten up, and burn numb, almost to where she can't feel herself. She sits on the bench and waits, frozen in filth, until the second bell rings, until she is officially late.

Milo never shows up.

Friday is 10,000 percent the opposite of Monday. No one ignores her. They can't. Now all her classmates look at her in sheer horror. Sarah falls into her homeroom seat. There is the squeak of chair legs and desk legs as those sitting close to her try to move away. Even the shunning can't penetrate the filth. It is body armor. Underneath it, she feels nothing.

With every step, the slightest movement or shift, her smell escapes. A scent sour and raw and sharp. The boys pull their shirt collars up over their noses. The girls press perfumed wrists against their faces.

It is beautiful.

Except she can tell they never expected anything less disgusting from her. There's no shock, no awe. Just a sense of destiny.

CHAPTER THIRTY-TWO

Danielle stands in the doorway of the pool office with one hand clutching her shoulder. "Coach Tracy?" She squeezes the words through her teeth.

Coach Tracy spins around in her chair, looking immediately concerned. "Danielle. What's wrong? Why aren't you in your bathing suit?"

"I think I hurt my arm yesterday in the weight room. I must have done too many lifts." Danielle startles as Coach Tracy rises to her feet. "I — I shouldn't have tried to show off. I'm thinking I'd better not get in the water today. You know. As a precaution for tomorrow's meet."

Coach Tracy presses a thumb gently into Danielle's shoulder muscle. Danielle sucks in a sharp breath on cue.

"This is a problem. You need to practice with your team so you get the timing down for the meet tomorrow. We still haven't worked on your flip turns." Coach Tracy presses a couple of other places down Danielle's arm. Danielle winces as she thinks she should. "I'm going to have to bring another swimmer up to fill your spot."

"I'm sure it will be better tomorrow, Coach Tracy. I swear. And I'll sit in on practice, so I won't miss anything. I just don't want to aggravate it. I really think I just need a day off from swimming, and it'll feel better."

Coach Tracy continues to prod her shoulder, but her touch feels different than it had moments before. It is less diagnostic and more playacting. "If you think that's what you need, I guess I can't argue with you. But I can't take the chance that you'll be better tomorrow."

Danielle is in pain as she walks out of the pool office. Except the hurt is in her chest and not her shoulder. It has been there all day. She can't get into the water today. Not when she'd spent so much time fixing her hair this morning. Not when she has plans for after practice, when she absolutely has to look her best.

Danielle takes a seat on the bleachers. She watches the rest of the varsity team dive into the water, along with Hope, whom Coach Tracy picks as her replacement.

About two hours later, Danielle sits in the locker room, waiting for Hope to get changed.

"Are you sure you still want to get pizza?" Hope asks. "Maybe you should go home and rest your shoulder."

Danielle folds up Hope's wet towel. "Pizza's not going to hurt my shoulder, Hope."

"But what if Coach Tracy sees you out with the guys? She might never let you swim varsity."

Danielle notices that the way Hope sometimes speaks makes her sound not like a best friend but like a little sister. And Hope sort of looks like a little sister, too, with her baggy sweatpants, shapeless T-shirt, and hooded sweatshirt tied around her waist. Her hair is up in a floppy bun, half-dried from her after-practice shower. Hope has really pretty hair, when she bothers to blow it out. Danielle thinks about suggesting that she should. But she doesn't want to keep Andrew and his friends waiting. And anyway, it isn't like Hope has something to prove to them.

"What could Coach Tracy possibly say? I have to eat dinner. It's not a big deal." And then, because maybe she's come off a bit harsh, Danielle adds, "I'm glad you're coming with me."

Bringing Hope along had been Andrew's idea.

He hadn't called her after the weight room incident, hadn't answered her texts. Probably, she figured, because he was worried about how angry she might be for the way he'd acted.

But the thing was, Danielle wasn't calling to yell at him. She had wanted to share the news that she was now a varsity swimmer. Okay, maybe it wasn't homecoming court, and it didn't have anything to do with whether she was pretty or ugly, but it was something Danielle knew Andrew and even his idiot friends could respect.

But more than respect, she wanted Andrew to be proud of her again. Proud to be with her.

So that morning, she'd woken up early and taken extra time getting ready. She'd used conditioner on her hair, and made the mental note that she should use it more often. She put on makeup and traded her T-shirt bra for one with padding. And finally, she put on the one sundress she'd packed for Camp Clover Lake, the one Andrew had once said made the boys in his bunk go crazy. It was too cold for cotton that thin, so Danielle paired it with a cardigan sweater and a pair of leggings.

And then she'd waited for Andrew at his locker before homeroom.

"Hey," he said, sounding tired.

"Guess what," she said, popping up on her toes. "I have news."

She waited for him to look at her. Andrew dug through his locker for his books. He used the door to hide his face.

And suddenly, the pride from her accomplishment twisted into something needy. "Your parents are still gone, right? Because I was thinking after school, I could come over again." She still wasn't sure how she felt about what they'd done on Wednesday, but here she was, ready to do that and more.

"Actually, a couple guys are going to grab pizza after practice," he said.

"Oh." It amazed her how much desperation could fit into a single syllable. "Where? Mimeo's or Tripoli's?"

"Probably Tripoli's. I don't know."

"I love Tripoli's. It's the best pizza in town." Andrew closed his locker door, and Danielle found herself practically standing on top of him. "I was actually thinking about having pizza tonight, too, which is weird."

"Do you . . . want to go?"

"Do you want me to go?"

He shrugged. "Why would I care if you ate pizza or not?"

"Well, then I'll go." It wasn't exactly the invitation she'd hoped for, but she knew that if she and Andrew were going to work, she was going to have to find a way to get along with his friends. It wasn't just about making Andrew see her as pretty. It was as important that Chuck and the rest of the guys saw her that way, too.

"Well, you should probably invite Hope to come, so you're not the only girl. It might be weird for you otherwise. And that way, you'll have someone else to talk to."

"Isn't that *your* job? You know, as my boyfriend?" He gave her a look, and Danielle backed off. She didn't want him to rescind the invitation he'd barely extended. "Okay. I'll bring Hope. We'll meet you at the corner after practice."

○ ○ ○

Danielle and Hope wait for twenty minutes at the corner, keeping an eye out for Coach Tracy's Jeep. When Andrew and his friends don't show, Danielle wonders if his practice is running late. The two girls walk over to the field.

It's empty.

Hope sighs. "I thought you said Andrew —"

"He must have forgotten. He's so focused on the homecoming game. It's all he talks about."

Hope doesn't say anything more on the five-block walk to Main Street, but Danielle is still annoyed with her. Already Hope is failing at her purpose: to make things less awkward for Danielle.

Danielle sees a break in the traffic and darts across the street. She knows Hope is behind her. A car honks, but Danielle doesn't stop. She has her eyes on Tripoli's Pizza.

The boys are inside. Andrew, Chuck, and a bunch of others. Two pizza trays have been cleared, save for three slices and a pile of uneaten crusts. The guys are being rowdy, laughing about something. But they quiet when Danielle walks through the door, Hope following at her heels.

Danielle goes right up to the table.

Chuck says, "Dan the Man!"

"My name is Danielle."

Chuck looks wide-eyed at the other boys. "Sorry, Danielle. Anyway, it's nice to see you, *dude*!"

The other boys laugh. But not Andrew. He stares down at the table.

"I thought you were meeting us at the corner," she whispers.

Andrew scratches at the cheese stuck to his paper plate.

"Right. Sorry. The guys practically carried me here after practice. They were starving. Plus, coach let us off early."

The other boys have their heads down, too, so she can't tell if Andrew is lying or not. And just as Danielle notices that none of the guys move to make room for her or Hope, she feels a hand touch her shoulder. "Here," Hope says, guiding Danielle backward. "I got us a table."

Danielle is shaking. She's never been so embarrassed. But what could she have expected? She practically forced Andrew to invite her along. If only she could go back in time and save face. There will be no easy exit now. She'll have to play it cool, or risk completely humiliating herself.

Danielle goes up to the counter and orders herself and Hope a slice and a soda each. When she sits back down, the boys' conversation is going again. She chews as quietly as she can and listens from her table.

"I don't care what those senior girls say. There's no way in hell I'm voting for Jennifer Briggis for homecoming queen," Chuck says. "It makes a mockery of everything. Any girl who gets picked ugliest in her class has no right to win. Point-blank." Danielle can feel Chuck's eyes on her, but she can't bring herself to meet his gaze. "And have you smelled that dirtbag Sarah Singer? It's like all the ugly girls in school are banding together to ruin homecoming!" Chuck sucks down the last of his soda, squeezes his hand around the can, and pushes the crumpled aluminum toward Andrew. "In other shitty news, I heard that Abby can't go to your homecoming party, bro. She's grounded."

Feet rustle underneath the boys' table. Another boy laughs so hard, he almost chokes.

Danielle stiffens. A party at Andrew's? After homecoming? Why hasn't he said anything to her?

"Shut up, Chuck," Andrew hisses.

Chuck groans. "Um, yeah. Like I was saying, Abby's so hot. Right, Andrew?"

Danielle can't breathe.

"I don't know what you're talking about."

Chuck stands up, gleeful, and points at Andrew. "Liar! You told me you jerked off to her the other night!"

Andrew whips a pizza crust at Chuck. The other boys howl.

Hope stands up so fast, her soda splashes onto her plate. "Let's go." But Danielle is paralyzed with embarrassment. "Danielle, come on!" Hope pulls her out from behind the table and pushes her to the door. "You're an ass, Andrew," she says on their way out.

Hope is booking it down the street away from the pizza shop as fast as she can, dragging Danielle along with her. But Danielle doesn't want to go. She wants to give Andrew a chance to explain himself. She tries to pull her hand free.

"Hope . . ."

"What happened to you, Danielle? Have you forgotten how to stand up for yourself?"

Hope has tears in her eyes when she says it. And, for Danielle, that hurts worse than anything else.

Andrew comes outside and jogs up to them. "Hey. Don't be mad, okay?"

Hope opens her mouth to go off on him again, but this time, Danielle steps in front of her. She chokes back her tears and says, "'Don't be mad'? Are you kidding? You're having a party after homecoming and you didn't invite me?"

"It's not even a party, Danielle! It's just a couple people talking about stopping by. I don't want anyone to come over. If my parents find out, they'll kill me. But Chuck is . . . Look, I didn't think you'd want to come. I didn't want to put you in that position to spend a night with Chuck. Not with all the crap he's been saying about you."

"Hmm. How thoughtful." Danielle crosses her arms. "Hey, just wondering, but did you stick up for me? Like, once?"

Andrew looks at his shoes. "I care about my friends, okay? I care about their opinions."

"So do I. That's why I've spent the whole week defending you to Hope. Telling her that you're a good guy, even though you've barely done anything to make me feel better."

Andrew holds up his hands. "You can't blame me for not knowing what to say. I don't know what you're going through."

It's probably true. But for as long as she's known him, Andrew has had a chip on his shoulder. He's always afraid that he doesn't measure up to Chuck and the rest of his friends. Football stuff, his clothes, his body.

He could have understood, if he'd tried. If he'd dug deep.

"I've gone out of my way to make you feel good about yourself. When have you done that for me?" A warmness is spreading through her body, limbering her up. "And this is how you break up with me? By humiliating me in front of your friends?"

Andrew finally looks at her. He mumbles, "I didn't break up with you."

It takes a second for his words to sink in.

Andrew still wants to be with her?

She searches his face for a glimmer of someone who remembers who she had been before Monday. The boy who had been proud to be with her, who had pursued her for weeks at camp. How could so much change in a week? Danielle hasn't only lost her sense of self, but she's lost her sense of Andrew, too.

She sees traces of sadness in the corners of his eyes and the edges of his mouth. *This is Andrew's Game Face*, she realizes. A mask to hide the embarrassment of how he's acted and the way he's treated her. It is a tiny glimpse that, underneath it all, he's sorry for how he's acted.

It is of some comfort to her.

But not much.

Because Danielle's Game Face is off. She's brave enough to lay herself bare, to put it all out there for him to see. The pretty and the ugly and the everything. She wants Andrew to do the same for her. To be real with her for once. To admit that, yeah, it sucks to have his girlfriend on the list. It's embarrassing. But he shouldn't let his friends treat her this way. He should stand up for her. To admit that his Game Face has been an act of cowardice, not strength.

"Go back to your friends," she says. "I can't do this anymore."

Danielle is surprised. Genuinely. At herself, for being the one to end it, and at Andrew, for walking away so fast.

CHAPTER THIRTY-THREE

It is Bridget's idea to rake the yard after dinner. She tells her family she wants to do it for the money, but that's a lie. She does it because she barely broke a sweat playing badminton in gym.

The repetitive work soothes her anxiety. Raking up the leaves with spindly metal fingers, tying up the garbage bag and dragging it across the lawn to the front curb. She moves as quick as she can, to keep her heart up, to keep burning calories.

Bridget hears a window open. She looks up to the second floor and sees Lisa sticking her head out.

Lisa calls down, "Need help?"

"Don't worry about it." Bridget leans against the rake. She feels a little dizzy.

"It's fine! I'm not doing anything."

Don't let her help.

You'll have less to do.

Fewer calories to burn.

"I'm not splitting the money," Bridget says curtly.

But Lisa has already closed the window. And a few minutes later, she's outside, next to her with another rake.

Bridget hates Lisa sometimes.

Bridget stays near the garage and she tells Lisa to rake near the fence. Even though there's an entire yard between them, Lisa keeps trying to make small talk.

"I heard there's a party at Margo's house tonight."

"Oh, yeah?"

"Aren't you going?"

Bridget's friends are going. "I don't think so."

"Why not? Is it because of the whole 'Vote Queen Jennifer' thing? Personally, I'm voting for Margo, even though, you know . . . people are saying she's the one who made the list."

Bridget had heard that. She tried to think about Margo, and what connections there were between the two of them, why Margo might have chosen her as the prettiest junior. The only thing she could come up with was that they'd both once kissed Bry Tate. "I don't think Margo did it."

Lisa shrugs. "It makes sense to me. If I made the list, I'd put myself on it. Why not?"

The girls finish raking the yard and head inside. Mrs. Honeycutt inspects their job from the kitchen window after dinner. Along with what Bridget is paid, Mrs. Honeycutt gives both girls extra money to get the ingredients to make ice cream sundaes.

"I'm not in the mood for ice cream," Bridget says to her mother.

"You're not in the mood for anything edible," Lisa pouts. She drags her finger into a dish of mashed potatoes, a portion that Bridget passed on during dinner, that has yet to be put back into the fridge.

Bridget wants to kill her sister. Instead, she thanks her mother and takes the car keys.

"What flavor should we get?" Lisa pulls open one of the glass doors in the freezer aisle. Cold pours out in a cloud.

"I don't care, Lisa."

"How about mint chocolate chip?"

Bridget shakes her head. "That won't make a good sundae. Just go vanilla." The word rolls around and coats her mouth with an imagined sweetness.

"But vanilla is boring," Lisa says.

Bridget wraps her arms around herself to keep warm. "If you don't like my suggestions, then why are you asking me?"

"Geez. Sorry."

While Lisa debates flavors, Bridget gets the rest of the supplies — sprinkles, whipped cream, chocolate sauce, and a jar of red cherries suspended in syrup. She is glad the ingredients are tucked inside boxes, sealed in jars. She meets Lisa back at the registers. She picked vanilla after all.

"Crap," Lisa says. "We forgot the bananas."

Bridget puts things on the conveyor belt while Lisa runs off. The cashier is an older lady in a store apron. She doesn't even look at Bridget while she scans the items. *Beep . . . beep . . . beep.*

As the trail of items rolls away on the supermarket conveyor belt, Bridget avoids eye contact with the multitudes of perfect women gazing at her from behind their glossy covers, ten or so beautiful specimens preserved and protected by metal magazine racks. Their smiles appear friendly enough, but Bridget knows it's a trap. Look too long and she'll start comparing the shade of her teeth, the circumference of her upper arms. Scan the bolded headlines and face a list of all the things wrong with her. It is a full-on assault, a gorgeous Greek chorus pleading, begging her to pay for their secrets.

The bag boy is maybe a few years older than she is, though Bridget hasn't given him a good enough look to tell for sure. Just a quick nod to indicate she prefers paper over plastic.

That's when she notices him staring.

She feels the bag boy's eyes slicing her up into parts, like the meat man in the bloody apron at the back of the supermarket. A pair of boobs, a hunk of ass, strips of thighs. The last thing he notices is Bridget's face.

The magazine models smile on approvingly, unblinking witnesses.

Bridget acts aloof, pretending she doesn't notice. But inside, she is sick over it. She doesn't like the attention. She doesn't want him to look at her. It makes her hands get clammy.

"Okay," Lisa announces when she returns. "We're set!"

It is as if Lisa can sense what is happening, because she peeks out coyly from behind her sister. It makes Bridget even more self-conscious. As soon as she gets her change, she heads for the doors and leaves Lisa to get the bags from the bag boy.

Bridget's cheeks are still red when she reaches the car.

"That boy was totally checking you out," Lisa says.

"No, he wasn't."

"He was." Lisa looks glumly down into her bag of ice cream. "I wish someone would check me out."

Bridget snaps. "Why do you keep saying this kind of stuff anyway? At the mall, and now, with this guy. It's like all you do is fish for compliments. Which, by the way, is incredibly unattractive."

Bridget sees Lisa's bottom lip quiver, but she pretends not to. She gets in the car and slams the door hard. Lisa doesn't get in the car right away. She just stands there, outside in the parking lot, her back pressed against the passenger window.

"Come *on*, Lisa! Your precious ice cream is melting!" Bridget screams.

Lisa finally gets in the car. Neither one talks on the ride

home, but Bridget can sense it. Lisa. She's going to say something. She's going to call her out.

When Bridget gets close to the house, she dials one of her friends. With her cell pinned to her ear, she waves at Lisa to take the bags inside. She goes straight up to her room and pretends to consider going to the party at Margo's house tonight. Really, though, she wants an excuse to get out of eating ice cream.

The conversation is wrapping up when she hears Lisa coming up the stairs.

Even though her friend hangs up, Bridget still holds the phone to her ear.

Lisa opens the door. She's made an ice cream sundae. It's big, with two spoons.

I'm on the phone, Bridget mouths.

Lisa sits down, her eyebrows furrowed.

Bridget keeps saying "mm-hmm" into the quiet phone. She watches Lisa set down the ice cream and walk over to the dress that's hanging up on the back of her closet door.

Bridget does not want her sister to see the tag, the size. She says "bye" real fast and then snaps her phone closed. "I told you I don't want any ice cream."

"I know," Lisa says calmly, as she lowers herself onto Bridget's bed. "But I want you to eat this with me."

Bridget can't bear the pain on Lisa's face. The begging. So she gets up and finds her book bag on the floor and starts rummaging through it. "Actually, I have homework to do. So —"

"Bridget. Just have a bite."

"I'm serious, Lisa. Leave me alone."

Lisa looks as if she might cry. Like she did when she was little and Bridget wouldn't let her touch any of the furniture in the dollhouse. "You're not eating. I know you're not eating. Like this summer."

Bridget sighs. "I want to look good in my homecoming dress, okay?"

"You still need to eat." And then, with incredible disappointment, she adds, "You were doing so well when we came home from the beach, Bridge."

Bridget hates that her sister knows. She hates that she isn't better at hiding things. "I will eat, Lisa. I promise. After the dance."

A tear runs down Lisa's face. "I don't believe you."

Bridget starts to cry, too. "I'm telling you. After the homecoming dance, I'll eat. I'll be back to normal again. I swear. You know how you keep talking about the list, wanting to be on it someday? Well, just think about things from my perspective. It's *a lot* of pressure."

Lisa keeps crying. It's like she hasn't heard anything Bridget just said. "You make me feel bad about myself, you know that? Every time I eat, I feel bad about myself now. I never used to be like that."

"Lisa . . ."

Lisa shakes her head. "If you don't start eating, I'm going to tell Mom and Dad."

Lisa wipes her face on her sleeve and walks out. She leaves the bowl of ice cream there to melt.

To Bridget, it's the meanest thing Lisa could have done.

CHAPTER THIRTY-FOUR

Abby sits alone in her bedroom, looking at her reflection in the dim television screen like a dirty mirror. When the smell of food reaches her room, she heads downstairs. No one calls her for dinner.

Her family is already seated at the round table. The food has been divided and served onto plates, save for Abby's steak, baked potato, and salad, which sit waiting for her on the counter. Abby begrudges the implication that she has shown up late, but serves herself without saying so.

Her parents unsheathe the newspaper from its blue plastic cocoon and divvy up the folds. Fern wedges her book open with a glass of milk and the pepper mill, and starts in on her steak. She is rereading the first book in the Blix Effect series in advance of the movie so every detail will be fresh in her mind. The book jacket is torn and weathered, almost every page dog-eared.

Abby takes her seat, squeezing past Fern's chair without saying excuse me, and she goes without sour cream for her baked potato because she'd need to ask Fern to pass it. She hasn't spoken to Fern, made eye contact with Fern, or even acknowledged Fern's existence since she told on her for forging her mother's signature on her progress report.

Despite the cold shoulder, anger simmers like a hot little coal inside Abby, and it shows no sign of dying out.

A radio on the kitchen counter is tuned to a news station at a low volume, making it seem as if there's a fifth guest invited to lead them in conversation. On most nights, the three other people look up from their reading and offer opinions on international conflicts or financial markets or scientific advancements. Never Abby. To her, the voice is white noise, like the cars pulling into driveways next door, the airplane flying over the roof on the way to the city. She typically eats with her cell phone cradled in her lap, so it can buzz intermittently with messages from her friends.

Tonight, Abby actually tries to follow along the bits of conversation that are tossed like a ball over her head, a game of keep-away. She chimes in, not forming an opinion of her own, but instead agreeing with the things her dad or her mom says. Her parents seem pleasantly surprised each time Abby speaks up. Fern doesn't say a word.

Abby waits until everyone finishes eating, and then politely volunteers to clean the table and do the dishes.

Her mom and dad frown across their dirty plates and rumpled papers.

"This is not going to change our decision, Abby," Mrs. Warner tells her.

"You lied to us, you lied to your teacher, and as a result, you won't be going to the homecoming dance," Mr. Warner says, peering over the top of his glasses.

Fern dabs at her mouth with a paper napkin and then lets the wad of thin paper drop onto her plate, where it blooms red with the juices from her steak.

"I know that," Abby mumbles. She hates that she let herself be deluded by Lisa, who had run to her locker after school and pitched the idea that if maybe she went overboard on being well behaved, they'd ease up on her punishment.

The severity of everything finally comes crashing down around her. She will not wear her dream dress. She will not get to dance with an upperclassman. She will not go to the party at Andrew's house. It is as if the night, an amazing memory that she could have looked back on forever, has already been ripped out of her diary.

And it is Fern's fault.

"Fern," Mr. Warner says. "When we talked with Mr. Timmet today, he told us that Abby has a test next week."

"We'd like you to help her start preparing this weekend," Mrs. Warner says.

Abby stands up and gathers the dishes, her heart lodged in her throat like a big, gristly piece of steak. It is humiliating to hear her family talking about her as if she isn't right there. She wonders what kinds of things they say about her when she isn't in the room. Things like "Poor, stupid Abby." And "Why can't Abby be more like you, Fern?"

"Actually, Mr. Timmet mentioned that to me himself after school today," Fern says, leaning back in her chair so Abby can take her plate. "But I'm going to the *Blix Effect* movie tonight. And afterward, everyone's going to the diner. So . . . I can't."

Mrs. Warner says, "Well, what about all day Saturday and Sunday?" And then, as Fern opens her mouth to respond, Mr. Warner adds, "What's more important, Fern? Helping your sister or a movie?" Fern doesn't answer, so he continues, "You'll tutor Abby for at least two hours tomorrow afternoon, or else no Blix Effect."

Abby picks up Fern's glass, even though there is still milk left in it, causing Fern's book to fall flat. "Why do you hang out in Mr. Timmet's room every day, Fern?" she asks. "Do you have a crush on him?" Abby watches, pleased, as Fern turns purple. "He's married, you know," she continues. "His wife's picture is on his desk. She's totally hot."

"Abby!" Mrs. Warner scolds. "Don't be so crass."

"What, Mom? Don't you think it's weird that Fern is, like, obsessed with Mr. Timmet? That she runs to his room every day after school, even though he's not her teacher anymore? I've never seen her talk to the boys in her class." Abby cups her hands around her mouth and fake-whispers, "I think she's into older men."

Fern bolts from the table. Abby smiles as Fern's footsteps pound up the stairs and down the hall.

"Abby, please. Leave your sister alone."

"You know Fern isn't as outgoing as you are. She feels more comfortable around adults."

"That's because she's a social reject!" Abby screams, hoping her voice will lift up through the ceiling.

After adding another day to her punishment, her parents retire to their respective offices.

Abby takes her time loading the dishwasher, sliding the plates in the cage so they nestle perfectly. She wipes down the countertops and the table and sweeps the floor. When the kitchen glistens, she flicks off the lights and the radio and glumly climbs the staircase.

When she reaches their room, Abby stands in the doorway and stares at her sister while Fern gets dressed to leave for the movie. With her oversize T-shirt, Fern barely looks like a girl.

Abby could help her. She could show Fern how to flatiron her hair, help Fern pick out better clothes. Maybe Fern could meet a cute nerdy boy at the movie tonight, someone who liked those stupid books as much as she did.

But Abby won't. She won't ever help Fern after what Fern has done to her.

As far as she's concerned, they are no longer sisters.

CHAPTER THIRTY-FIVE

Candace is dropped off at Lauren's a few minutes early. She stands on the sidewalk and stares at the old house, white paint peeling from the shingles, bushes overgrown and shapeless, dead leaves blanketing the grass. She thinks with deadpan sincerity, *This is the girl who has stolen all my friends.* She reaches for the flowers in her backseat and prunes away any wilting petals.

It is her mom's habit to show up with a small gift for the hostess. Candace has never done it before herself, even though she's eaten dinner a million times over at her friends' houses. But this invitation is different. There is a mission at hand.

"My mom wants to meet you," Lauren had said when she'd called yesterday. "Can you come over for dinner tomorrow? Please."

"Why does she want to meet *me*?"

"She's . . ." Candace could practically hear Lauren's brain firing as she chose her words, "very protective." Then Lauren sighed. It made a staticky sound, the phone pressed too close to her mouth. "And she won't let me go to your party unless she meets you."

Candace bit her lip. She wasn't entirely sure if she did want Lauren at her party. The girl was nice and all, but the invitation had been more about making peace with the rest of her friends. "What's in it for me?"

"If I don't go, none of the other girls will, either," Lauren said matter-of-factly. "So, will you come? Tomorrow night?"

Candace rubbed her eyes. At times, Lauren was totally clueless, like a girl raised in the wilderness. And then, at other times, she seemed to know exactly what was going on.

"A Friday night? I'm supposed to meet up with some people." Candace whined, mainly to show Lauren what a sacrifice this was. She didn't have plans. "Fine. Sure. I guess I can go out afterward."

After Candace had hung up, she was surprised to feel flattered. Though the invitation had been one of desperation, Lauren still trusted her to act as a representative of her friends, despite what the list had said about her, and all the mean things the girls were certainly filling Lauren in on.

So Candace decided to really do it up. She'd wear a nice skirt and a cardigan sweater. She'd bring flowers.

And anyway, Candace had been curious about Lauren's home life and she wanted to see for herself. She still wasn't convinced that the girl wasn't in a weird religious cult. And, for the life of her, she couldn't understand what it was about Horse Hair that had made her friends fall head over heels.

At exactly a minute before seven, Candace rings the bell.

Lauren brightens when she opens the door and sees the flowers. It's cute. "These aren't for you," Candace says, pulling the bouquet back. She glances past Lauren and gets a quick look at the living room. One floral couch with a sag in the middle of each cushion, a heavy oak coffee table, a gold lamp that Candace decides is the ugliest she's ever seen. There are no photos or candles or pretty little vases like there are on Candace's fireplace mantel. It smells bitter and lemony, like cleaning fluid. The curtains have been drawn open, but there is weatherproofing plastic on the old windows, sealing the stale air inside.

Mrs. Finn comes out of the kitchen, an even paler version of Lauren. Everything about her seems tired, from her flat hair to her dull pants and stale blouse to the tips of her toes striped by the dark seam of her panty hose.

Mrs. Finn is so different from Candace's own mom. She wears no makeup, and is dressed more like a grandmother. That said, Candace hates when her mom borrows one of her tops to wear out on a date with Bill. But at least her mom tries to look good. Mrs. Finn could maybe be pretty with a little effort. But it seems like Mrs. Finn gave up on herself a long time ago. Candace doubts Mrs. Finn has been on any dates in a long time.

"Hello, Mrs. Finn. These," she says, presenting the flowers, "are for you." Lauren beams at Candace, and Candace gives her a look to quit it. She's nervous enough as it is.

Mrs. Finn nods, and motions for Lauren to take them. "Dinner's running a little late," she says. "I've just started at a new job, and, well . . ."

"Timing got away from us," Lauren says. "I know you said you have plans later. Is that okay?"

Candace doesn't want to stay any longer than she has to. But she smiles and says, "Sure. No problem."

The dining room is set for a formal guest, with tap water poured into crystal goblets. Lauren can't find a vase, so she puts the flowers into a tomato sauce jar and sets them in the middle of the table. "I'm going to help my mother in the kitchen," she says. "I'll be right back."

"Okay," Candace says, and sits alone for what feels like an eternity. She thought this dinner was supposed to be about getting to know her, and here she is, sitting in a dark room by herself.

Finally, Mrs. Finn brings out a pot of spaghetti. Lauren serves everyone, smiling like a robotic housewife.

"So, you grew up in this house, Mrs. Finn?" Candace says, just to get the conversation going.

"Yes."

"Did you go to Mount Washington High?"

"I did. Though it looks much different than when I was a student."

"I'm sure a lot of things are the same," Candace says, thinking of the musty library couches, the dusty old trophy cases, the impossibly uncomfortable auditorium seats.

"I'm sure you're right," Mrs. Finn says.

It only takes one bite for Candace to know that the spaghetti hasn't been fully cooked. She sets her fork down and concentrates on the garlic bread.

"So, tell me about yourself, Candace."

Candace takes a sip of water and folds her hands in her lap. "Well, I'm a sophomore, like Lauren. I live on Elmwood Lane, across town, with my mom."

"What does she do for a living?"

Candace lights up. She likes telling people about her mom's job. Ladies, especially. They always press her for secret beauty tips. "She's a professional makeup artist. For the local nightly news."

Mrs. Finn looks surprised, but not exactly impressed. "My. That's not the kind of job you hear about every day."

"She used to work at a makeup counter at the department store," Candace explains. "And she did a makeup consultation for one of the newscasters. Like a makeover, you know? Anyway, the lady loved it and recommended Mom for the job."

"That's very nice," Mrs. Finn says. And, before Candace has a chance to pick up her fork again, she adds, "So what kind of books do you like to read?"

"Sorry?"

"What kind of books do you like to read?" Mrs. Finn repeats. "Lauren loves to read."

Lauren nods. "I do."

Candace hadn't read a book in months. Not even the one her English teacher had assigned, *Ethan Frome*.

"*Ethan Frome*," Candace says.

"I love *Ethan Frome*!" Lauren cries. "It's so romantic and sad. I mean, can you imagine being forced to live with your wife and the mistress you've unintentionally crippled?"

Candace smiles stiffly. "No. I can't."

"What else have you read recently? For pleasure?"

Candace takes a sip of warm tap water and sets down her glass. "Ummmmm . . ." she says, drawing out the *m* sound as long as she can.

"Mom," Lauren says, a little quieter. "You're putting her on the spot."

"I guess I read a lot of magazines. More than I do books." Candace lowers her eyes. "It's bad, I know."

"It's not," Lauren says, defending her. "Magazines are great. I love magazines."

"Lauren tells me that you have a lot of friends in your class. What do you think attracts people to you?"

At this moment, nothing. "I really don't know. Maybe because I'm honest?"

"Honesty. I like honesty. That's good, because I have an honest question to ask you. And it's not if you are enjoying the dinner, because you are clearly not." Mrs. Finn laughs, but Candace and Lauren don't. They just stare at each other nervously. "I'd like to know why you think everyone is suddenly gravitating toward my daughter."

Candace surprises herself with her answer. Instead of saying that Lauren is pretty, she chooses "Because she's nice" instead.

"Thank you so much for doing this," Lauren says, walking Candace to the door. "I hope it wasn't too terrible," she adds in a low whisper. Lauren herself looks tired, drained. Like this wasn't any fun for her, either.

"Not at all," Candace says, even though she feels completely awful about herself. Mrs. Finn wasn't interested in getting to know her. She only wanted to prove she wasn't worthy of her daughter's friendship.

Don't worry, Candace wants to shout over her shoulder. *We're not friends. Not even close.*

Lauren's hand touches her shoulder, gentle. "I know this has been a hard week, but the girls will come around. And I'll put in an extra good word for you with them."

"Thanks," Candace says. She means it, almost too much.

On her way down the front walk, something comes over Candace, and she slows her pace. She thinks about asking Lauren if she wants to come hang out with her for a bit. First off, Lauren could use a couple of hours away from Mrs. Finn. But also, Candace has this sudden, urgent need to talk to her. She wants Lauren to know she's not a mean girl. She wants to apologize for being a bitch in the bathroom on Tuesday, when Lauren had only tried to be nice. She wants to rewind tonight, start dinner over and perform better in front of Mrs. Finn.

She turns around, but Lauren has already started to close the door between them. Before it slams shut, she calls out, "Have fun tonight, Candace."

Oh, right. Her fake plans.

"I'll try," Candace says, even though she won't.

CHAPTER THIRTY-SIX

Jennifer counts fifty-eight, fifty-nine, sixty Mississippi seconds, and rings the doorbell for the second time. And, for the second time, it doesn't open.

She hasn't visited Margo's house in four years. Not officially, anyway. She's driven by every so often, for no real reason other than to see that it was still standing. Jennifer leans over the side railing and peers up at Margo's bedroom window. The glass is dark, reflecting only the spindly limbs of a bare tree in the front yard and the slack wires stretching from pole to pole.

Jennifer presses her ear to the front door and rings the bell for the third time. She strains to hear the chime, but the bell is either busted or buried underneath the music and the laughter of the people inside. She knocks a few times. Then pounds her fist. Shadows move around behind gauzy window curtains.

There used to be a key hidden under the doormat. Margo was always forgetting hers and getting locked out, and she'd show up at Jennifer's house a few minutes after having said good-bye on the corner to watch cartoons or talk shows until someone came home to let her inside. That was in eighth grade, before things started to get weird. Margo eventually convinced her mother to leave a key under the mat. Margo hardly ever came by after that.

Jennifer crouches down and lifts the wiry grass mat. There's nothing but brittle bits of dead leaves and dirt underneath. A minivan drives down the dark street. The driver glances at her, before turning into a nearby driveway.

Jennifer fights off shivers. What if she accidentally alerts a neighbor to the party and gets Margo in trouble?

She digs through her purse for her cell phone. As soon as she touches it, Jennifer realizes that she doesn't remember Margo's number. No one bothered to give her Dana's or Rachel's. All Jennifer got were instructions to show up at eight.

The guest of honor lets out a deep breath.

Was it a real invitation? Or did they just pity her?

Does it matter?

Then again, it is a quarter to nine, so she is late. They could have thought she'd backed out. Margo was probably hoping.

It had taken Jennifer longer than she'd thought to fix her hair — half up and done in loose barrel curls. She'd worn it exactly the same way in her prettiest picture, taken when she was nine at her grandparents' anniversary party. Margo had gone with her, and when someone wheeled out a sheet cake, the two girls sang a verse of their wedding song in front of everyone. They'd practiced for the moment all summer long. In the picture, both girls were in spring dresses, standing together on the low stage in the church basement, mouths open. The picture stayed up on the mantel in her family's living room, even after their friendship ended. Jennifer wanted it there, a reminder that she had been pretty once. Back when looks didn't matter.

Jennifer's voice was much nicer than Margo's. Everyone at the party had said so, not only her grandparents.

Anyway, when Jennifer had asked to borrow the family car for the night, she'd felt good. She'd spent the afternoon at the mall, trying on armfuls of clothes before settling on the tight black sweater and purple wool pencil skirt that Rachel and Dana had suggested she buy.

"Where is this party?" Mrs. Briggis had asked.

"Margo's house." Her parents had both looked up, but Jennifer waved off their concern. "It's fine. We're over that now."

"You're a good girl, Jennifer."

When her father and mother kissed her good-bye, neither noticed the bottle of vodka tucked in her purse.

Despite the timing snafu, there is still a detectable flutter in her chest, anticipation of how wonderful this night could be. It doesn't matter if four years on the ugly list is what finally got her here. She is here now and she is going to make the best of it that she can.

If only to prove Margo wrong.

Driveway gravel crunches behind her. Jennifer spins and faces a pair of headlights. The engine quiets, and the brightness clicks off a moment later, leaving two white stars in her eyes. When they fade, she sees Margo.

Margo's hair is damp from a shower. She isn't dressed up, either. Just a pair of jeans, a fitted cheering T-shirt, a cardigan sweater, and her Keds. She takes two plastic grocery bags from the backseat.

"Why are you standing outside?" Margo asks with the sort of cold laugh that older sisters are good at. Full of knowing better. Before Jennifer can answer, Margo steps past her and twists the doorknob. The front door is unlocked.

Jennifer steps inside. It is warm inside, muggy, and it makes Jennifer's fingers red and stingy. It's brighter than she'd thought the party would be, bright as a high school classroom. No dim lighting, no candles for ambiance. She peers past the coatrack into the formal living room. It looks the same as she remembers, gray walls with white trim, identical couches facing each other in front of the fireplace, and a maroon oriental rug with fringe. She takes a second look. No. The rug is new. There are kids sitting on the couches, on the floor, and also perched on coffee tables and slanted against the bookshelves.

The front door closes behind Jennifer, and everyone who notices her smiles hello. But there is no one posted at the door checking the backs of people's homecoming tickets to make sure they'd voted for Jennifer, as Dana and Rachel had promised there'd be.

Jennifer follows Margo into the kitchen. Dana and Rachel are sitting up on the center island, drinking fruit punch out of plastic champagne glasses. They share a cigarette.

"Margo!" they shout. "Did you get snacks?"

"Yup," she says. She unpacks one bag and stuffs the rest in the cabinet that Jennifer remembers used to hold cereal. "We're hiding these from the boys. Pigs."

"Hey, Jennifer," Rachel says, almost like she'd forgotten Jennifer was coming. "Glad you made it!"

"Do you want a drink?" Dana asks. The upper part of her lip is stained red. "We invented this stuff called Punchy Punch. It's pretty sweet, but it's better than the nasty cheap beer the guys buy. And it gets you drunk way faster. Here, Margo. Get Jennifer some."

Margo pours herself a glass, and then one for Jennifer, half-full. She hands it to Jennifer, but does not make eye contact.

"Oh. I brought this." Jennifer pulls the bottle from her purse. "I don't know if it's any good," she says shyly.

Dana takes the bottle and checks the label. "Nice. It's great, actually." She smiles. "Thanks, Jennifer."

Margo brings up cheering, a last-minute formation change or something, and Dana and Rachel start discussing it with her. They aren't excluding Jennifer, but it's obvious she can't participate in the conversation. Surely, this is part of Margo's plan to make her feel so uncomfortable that she'll leave. Well, that's not going to happen. Jennifer hangs her jacket on the back of a kitchen chair and stands there, smiling, downing her Punchy Punch. Jennifer even asks Margo for a refill. She is not going to let Margo·make her feel unwelcome, even if it is Margo's house.

After all, Jennifer used to come here all the time.

"Is the bathroom still upstairs?" Jennifer asks, setting her just-emptied glass down.

"Yeah," Margo says, in a voice that adds *of course it is.*

Jennifer takes the stairs slowly. Framed pictures of Margo and Maureen line the walls. Jennifer knew Maureen didn't like her. It made coming to this house, especially near the end of their friendship, pretty uncomfortable. Especially because Margo really looked up to Maureen. She always had, even though Maureen wasn't all that nice to Margo, either.

When she gets to the landing, Jennifer stares down a hallway full of closed doors. She can't remember which one leads to the bathroom. She tries one and opens it to Mr. and Mrs. Gable's bedroom. They are inside, lying on the made bed, watching television. Mrs. Gable gasps, literally gasps at the sight of Jennifer, and she nearly spills her large goblet of red wine on the white duvet.

"I'm so sorry," Jennifer says, quickly backing up. "I didn't know you guys were home."

"We're in seclusion," Mr. Gable deadpans.

"Better we are here, if things get out of hand." Mrs. Gable sets her wine on the nightstand and beckons Jennifer forward. "So how are you, dear? It's been so long. We've missed you. Are you doing well? How are your parents?"

"They're fine. How's Maureen? Is she liking college?"

"Who knows with that one? She hardly ever calls." Mrs. Gable glances around the room, her eyes settling on a laundry-cloaked chaise lounge. "Do you want to come in and chat awhile?" She bites her lip, and then says, "I always ask Margo about you. How you're doing and whatnot."

Jennifer's throat tightens up. Margo's parents were always good to her. She misses them. And she likes that they've missed her, too. It's cruel, the way things worked out.

Jennifer watches Mr. Gable discreetly squeeze his wife's thigh. "I'm sure Jennifer wants to get back to the party."

"Right. Of course."

"I'm actually looking for the bathroom. I've forgotten which door it is."

Mrs. Gable seems sad that Jennifer didn't remember. "Third on the left. Right across from Margo's room. It's really so good to see you, Jennifer. Don't be a stranger."

Jennifer promises she won't, and closes the door. Her hands are sweating and she wipes them on her skirt. She walks down the hall, reaches for the bathroom doorknob. But instead of opening it, she turns around and stares at the closed door to Margo's bedroom.

The urge to see it is overwhelming.

She listens to hear if someone might be coming. There's nothing but party noise downstairs.

She takes one step. Then another. She opens the door and inches inside.

Jennifer always loved Margo's room, and it looks exactly as she remembers. It was made for a princess: canopy bed, huge armoire, a window seat where they'd sit and talk for hours. There are stuffed animals propped up with the pillows on her bed.

Even though Jennifer is where she shouldn't be, even though she and Margo aren't friends anymore, it comforts her to be back in this room again. Despite the fact that eighth grade was forever ago, and that Margo would probably always pretend otherwise, they *had* been friends.

Margo's cheerleading uniform hangs from a bedpost inside a plastic dry-cleaning bag, ready for tomorrow's football game. And from the door of the armoire Jennifer thinks she spots Margo's homecoming dress.

She tiptoes across the thick cream carpet for a closer look.

After a minute of simply staring, Jennifer rubs the hem stitches between her fingertips. The style is not what she expected Margo to choose for senior-year homecoming. She imagined something fun and flirty, carefree. With a skirt that would lift when she'd spin on the dance floor. This dress is tight, dark, sophisticated. And, in Jennifer's opinion, totally wrong for homecoming. Though she concedes that the green will look great with Margo's skin.

But the dress? It's like Margo has something to prove. That she's too good to care about being homecoming queen, about high school stuff. That all this is below her.

Except Jennifer knows the truth. Or at least, she did. Margo *does* care about what people think of her.

Before she can think better of it, Jennifer opens Margo's armoire. The insides of the doors are covered in peeling stickers — rainbows, horses, glow-in-the-dark stars. Clothes hang from the dowel rod and sit folded in messy, teetering stacks at the base. Jennifer can't see to the back, to the place where Margo used to hide things she didn't want anyone to find.

She reaches her hand deep inside and feels around.

"Oh my god."

Jennifer whips around and sees Margo standing in the doorway.

"What the hell are you doing in my room?"

Jennifer can't breathe. "Nothing, I —"

"Oh my god," Margo says again, though this time it's with less shock and more anger. She charges forward and slams her armoire doors shut, almost severing Jennifer's fingers in the process. "You're lucky, you know that?" Margo is shaking, and she flaps her hands as if she were wicking off the overflow of energy. "If it weren't for everyone else here right now . . ." Margo trails off, but Jennifer watches her hands clench into fists. "You'd better go back downstairs right now," she says in a low growl. "And if I see you up in my room again, I don't care what people say about me, I'll drag you by your hair and throw you out the front door."

Jennifer sprints past Margo and charges downstairs. Dana and Rachel are still in the kitchen. That's surely where Margo is headed, to tell on her. She doesn't know where to go.

"Hey! We need an Asshole in here!"

Jennifer follows the voice into the dining room and finds a large table encircled by senior boys. Empty beer cans are everywhere.

"I'll play," she says, quickly taking a seat. Her heart is racing, and as she is dealt in, Jennifer keeps glancing toward the kitchen, expecting Margo to burst in at any moment and make good on her threat.

Jennifer briefly looks at the cards in her hand, as if she has a clue how to play. While Justin shuffles the cards and deals the next round, he goes over the rules of Asshole, but Jennifer doesn't pay much attention, aside from the basic function that she must get rid of her hand as quickly as possible.

"Asshole needs to sit left of the President," Justin says.

Jennifer stands up, her legs unsteady, and trades seats with a boy sitting next to Matthew Goulding. Like a seasoned poker player, Matthew studies his hand stoically with a ball cap lowered over his brow.

He is Margo's longtime crush. Or at least, he had been when Jennifer was still in the loop. She thinks back, cycling through the gossip and whispers from the last four years. Have they ever hooked up?

No, she doesn't think so.

They play a few rounds. With each new hand, Jennifer has to give her best two cards to the President. And the President gives her his two worst cards. It is designed to be almost impossible to rise up from the very bottom.

Jennifer plays dumb about the valued cards in her hand. From the little she's picked up, she knows that aces and twos are the cards to have. But instead, she inches her chair close to

Matthew and flashes him her whole hand, letting him pick through whatever it is he wants.

Jennifer can hear the party going on in other rooms: video games being played by boys, girls arguing over the music, the sliding glass door leading to the deck opening and closing. But she is content to stay right where she is.

An hour goes by, and Jennifer has lost every round. She has the most cards of all the players. Not that she minds. The last time Matthew won, he'd given her a two card, which was the most valuable. Plus, she's got a nice buzz going.

Ted, another senior who is playing with them, is clearly drunk. He's spilled his beer twice, and during the last hand he leaned back too far. His chair tipped out from underneath him, and his head cracked against the wooden hutch. Ted didn't seem hurt, though. He couldn't stop laughing.

After Matthew wins again, he says, "Okay. This is getting boring," in a friendly way, and hands her a leftover two card. For the rest of the round, he helps Jennifer. They become a little team. She shows him her cards, and he points or nods at the ones she is to throw down. She keeps watching, hoping Margo will walk in and see them there. The others around her still win, but Jennifer manages to come in second to last.

"I didn't lose!"

"Congrats." Matthew rises to his feet. "You're now Vice Asshole."

Jennifer glumly watches him go.

Justin says, "We need more beers." He says it and looks at Jennifer. "Vice Asshole gets the beers." He points to a door inside the kitchen. "There's a fridge in the basement."

"I know that," Jennifer mutters.

She squeezes past the other card players at the table and goes into the kitchen. As she does, she catches sight of Matthew outside on the deck through the glass door. Matthew hops up on the corner of the table. He is smiling, talking to Margo.

Each step down into the dark, cool basement falls with a thud. There are laundry machines, Mr. Gable's tools, and an old yellow refrigerator that Margo's family put down here when they had their kitchen redone. Jennifer and Margo used to play school in the basement, but the teaching charts and fake tests are gone from the walls.

She opens the fridge and tries to figure out how best to carry the most cans back upstairs. The basement door opens and shuts.

"Hey," Ted slurs. He holds the banister as he descends the stairs slowly, calculating each step.

"Hi."

Ted walks up behind her and perches his arm up on the open refrigerator door. "You getting beers?"

"That's my job!" she says, immediately regretting the cheeriness in her voice. People are not supposed to like the job of Vice Asshole.

"Here," Ted says, like an offer to help her. But instead of taking the cans, he guides Jennifer toward the washing machine. The fridge door shuts, leaving them in darkness.

Ted closes his sleepy eyes before he leans in, and it takes a bit of adjusting, but his mouth lands over hers. It is wet and warm and slightly sour. His arms go around her waist and he pulls her against him.

Jennifer closes her eyes. It is her first kiss. She knows Ted is wasted, but it's okay. This was a boy who, last year, threw a hot dog at her. And now, he is kissing her.

And if Ted will kiss her, maybe other boys will be interested in her, too.

Her kissing gets suddenly more inspired. She thinks of the things she's seen on television, the way women run their fingers through a guy's hair, so she does that. Ted seems into it, kissing her hard and fast, his nostrils pumping out hot air, muscles tightening.

The basement door opens and then closes. And then opens again. Each time, a wedge of light finds them.

Jennifer knows whoever is looking can see her and Ted. She brings her arms up around his shoulders, parts her legs as much as her pencil skirt will allow and lets Ted's leg slide in between hers. Interlock.

A boy laughs. It sounds like Justin. He says, pretty loud, to the people upstairs. "Whoa! Ted *must* be wasted. He's making out with Jennifer Briggis!"

Ted peels his lips off of Jennifer. "Shut up, dickhead," he calls out. But not in a way like he's angry. Like he thinks it's funny.

The door slams shut again, and they are finally back in the darkness. "Don't listen to him," he says, and pushes her hair back. "I'm not that drunk. Seriously."

She looks up at him, searching his glassy, watery eyes for a glimmer of truth. And when she doesn't find it, she closes her eyes and keeps on kissing him.

CHAPTER THIRTY-SEVEN

Margo and her friends only smoke when they drink. They never buy the packs themselves, just bum them from real smokers. Still, Margo knows she shouldn't do it. Honestly, she is *thisclose* to a full-blown addiction.

But after her fight with Jennifer, it is all she wants. She goes outside onto her deck and smokes four in a row all by herself. Well . . . mostly she lets them burn down in her fingers, only taking a drag every few minutes.

She is too mad, her chest squeezed far too tight, to inhale.

A replay loops in her mind, the moment of going upstairs and finding Jennifer rummaging through her things. Paranoia sets in, and her hands shake, the smoke wiggling up to the sky in a frantic curl. How long had Jennifer been in her bedroom? What had she been after? What had she hoped to find?

And then it hits her.

Jennifer had been looking for the Mount Washington embossing stamp.

Finding the stamp would be Jennifer's ultimate vindication. She'd walk downstairs with it over her head for all Margo's friends to see. It would practically guarantee that Jennifer would be voted homecoming queen. And, as a bonus, Margo would spend her senior year friendless and alone, the way Jennifer had as a freshman. Karma, full circle.

Is that what she deserved?

Obviously Jennifer thought she was a horrible person. But Margo can't believe that Jennifer really, truly, thought she'd been the one who wrote the list. Maybe it was crazy for Margo to think otherwise, after everything that's happened, but Jennifer should know her better than that.

The glass door behind her slides open. Margo turns and sees Matthew.

He pauses, half-outside, half-inside. "Hey. I came out to get some air. But . . . you look like you want to be alone."

"It's fine," she says, turning back to the yard. She thinks about putting her cigarette out, because she knows Matthew doesn't like smoke, but it seems fruitless at this point. Everyone already seems to think the worst of her anyway.

Still, Margo is glad for his interruption, eager to think about something other than Jennifer. But that's exactly who Matthew brings up.

"Jennifer Briggis depresses me big-time," he says, hopping up on the patio table. "I've never seen a person try so hard to be liked."

I'm the same way, Margo thinks, staring off into the dark, "At least half the people here tonight think I put Jennifer on the list. They think I made it."

"Yeah," he says, swinging his legs. "I know."

Matthew's confirmation makes Margo go wobbly. She grips the deck railing to steady herself. "Jennifer thinks I did it. I guess I can't blame her." Her eyes well up, and everything goes blurry. "She has every reason to hate me." Margo spins around and looks at Matthew. "I was terrible to her."

It is the first time she's said it, without a caveat, excuse, or blaming someone else. She begins to cry.

Matthew climbs off the table and stands next to her. "You okay?"

She wipes her face on the sleeve of her cardigan. "You must think I'm an idiot, crying over this stuff."

To her relief, Matthew shakes his head. "I don't. Actually, I'm proud of you for saying your piece to Dana and Rachel about the whole 'Vote Queen Jennifer' thing." He rubs her shoulder. "For the record, I think it's a terrible idea, too."

"Dana and Rachel have their hearts in the right place," Margo says. But her own heart? She's not exactly sure.

"I guess. But it's crazy to me that Jennifer's going along with it."

"Of course she is. She wants to feel beautiful. Every girl inside my house does. That's why we all get so wrapped up in the list, in homecoming." It sounds like Margo is sticking up for Jennifer, but really she's defending herself. For caring about the list, for being upset that she might not get to be homecoming queen.

"I don't think that's it," Matthew says. "You girls want *everyone else* to think you're beautiful."

She says, "Maybe," though it is definitely true. It just sounds so pathetic.

"I don't think you made the list, Margo. If that makes you feel better."

"It does." Another couple tears fall. Margo blushes. "I'd better get back inside." Margo grinds out her cigarette into the wood and looks at him. "Can you tell I've been crying?"

Matthew reaches out and touches her cheek, catching her last tear on the tip of his finger. "No."

"Thank you for saying that, and for listening to me." She heads for the patio door, her heart racing.

"I'll dance with you tomorrow night, even if you don't win," he calls after her.

A dance with the boy she's loved forever. It is wonderful to look forward to something that has nothing to do with the list or being homecoming queen, something that has no guilt or sadness attached to it.

It is only good.

The party starts to break up around midnight. Every time Margo has made a lap for trash, she has kept an eye out for Jennifer. Not to apologize, exactly. Because, when it comes down to it, Jennifer shouldn't have been in her room. But she'd maybe smile or something small like that, to make things a little more civil. But she hasn't seen her for hours.

Dana and Rachel help her clean up. The three friends are in the kitchen, rinsing out empty beer cans and putting them in the recycling bags, when the basement door creaks open. Jennifer and Ted emerge from the darkness.

The curls in Jennifer's hair have mostly uncoiled and it is mussed in the back. Ted is red-faced and squints at the light. "Shit," he sighs, and quickly stumbles off.

Dana, Rachel, and Margo avoid looking at each other.

"What time is it?" Jennifer says, and then makes a weird swallowing noise.

"Um, it's after midnight," Dana says. "How long were you guys down there?"

"I gotta go." Jennifer tries to take a step, but it looks as if she can't decide which foot to put forward, and she sort of wobbles unsteadily on her boot heels and doesn't move forward at all.

Margo gets a heavy feeling inside, just like the Punchy Punch, thick and syrupy.

"You can't drive," Dana says. "Where'd Ted go?"

Rachel looks out the window. "Um, I think he just left."

"What a jerk," Dana says, quickly wiping her hands on a kitchen towel. "I'll take you home, Jennifer. You can leave your car here and come get it tomorrow. You ready, Rachel?"

"Ready. We'll see you tomorrow morning, Margo. Thanks for everything."

Jennifer teeters past Margo without making eye contact. "Yeah. Thanks. For everything."

SATURDAY

CHAPTER THIRTY-EIGHT

It's impossible to sleep with a broken heart.

Every which way Danielle rolls in her bed, a shard pricks and tears and pokes at her insides, leaving behind another fresh wound.

At six thirty, she gives up and trades her pajamas for her Speedo and her team-issued sweat suit.

Mrs. DeMarco drives her to school wearing her fuzzy blue bathrobe stuffed bulkily under her coat.

The school parking lot is empty.

"Did you get the time wrong?"

"Maybe," Danielle lies. "But don't worry, Mom." She unbuckles her seat belt. "They'll be here soon. Go back to bed."

She waits on the driveway curb, rubbing her hands together to keep warm. When Coach Tracy's Jeep appears, Danielle chases it into the lot. Before the engine goes off, Danielle has her face up to the driver's-side window. "Good morning, Coach Tracy." Her breath leaves a cloud on the glass. Danielle wipes it with the sleeve of her sweatshirt, then opens the door like a valet.

If Coach Tracy is surprised to see her, Danielle can't tell. All she says is, "What are you doing here?"

"I woke up this morning and realized that my shoulder feels pretty good. Great, actually." She pivots so she is parallel to the Jeep, hitches forward at her hips, and rolls her arms in a spirited butterfly stroke. "So I thought I'd let you know that I'm ready to swim on the relay, if you need me."

"That was a quick recovery," Coach Tracy deadpans. "But your spot's been taken. You know that."

"Right." Danielle takes a breath and steadies herself. "But I came anyway, because I wanted to prove to you how much this opportunity means to me. And to promise that I'll never miss another practice again this season." She pauses. "And . . . you know . . . to say that I'm sorry about yesterday."

Danielle was hoping that if she owned up to what they both already seemed to know, Coach Tracy would give her another chance. She waits for her coach's face to soften, but it tightens instead.

"I'm trying very hard not to take what you did personally, Danielle. But you need to understand that I find faking an injury particularly insulting." Coach Tracy's eyes get wide and intense. "I can never swim the way I used to. I could have gone to the Olympics. But even worse than that, I lost a big part of my identity, one of the things that made me special, because of what happened to *my* shoulders. Can you understand what that might feel like?"

Danielle drops her head. She wants to tell Coach Tracy everything — about the list, about how she was teased this week, about her breakup with Andrew. She tries to speak, but her voice cracks. And anyway, Coach Tracy isn't finished. She cuts Danielle off.

"Obviously you weren't ready to handle the responsibilities and the honor of being a varsity swimmer on my team," Coach Tracy says. "But since you're here, you can grab the team towels from the back of my Jeep and load them onto the bus. And the water bottles, too. Do everyone a favor and make sure they stay filled throughout the meet."

Danielle isn't sure whether to feel lucky or sad. But she does as she is told and then boards the school bus that will take the swim team to their meet. The other varsity team members climb on. Most of them have their sweatshirt hoods pulled up, headphones in their ears. No one asks about her shoulder injury. And Danielle doesn't tell them that she's been demoted from varsity swimmer to team equipment manager.

Hope arrives and looks pleasantly surprised to see Danielle. Danielle tries not to feel jealous that her best friend has her varsity spot. After all, it's nobody's fault but her own.

"Do you mind if I sit next to you?" Hope asks.

Danielle scoots over. But it is hard to look at Hope. She is still completely humiliated by the way she'd acted with Andrew.

"How are you feeling today?"

"Not great," Danielle says.

"Did Coach Tracy say that you can swim?" Hope whispers.

"No."

"I'm sorry, Danielle."

Danielle pulls her sweatshirt hood up like the others. "Yeah. Me, too."

The swim meet is a nail-biter. The score goes back and forth, each school having the lead for a single relay, only to lose it again the next heat. Danielle sits in the bleachers, handing out towels and water to the other team members. She reminds Hope to stand up every so often to do jumping jacks or squats to keep warm, like she's seen Andrew do on the sidelines.

As quickly as Andrew creeps into her mind, Danielle tries to push him back out. It is sad knowing she'll have to give herself this new reflex. Despite his glimmers of regret, she can never ever forgive Andrew for what he's done. How he's humiliated her, worse than any list or any stupid nickname. Though she knows she is strong physically, she wonders if she is strong enough to get over him.

When it comes time for the four hundred freestyle relay, Mount Washington has earned a bit of a lead, courtesy of the boys' individual freestyle, in which they take first, second, and fourth places. There is a chance that, with a strong finish, the girls can sew it up. Coach Tracy comes over. "Alright, Hope, I'm switching you out of this race and into the two hundred freestyle in the next heat." She turns to Danielle. "Let's go. I'm putting you as anchor." And then she adds, before cramming her whistle into her mouth, "Prove me wrong."

A bolt of energy jolts through Danielle. She wants to cry, to thank Coach Tracy, but there will be time for that afterward. After she proves herself.

Danielle quickly sheds her tracksuit. She's never felt nervous before a swim, but now every muscle is twitching. Hope gives her a good-luck hug and tucks a stray hair underneath Danielle's swim cap.

She follows the other girls up to their lane. She'll be swimming with two seniors (Jane, who'd been her partner in the weight room, and Andrea) and one junior (Charice). Danielle knows they're the three best female swimmers in the school. She can't help but wonder if she's good enough to be racing with them.

They gather in a little group and Jane gives everyone a quick pep talk, but Danielle isn't listening. Instead, she is looking at the girls in their bathing suits. They have the same kinds of broad shoulders and muscles as she does. And Danielle suddenly feels like she is exactly where she should be.

After the third girl leaps into the water, Danielle pulls her goggles down, climbs on top of the stand, and readies herself for the last leg. They are a second or two behind the other school.

Her mind goes white as she breaks through the surface of the water. She pushes all the pain out of her arms, kicks the hurt free from her legs. She swims her broken heart out.

Danielle and Hope climb onto the team bus and share a seat near the front. The vibe is completely different from what it had been in the morning. Everyone is in a celebratory mood, stomping their feet and clapping their hands. The whole team sings the Mount Washington fight song at the tops of their lungs while two of the varsity boys do a jig in the aisle.

Danielle's relay team came in first, and she tied a school record for the fastest leg. Though Danielle knows somewhere inside of her is a beam of happiness at her accomplishment, she can't reach it. She simply feels exhausted. Everything she'd had to give is gone. There's nothing left inside her, certainly no strength for celebration. She only wants to climb into bed and sleep for the rest of the weekend.

Jane leans over their seat. "Danielle! Our MVP!" She points over her shoulder at the back of the bus. "You guys know Will Hardy, right? He lives in the redbrick house a block behind the school parking lot. The whole varsity team's going over there before the homecoming dance to pre-party and take pictures, and then we'll walk to the gym in a big group. You both should come."

"Wow, thanks!" Hope beams a huge smile at Jane, and then gives a knowing look to Danielle. "We'll be there."

Danielle pulls her hands inside the sleeves of her sweatshirt. "Actually, I don't think I'm going. But thanks so much for inviting me."

Jane's mouth drops open. "What? Why aren't you going to the dance?"

"I'm exhausted. I only slept about five minutes total last night."

"Tired?" Jane makes a face. "So take a nap. The dance is eight hours from now."

"Yeah. I just don't think I'm feeling up to it."

Danielle can tell Jane is confused and looking for a bit more of an explanation. But she isn't ready to tell people what happened. It's still too hurtful and raw.

Hope sighs. "She and her boyfriend just broke up," she tells Jane. "He's been a jerk to her because of the list, and yesterday he invited her out for pizza and then let all his friends make fun of her." Hope takes a breath. "And then she found out that he is having a party and didn't invite her."

"Hope!" Danielle says.

Jane purses her lips. "Who is this a-hole?"

"Andrew Reynolds," Danielle says. Jane shrugs blankly. "He's a sophomore."

"Well, this Andrew guy got off lucky, because he deserves to have his balls kicked." Jane spins around and faces the back of the bus. "Andrea! Charice! Come here and help me convince Danielle that she needs to come to the homecoming dance."

Andrea and Charice move to the empty seat across the aisle. "What? Why won't Danielle come to the dance?" Charice asks.

"Her ex-boyfriend, Andrew Reynolds," Jane says.

"Who's that?" Andrea asks.

"Does he go to Mount Washington?" Charice asks.

"Yes," Danielle says, surprised that the girls don't know him. Then again, why would they? Andrew is only a sophomore. "He's on the varsity football team."

"But he doesn't play," Hope clarifies. "He's kind of short. And his eyes are really close together. Like someone's pushing in on his ears and squishing up his whole face."

Andrea brightens. "Oh, that skinny kid with the bad skin?"

Danielle shakes her head. "His skin's not *that* bad. It's from his helmet." Though, thinking about it, Danielle remembers that Andrew also has bacne. She never gave it much thought beyond simply noting its existence the first time they went swimming in Clover Lake together. It hadn't mattered to her. She liked him for who he was.

And while she is flattered by what the girls are trying to do, there is one big reason she doesn't want to go to the dance. She takes a deep breath and explains.

"I don't think I could handle seeing Andrew dance with another girl."

Six weeks ago, they'd danced together on the last night of camp. The deck that stretched off the back of the mess hall had been transformed by strings of white lights that didn't shine nearly as brightly as the stars in the sky, but still managed to add something special.

The camp director acted as the DJ with rented speakers and

the stereo from his office, and he played a mix of oldies, pop songs, and silly things like "The Hokey Pokey" and "The Electric Slide." It was only the girls who danced, in small circles with one another. Every so often, one of the boys would bust out in a running man or funky chicken for a laugh, but the rest stood around and watched.

Andrew wasn't much of a dancer. Honestly, neither was Danielle. And anyway, the night was for the campers, not the counselors. So they stood together behind the buffet table, refilling cups of fruit punch, making sure the kids didn't throw pretzels at one another, and stopping the girls from spinning one another around too fast. The other counselors, the veterans, leaned against the railing, miserable that the best part of their summer was a few songs from ending.

Danielle hadn't been sure what the night had meant for her and Andrew. Once they'd finally gotten together, her feelings for him had developed fast. Though maybe not that fast, considering how much time they spent together: three meals a day, every scheduled activity. They'd watched all the VHS tapes in the camp's media closet, up to the letter *W*, and Andrew had thought to take a picture of what movies were left so they could finish things out at home. Clearly, that boded well for them. But Danielle also knew things would be different. They'd both have friends, sports, and schoolwork to compete with.

She told herself she'd be fine either way. She told herself that a lot in the last days at Clover Lake, hoping to brainwash herself into believing it.

And then, without warning, Andrew leaned over and whispered, "I'm so glad I don't have to say good-bye to you tomorrow."

"Me, too," she whispered back.

The night suddenly took on a different feeling. It was the last night for the kids, for the veterans, for everyone but Danielle and Andrew. Tomorrow morning, they wouldn't have to climb on two buses that would drive them in opposite directions. They'd ride back to the same place.

It wasn't the end of anything, but the beginning of everything.

The camp director took the microphone and announced that it was the last song. Danielle didn't even have a chance to react before Andrew's hand was laced in hers, pulling her onto the dance floor. A couple of the kids pointed and made goo-goo faces at them, but it didn't stop Andrew from putting his hands on her waist, threading his fingers through the loops in her shorts. She put her hands on his shoulders.

"You're beautiful," he said.

His words, in memory, take on a hollow sound inside Danielle, as the reality shadows everything that had been bright and light and possible.

Had she looked beautiful to him that night?

She'd certainly felt beautiful, even with the bug bites and the chipped purple polish on her toenails and the horrible tan lines from her lifeguard suit. She'd felt beautiful that whole summer. But it seemed like so long ago.

Toward the end of the song, Andrew crushed her toes underneath the rubber tread of his running shoes. That hurt for sure, but not as badly as it would to see him stepping on someone else's feet.

Jane snaps her fingers. "Hello! Danielle! Andrew's going to be the jealous one when he sees you dancing with senior guys."

Danielle laughs. "I don't know any senior guys."

"Yes you do!" Jane turns around and calls out for Will. "Will, aren't you going to dance with Danielle tonight?"

"Sure," Will says, smiling at her with a set of very white and very straight teeth. "I got moves. Lots of moves." He does the running man down the bus aisle, back to his seat.

"I saw him checking you out at the relay," Andrea whispers.

"Yeah, right."

Charice leans forward and pinches Danielle's cheek. "You're hot, girl! What are you even worried about?"

Jane folds her arms. "Look. We're picking you both up at seven. End of story."

Danielle laughs. "I don't have a dress or anything."

Hope nudges her. "Yes, you do. That pink one you bought."

Danielle had put it on last night as part of her pity party after the whole Andrew incident. The dress didn't really fit. Not just the material, but the style. It wasn't her at all. "I'm not wearing that."

Jane points at Andrea. "She's got dresses out the ass."

Andrea flips her hair. "Yup. It's true. I am an admitted clothes whore. I can bring a few things over. I think we're about the same size."

"Thanks," Danielle says, starting to feel excited. She'd noticed Andrea's clothes before. She always had something pretty on.

"So you're in?"

Danielle nods and smiles. "I'm in."

CHAPTER THIRTY-NINE

Margo stands at the sink eating a quick bowl of cereal. The homecoming game is in a few hours. She has her cheering uniform on, her hair pulled up with a curl of white ribbon. The kitchen looks as good as it does after the cleaning lady visits, with no trace of last night's party, aside from the starchy smell of flat beer wafting up the drain, the three over-stuffed bags of recycling set out on the deck and now slouching against the glass patio door, and a faint haze of cigarette smoke in the air.

Rachel and Dana should be here any minute.

Margo walks to the front window and parts the curtains. Jennifer's car is still parked in the driveway. Margo prays Jennifer will come and get it when she's not here.

The phone rings. She thinks it might be the girls letting her know they are running late, but it isn't. It's Maureen.

"Hey," Maureen says, with an awkward pause to acknowledge that they haven't spoken for an entire month. "Is Mom there? She's not picking up her phone."

"She's out shopping with Dad, and then they're going to the homecoming game."

"Oh, right." Maureen says it flatly. "How's that going?"

Margo thinks about not saying anything, but in some ways, Maureen is the best person she can talk to about it.

"Honestly, not great. There's this whole big movement going to get Jennifer Briggis elected as homecoming queen."

Maureen lets out a deeply annoyed breath. "Don't you think that's mean, Margo? Hasn't the girl suffered enough?"

"I don't have anything to do with it." Margo really doesn't appreciate her sister's tone, considering how Maureen had talked about Jennifer back in the day. "In fact, I'm one of the only ones not doing it, even though everyone in school thinks *I* made the list this year."

"Wait. What list?"

"You haven't even been out of high school for four months, and you've already forgotten the list?" Margo checks her watch. The cheerleaders are supposed to be at Mount Washington High in five minutes so they can board the bus with the football players and lead the Spirit Caravan. They'll be cutting it close.

"I haven't forgotten," Maureen snarks back. "But last year's was supposed to be the final list."

Margo squeezes the receiver. "How do you know that?"

It takes a while for Maureen to say anything. And in the pause, Margo slowly lowers herself down on the arm of the sofa, because she just has this feeling. Finally, Maureen sucks in a breath and says, "Because I made last year's list."

A horn honks outside. Dana and Rachel. Her ride.

"What do you mean you *made* last year's list?" Margo says quickly, because she's out of time. "You were *on* last year's list."

"I know." Margo hears her sister shift the phone from one side to the other. "I put myself on it."

"But —" The car horn beeps again. Margo curses under her breath. "Hold on a second, okay?" she says to her sister. "Just hold on. And don't hang up!" She sets the phone down on the couch and swings opens the front door. "I'll meet you at the school," she screams to Dana and Rachel. "Go ahead without me!"

"What? Why?" Dana yells back.

"You'll miss the Spirit Caravan!" Rachel chimes in.

"Then I'll see you at the football field!" Margo tells them. Dana and Rachel are completely baffled as to what reason she might have to skip out on the Spirit Caravan, but there's no time for Margo to lay everything out. "I'll explain later," she calls, waves good-bye, and then slams the door. She runs back to pick up the phone. "You there, Maureen?"

"Yeah," she says in a tired voice. "I'm here."

Margo goes to the window and looks outside. Dana and Rachel are gone. "Alright," she says, sitting cross-legged in the center of the living room rug. "What happened?" She doesn't say another word. She doesn't even breathe.

"It was the end of my junior year, and I was cleaning out my locker. I picked up this plastic bag and it was weirdly heavy. There was something wrapped up in brown paper inside. I unwrapped it and realized it was the Mount Washington stamp. There was no note in the bag. No instructions or any clue as to who'd put it there or why. I even went through the trash can, through all the old papers I'd just tossed, in case I missed it. I have no idea how long the bag had even been in my locker. But I definitely knew I had a serious opportunity.

"So all summer long, I thought about who, exactly, to put on the list. It was a serious power trip, and I became obsessed with evaluating everyone I saw. My friends, your friends, the little freshmen on orientation day. It was a massive secret beauty contest, and I was the only judge. Though, truthfully, I was only thinking about the pretty girls. The ugly ones were just . . . afterthoughts. Except Jennifer. I sort of decided from the very beginning that Jennifer would be on the list."

"Why?"

"Because anyone other than Jennifer would have been a let-down." Margo lets the words seep in. Maureen continues, "I did think about picking you as the prettiest junior, Margo. But I went with Rachel, since I thought it would raise red flags. You know, to have both of us on there the same year."

"You could have picked me and not yourself," Margo notes.

"Hmm. I guess that's true. But I thought I deserved it."

It's funny, but Margo had felt the same way. She never questioned her sister being on the list, being homecoming queen. But knowing it was Maureen herself behind it — well, it made things different.

Maureen goes on. "The thrill of being prettiest senior lasted for, like, a minute. My friends were jealous. They treated me weird. They thought they deserved it more than me. Which maybe they did, but I started to think maybe they weren't my real friends at all. And every time I saw Jennifer trying to be a good sport about everything in the hallway, I felt guilty. Have you ever read that Edgar Allan Poe story about the heart that beats under the floorboards? That was basically my life. That's when I got the idea. To confess.

"I went to see Jennifer after graduation. I told her what I did, and that I was going to make sure that she wouldn't be put on the list next year. There would be no list. There'd be no four years in a row. I made this big deal of throwing the embossing stamp in the trash right in front of her. I told her I was sorry, and that, if she told on me, I wouldn't blame her for it."

"Wow. That's . . . wow. But wait. Who were you going to give the stamp to?"

"You, I guess." And then Maureen adds, "But I never would have told you it came from me."

Margo's mind spins. Who would she have put on the list, if she'd had the chance? For as badly as she wanted to be homecoming queen, could she have put herself on it?

An interesting hypothetical, yes. But it didn't matter. What did is that Margo is innocent. And now she has proof that Jennifer's the guilty one.

Margo says, "So after you left, Jennifer must have pulled the stamp out of the trash and she put herself on as the ugliest senior." She wonders why Jennifer would do that.

"Yeah," Maureen says. "And she put you as the prettiest."

Even though the Spirit Caravan has surely started making its way back down the mountain and to the football field, Margo drives to Jennifer's house. She can't let this go one second longer.

To think, the whole time, Jennifer knew. She knew people suspected Margo was behind the list, but she never hinted otherwise, never said a word to defend her. Jennifer had been glad to let Margo take the fall, have her reputation ruined, to have Margo's friends and complete strangers think the absolute worst of her.

Margo hates that she ever felt sorry for Jennifer. She wishes she could go back in time and erase her conversation with Matthew. Not the end of it, obviously, but definitely the parts where Margo made herself look bad. She can't wait to call Jennifer out, to force her to own up to what she'd done. And to all the people who thought she was guilty, she'll say, *I told you so.*

But as she pulls along the curb in front of Jennifer's house, a wave of nerves catches her by surprise. She and Jennifer are about to have it out, the way they probably should have back in eighth grade. Only this time, it will be way more messy, way more painful.

Mrs. Briggis answers the door. It is the first time Margo has seen her since the day her friendship with Jennifer ended. She steels herself for the coldness, but there isn't any. "Margo! What a nice surprise!" Mrs. Briggis looks over her shoulder. "Jennifer's still asleep. I don't think she's feeling very well."

"Do you think I could go up and talk to her? Just for a second? It's about tonight."

"Of course. She's really looking forward to the dance. It was so nice of you girls to take her out shopping and convince her to go. I know if she never went to a single high school dance, she'd regret it forever."

Margo looks down at her feet. "Yeah."

Margo takes the stairs two by two and enters Jennifer's room without knocking. Jennifer is asleep in bed. Her party clothes, the ones she'd worn last night, are in a heap on the floor.

The walls are painted a cheery lemon yellow, which Margo thinks is new, though she can't remember what color they used to be. The bunk beds are gone, replaced by an iron frame with rose-colored glass spheres mounted to the posts. She can't see Jennifer, just her lumpy form underneath the quilt Jennifer's grandmother had sewn as a present for Jennifer's eleventh birthday. Margo loved that quilt. The pink squares with the strawberry print were her favorite. Jennifer liked the ones with the shamrocks best.

Margo has not thought of Jennifer's grandmother since they stopped being friends, and she realizes that she's probably dead. She'd been very sick all through eighth grade, deteriorating. Jennifer used to call her at the nursing home and sing to her over the phone.

Margo inches forward. "Jennifer!" she whispers. "Jennifer, wake up."

Jennifer wriggles out from under her covers and squints at Margo. "What are you doing here?"

"I know you made the list, Jennifer. My sister told me everything." Margo crosses her arms and waits for the moment. That *uh-oh* moment to register on Jennifer's face.

Jennifer rolls over. She's hurting, Margo can tell. Probably from everything she drank last night. There's a glass of water on her nightstand. Jennifer takes a few big gulps, and then says, "Oh."

No *uh*. Just an *oh*. That's it.

Margo glances around the room for the Mount Washington stamp. For proof she can take back and show everyone. But Jennifer's room is messy. She probably has it hidden. So she turns back to Jennifer. "Why did you put yourself as the ugliest senior? It was to frame me, right? Or maybe you were just looking for people to pity you."

"Why shouldn't people pity me?" There's no sarcasm in Jennifer's voice. It's just an honest question.

"Umm, because it's your fault you're on the list! You did it to yourself!"

Jennifer shakes her head, as if Margo isn't following. "Yeah, *this* year. But what about the three other years of high school?

Maureen told me she put me on the list because anyone else would have been a letdown. And you know what? She was right. If I'd put anyone else's name on that list, people would have said, *It should have been Jennifer.*" Jennifer closes her eyes and winces as she sits up. "Look, I had no idea this 'Queen Jennifer' stuff was going to happen. I'm as surprised as you are about that."

"So then why did you put yourself on the list?"

"Because being on the list makes me somebody. People know who I am. I don't know why you're so upset with me. I picked you for prettiest, didn't I?"

Margo laughs. She can't help herself. On Monday, it had felt like the entire school had voted her the prettiest. Like it was *a fact.* But no. It was only Jennifer.

"You *are* the prettiest, Margo." Jennifer continues, "And I didn't want to take anything away from you. But when Dana and Rachel started being friendly to me, I wondered if . . . I don't know . . . maybe we could be friends again, if I could prove that I fit in with your group." Jennifer closes her eyes and shakes her head sadly. "But it was clear you weren't interested in that."

It's true. Margo wasn't.

But why was Jennifer? Didn't Jennifer hate her?

And then Margo remembers. Last night. In her bedroom.

"What were you doing in my room last night? What were you looking for? You were the one who made the list, so clearly the stamp wouldn't have been in my armoire. What had you wanted to find?"

Finally, the look Margo has been waiting to see arrives. The corners of Jennifer's mouth sink. She's embarrassed. Humiliated. But over what?

Jennifer lowers her head. "Your diary."

Margo gasps and steps backward until she hits the door. "You read my diary?"

"It's not like I did it all the time. Only when you started acting weird. I was trying to find out what was going on with us, because you wouldn't talk to me about it."

Everything starts to click in Margo's head. "You always knew the perfect things to say to make me feel bad about myself. Now I know why."

It always struck her as odd, the way Jennifer would randomly bring up things she'd only just confessed to the pages. Like when she lamented the size of her chest. Or the things she'd secretly do with Dana and Rachel. Or being in love with Matthew Goulding. Or how she was seriously afraid of Maureen sometimes. There were pages and pages devoted to her inner turmoil about ending her friendship with Jennifer.

Margo takes a deep breath. Jennifer must have known the friendship was going to end before Margo found the courage to do it. Which maybe should have made her feel less guilty, that Jennifer hadn't been blindsided by it the way she'd assumed. That she knew it wasn't just a pretty girl leaving her ugly friend behind. Instead, Jennifer knew the guilt, the worry she'd had about hurting Jennifer's feelings.

Jennifer continues, "I thought if I could knock you down a few pegs, you wouldn't leave me for Rachel and Dana. But you still did."

Margo realizes that senior-year Jennifer has the same flawed logic that eighth-grade Jennifer did. She wants to leave the room now — leave the house, leave Jennifer, in the same way she did back then. The only difference is that her younger self wasn't entirely sure of her reasons. But this time, Margo is all too aware of why she wants to go. And she doesn't feel sorry about it one bit.

There's just one thing she needs before she goes.

Margo swallows. "I want that stamp."

"Are you going to tell everyone I did it? Is that your plan, to make sure I don't win?"

"This isn't about homecoming queen, Jennifer! God! Of course I'm going to tell on you. Everyone thinks I did it."

"Oh, I feel *so* bad for you." Jennifer rolls her eyes. "You know you didn't do it. What does it matter what everyone else thinks?" Jennifer smirks. "That's right. You haven't changed, either. You still care what people think of you."

"Give it to me, Jennifer. My sister told you she wanted the list to end."

Jennifer purses her lips. She lies back down on her bed. "Tell you what. You want the stamp? You want to end the list? Then I'll give it to you tonight, at the end of the dance."

"No deal."

"Then no stamp."

Margo puts her hands on her hips. "Fine. I don't need the stamp. But I'll tell. I'll tell everyone."

"You won't be able to prove it. I'll just deny it." Jennifer rolls over to the wall. "And I'll hand it off for next year," she threatens. "I already know who I'm going to give it to. And there'll be nothing you can do to stop it."

Margo considers this. "You'd really do that? What about the other girls?" she asks. "The ones you picked as the ugliest? You'd let them go through what you did?"

"I picked those girls for a reason, Margo. I picked *everyone* for a reason. And anyway, they can deal with being put on the list one time. Look at me. I survived." Jennifer sighs. "Just give me tonight, Margo. Give me one night, one chance to not be the ugly girl. Please. If you do, I'll give you the stamp. If you don't, well . . . you can try and get me in trouble. But, remember, you'll be putting Maureen at risk, too."

Margo knows she doesn't owe Jennifer anything. Not anymore. But at the same time, she has no desire to wrestle the stamp out of Jennifer's hand, or to spread the truth when the truth will only come back to haunt Maureen.

This is bigger than just her and Jennifer. The greater good is at stake. The chance to end the list once and for all. And, suddenly, that's what matters to Margo. Not homecoming, not redeeming herself to her classmates, but making sure no one has to go through this ever again.

"Tonight," she tells Jennifer. "I'll give you tonight. Then it's over."

CHAPTER FORTY

It is the worst Saturday of Abby's whole life.

Lisa sends her text messages throughout the football game so she can follow the score. It is sweet of Lisa to do, but it also makes it harder for Abby, having to read tiny versions of the play-by-play action that she doesn't get to be a part of.

The game is not going well, at least not at first. Apparently, the coach gets so desperate, he lets a few of the second- and third-string kids play. Mount Washington manages to fight their way back within one. With the clock ticking down, Andrew drops a Hail Mary pass that would have won the game. Lisa spots him afterward, being ignored by his friends.

She feels bad for thinking it, but Abby is glad the team loses.

Maybe Andrew will be so upset that he'll cancel his party. Or maybe Jennifer and Margo will duke it out over the homecoming crown and Principal Colby will call off the dance. Or Sarah's smell will be declared an environmental hazard and the whole gym will be shut down.

There is always hope.

The rest of the afternoon is beyond boring. Abby doesn't know what to do with herself. So when the time comes that she would have been getting ready for the dance, that's exactly what she does.

She takes an extra long shower and shaves her legs. She blows out her hair and uses her fat curling iron to give the ends a little bounce, like Bridget had done for her and Lisa at the beach.

Then she opens her makeup bag and does her eyes. A little eyeliner on her top lids, some shadow at the creases. She spreads petal pink blush on the rounds of her cheeks. Pink would have looked best with her dress, the dress she never bought. She traces her lips and then spreads a thin layer of lipstick in between the lines.

Abby texts Lisa a few times, asking to see a picture of Lisa dressed up. Lisa doesn't write back. Probably because she's too excited, or maybe because Bridget is doing her hair for her. Though typing the words makes her want to cry her eyes out, Abby manages to send one last text:

Have fun tonight!

Then she turns off her phone. She thinks about taking a Benadryl so she can fall asleep. She doesn't want to spend the night staring at the clock, imagining all the fun happening without her.

She comes out of the bathroom and walks into her bedroom. Fern is sitting at her desk with *The Blix Effect* and a notebook.

"Well, are you ready or what?" Fern asks impatiently.

"You've read that book ten times, saw the movie yesterday, and are about to see it again. You don't have the story down yet?"

"Hello! I'm killing time while you've been playing beauty parlor in the bathroom." Fern finishes scribbling something down, and then looks up at Abby, surprised. "You do remember that you're not going to the homecoming dance, right?"

A thunder rumbles inside her. "Shut up," Abby says, and climbs into her bed and pulls the covers over her head.

"Nice. Real nice." Through a little gap in the fabric, Abby watches Fern sneer at Abby's side of the bedroom, scoffing at the mess. She sighs the way their mother would sigh, only it sounds much lighter coming from Fern's mouth, like a girl playing dress up. Fern moves the books from her desk to her tightly made bed. "Sit here," she tells Abby. "And maybe you should take advantage of being grounded and, you know, clean your side of the room tonight. It's disgusting."

Abby kicks off the covers, trudges over, and falls into Fern's chair. Fern crouches next to her on the floor. Abby opens her textbook and takes out Monday's still-unfinished worksheet. It is wrinkled and Fern seems annoyed by it, which makes Abby happy. But mostly, she would rather fail than suffer through this.

Abby watches Fern's eyes sprint across the page. She secretly hopes Fern won't remember this stuff, but Fern quickly announces, "Alright. So you need to calculate the rate of the seafloor spreading."

Abby stares at the map in her textbook. There's a star on North America, another star marking Africa, and a spread of blue for the Atlantic Ocean.

Fern continues, "The seafloor was approximately two thousand two hundred kilometers between North America and Africa eighty-four million years ago, and it's four thousand five hundred and fifty kilometers today." Abby starts to write that down, but Fern says, "You don't have to write that down, Abby. It's already on your worksheet."

"Fine." Abby crosses her legs at the ankle and rubs the bones together.

Fern waits a few excruciating seconds before asking, "So what's your next step?"

Abby stares into the ocean. The blue seems to get darker as the paper dips into the spine. "I subtract?"

"Well . . . yes. But your figures are in kilometers, and you need to answer in inches."

"Why does it have to be in inches?"

"Because the seafloor grows so slowly, the number would be insignificant in kilometers. And also, we don't use kilometers in this country."

There is a tone to Fern's voice. It is teacher-y and confident, making the words sound pointy and crisp, like the tip of a freshly sharpened pencil.

"If the answer is so *insignificant*" — Abby's tongue clumsily pushes out the word — "why does it matter?"

Fern looks slack jawed at Abby. "Because moving plates cause volcanic eruptions, they cause tsunamis. I mean, Mount Everest grows an inch a year. That's something you'll want to keep track of."

"An inch? Wow. You don't say."

Fern ignores her. "One kilometer equals point six two miles, and there are five thousand two hundred eighty feet in a mile, and twelve inches in one foot."

"You know that by heart?" Abby laughs heartily, even though it isn't that funny. But she likes turning the tables on Fern.

"Those are basic conversions," Fern says back. "Now, to solve it, set up a cross multiplication." She stands and goes over to her bed, flopping down on it as if she were already exhausted.

Abby grips her pencil and writes "cross multiplication" down on her notebook with the hope that seeing the words might spark her memory.

It doesn't.

Fern opens *The Blix Effect* like she is going to read it, but Abby can feel her sister's eyes pinned to her. "Multiply by a ratio of one, Abby."

Abby drops her pencil. "I don't know how."

Fern's face wrinkles. "That's eighth-grade math."

"Don't you remember? I was stupid last year, too." Abby stands up.

"You're not stupid, Abby."

"Whatever, Fern." Abby lies back down on her bed. "I know you don't want to help me, so forget it."

Fern walks over and stands with her hands on her hips. "You're a brat, you know that?" Fern says. "I have a stack of homework I have to do myself, and here I am spending my time trying to help you and you couldn't be more ungrateful!"

"What does it matter? I'm missing the dance."

"Are you kidding me? Hello! If you're doing as badly in your other classes as you are in Earth Science, you could get left back, Abby. Do you want to be a freshman again next year? How do you think that will affect your precious social standing?" Fern licks her lips. "Or maybe you could be the prettiest freshman girl *again* next year! Wouldn't that be *totally awesome*?"

Abby rolls over and stares at the wall. Getting left back is a huge, very real fear of hers. And Fern knows that. She knows that, and now she is throwing it in her face. "You're a horrible sister!" Abby screams at the top of her lungs.

Fern startles. She backs away from the bed. "What? Was I not just helping —"

Abby rolls onto her knees and jabs a finger at her sister so hard, the mattress springs bob her up and down. "Don't you even feel a little bit bad about ratting me out to Mom and Dad?"

"Is that why you brought up Mr. Timmet? To get back at me?" Fern shakes her head. "I hate to break it to you, Abby, but this is your fault. Quit feeling sorry for yourself. And quit blaming me."

"You want to punish me for the list. You're jealous!"

Fern's face gets tight. "That's pathetic."

It is as if Abby has reached the top of a steep hill, and now she tumbles down without any chance of stopping. "You are. You're jealous because I'm pretty and you're ugly and EVERY-ONE KNOWS IT."

For a second, it is a relief. To have said the thing she felt, to have said the best thing to hurt Fern. But in the next moment, Abby can't breathe.

It happens fast. Fern's face goes white, and then the tears pour out, as if they've been collecting there the whole time, waiting for the opportunity to fall. "Obviously, Abby! I know I'm ugly. I was on the list, too."

It scares Abby to hear Fern say this. To hear Fern call herself ugly. "No, you weren't. The list didn't mention you by name. And like you said, no one thinks we're sisters, anyhow."

Fern wipes at her eyes, but it doesn't help. "I'm not talking about this year's list." She looks away, ashamed. "I was on last year's list. I was the ugliest sophomore."

"What are you talking about?" Abby says, but she thinks back and starts to remember. Last year, she'd overheard Fern in the kitchen with their parents. Fern had been upset that some-one had called her ugly.

Abby now understands that "someone" was, essentially, the entire school. Well, one person speaking for the entire school.

Their parents quickly leaped to Fern's defense. Looks didn't matter; Fern was smarter than the majority of her classmates; intellect was what counted; a million other compliments Abby never received. They had wanted to call the school to complain, but Fern forbid them to.

No wonder Fern had been so bitchy to her this week. And while Abby definitely feels bad, Fern should have told her. "How was I supposed to know that? You said the list was no big deal."

"It isn't a big deal," Fern clarifies, her voice startlingly emotionless despite the tears. "I don't need a stupid list to tell me what I already know."

Abby opens her mouth, but no words come out. She doesn't know what to say.

"And I'm not sorry for telling on you, Abby. It's crazy to me that you think this list is the only thing you've got going for you. I seriously don't understand how someone like you has such horrible self-esteem."

It is the first nice thing Abby can remember Fern saying to her. "Well, you're not ugly, Fern." She would have said it back then, too. If she'd known.

"I am ugly. I know it."

To hear Fern, so sure of herself, makes Abby want to cry. It makes her feel so ashamed for thinking it. She never meant it. Not really. "You're not."

"And you're not stupid."

Abby shakes her head. "Trust me, Fern."

"Trust *me*, Abby."

They are clearly at an impasse. Abby realizes they both firmly believe they are one thing and not the other. But they also have each other's backs, like real sisters, for what feels like the first time ever.

Fern sits down on the floor. "Look, I'm just going to stay home and help you with this. I don't need to see *The Blix Effect* again."

"No, Fern. You should go. I'll see where I can get on my own with this and you can check it when you come home. Do you want me to do your makeup?"

"Give it a rest," Fern says, and they leave it at that.

CHAPTER FORTY-ONE

Lauren climbs out of the back of her friend's pickup truck. It is overstuffed. Most of the girls are crabby about Mount Washington's football team losing yet another game. But not Lauren. She's smiling ear to ear, having had the time of her life. She loved the burn of the wind on her cheeks, that her hair is a tangled mess, that she'd cheered her throat raw.

"So we'll see you at Candace's house in a few hours?"

"Yup! See you there!"

"Do you need a ride?" the girl driving asks.

"No, I'll be okay."

"I'm not even excited to go over there," someone groans.

"Let's go as late as we can. I don't want to be hanging out there all night."

Lauren realizes this is the perfect time to discuss Candace. "Come on," Lauren says. "It'll be a fun way to start off the night." The girls still seem doubtful, so Lauren adds, "Candace was really nice to me last night and it's not because she likes me. It's because she misses all of you."

"You shouldn't defend her, Lauren."

"I'm not defending her, exactly. I'm just saying that maybe she's changed."

"She's using you to make herself look good in front of us."

Lauren wants to say no, because she truly doesn't think that's it. But she doesn't say anything. She feels bad for Candace, because Lauren hasn't changed anyone's mind. But she did what she could. She tried. And Candace will still have a chance, at her party.

Her mother is in the shadowy part of the kitchen, looking over some papers.

"We lost!" Lauren announces cheerfully. "But it was the most fun I think I've had in my whole life." She goes to the sink and gulps down a glass of water. "The game was so close, Mommy. We lost it in the last minute, when one of our guys dropped a pass. But it was so exciting! Much more exciting than football on television. And our high school band is amazing. They played songs throughout the game, songs that everyone knew the words to. And all the girls sat together on the bleachers underneath blankets. It was just . . . perfect."

Lauren crashes down next to Mrs. Finn. She glances down at her mother's papers. One of them is the list. The copy that's been in Lauren's book bag all week.

"We need to talk," Mrs. Finn announces.

"You went in my bag," Lauren says, backing up slowly until she hits the counter. "I can't believe you went into my bag!"

"What kind of people are you friends with, Lauren?" Mrs. Finn taps the paper.

"My friends didn't do this."

"Then who did?"

"I don't know, Mommy!"

"They certainly don't speak kindly about Candace. In fact, they pretty much confirmed my impression of her."

Lauren shakes her head. Candace had been nothing but kind and respectful last night. Which was more than she could say of her mother. "Mommy —"

"Why didn't you show this to me right away?"

"Because I didn't want you to worry. I've met a lot of really nice girls. My grades are good. Everything's okay. Everything's great, actually."

"You think those girls care about you?" Her mother runs her quivering hands through her hair. "You've changed, Lauren. I don't like who you are choosing to spend time with. And this" — she crumples up the paper — "is beyond anything I would have thought you'd get involved with."

"Mommy . . . I haven't changed."

"I'm quitting my job."

"What?"

"This isn't working out for us, Lauren. I'm going to pull you out of Mount Washington as soon as possible. I figure if I sell the house, which is too big for the two of us anyway, I'll have enough money to carry us through the last two years of high school."

The kitchen walls close in. "I want to stay in school."

"I was always afraid of the way other people would treat you, never that you'd become some kind of mean popular girl. I can't even begin to say how disappointed I am at the choices you've made."

"You don't like it because you don't control my life anymore. Because I'm not afraid of school and other people." With a shaky hand, she holds on to the back of a kitchen chair. "I've got to go get ready."

"You're *not* going to the dance!"

Lauren sits down, shocked but still obedient. A second later, though, she stands back up.

"You can't do that! I haven't done anything wrong!"

"This is my right as a mother, to intervene when I see my daughter going down the wrong path."

"Mommy, please. It's the homecoming dance. Everyone's going to be there."

"Lauren, I've said what I need to say."

Lauren storms up to her room. She slams the door and falls on her bed, sobbing. It isn't fair. She knows that the list had made a lot of girls unhappy, but it is different for her. The list has given her confidence. It's made people take a chance and approach her. Sure, maybe if the list had never been written, everyone still would have viewed her as the homeschooled girl, but things are different now. She is different now.

Later, Mrs. Finn comes up to deliver dinner. Neither speaks to the other. Lauren eats a little, but not much, and when her mother returns to collect the tray, Lauren has her curtains drawn, her lights out. Again, she says nothing.

But as soon as her mother closes the door, Lauren climbs out of bed wearing the dress she'd worn to her grandfather's funeral. It is long, black, and surely wrong for the dance. She puts her shoes in her bag, along with a camera. She shimmies open her window, drops out, and runs barefoot across the grass.

CHAPTER FORTY-TWO

It is time to see if the dress fits.

Bridget walks slowly down the hall, robe tied tight around her, a glass of ice-cold water in her hand. She takes a sip, barely gets it down. The fear has collected in her throat like a too-big bite of something gone bad. Moldy bread, sour milk, rotten meat.

With each step closer to her bedroom, Bridget thinks of the things she swallowed this week. The bagel, the bottles of cleanse, the pretzels, a forkful of salad at the mall. It adds up, in her off-kilter mind, to a hundred Thanksgivings.

If the red dress doesn't fit, if she is too big for it, what will she do? There's nothing else in her closet to wear. And even if there were, it would be impossible for her to have a good time, knowing she failed. All her sacrifices, all the hunger pains, will have been for nothing.

As Bridget passes the bathroom, she hears Lisa through the closed door singing along to the radio while brushing her teeth. Though she's doing it earnestly, Lisa's voice is garbled by the brush and the foam and it makes the whole thing sound wonderfully silly. It breaks through the darkness, the emptiness, inside Bridget. She stops, delays the judgment awaiting her for a little longer, and quietly opens the door a crack.

Steam seeps out and she sees Lisa dressed in a tank, shorts, and her slippers. Her black hair, wet and shiny like oil, hangs down her back, and the dripping water has made the portion of tank top covering the small of her back see-through. White bubbly paste blooms at the corners of Lisa's mouth, and she bops from side to side, the toothbrush her microphone, the fluffy bath mat her stage.

Bridget hasn't seen much of her sister today. Bridget decided to bail on the Spirit Caravan and the football game. She was too tired, and what little energy she had she wanted to save for the homecoming dance. Also, she knew it would be hard to pass up the snacks. Her friends love to hit the snack shed — nachos, soft pretzels, hot dogs, popcorn, cardboard boxes balanced on their laps, hands reaching across one another.

Anyway, Lisa barged into her room, looking for something. Even though Bridget was clearly sleeping, Lisa turned on the light and made lots of unnecessary noise. When she noticed the ice cream bowl that had been left last night, melted soup covered by a skin of curdled milk, she snorted. "This is disgusting, Bridget," she said.

Bridget knew why her sister was being so sharp. It had all come out last night. Lisa was worried about her. And even Bridget couldn't deny . . . it was for good reason.

So instead of getting mad at Lisa, Bridget rolled over and told her to take her spot in the backseat of her friend's car. Do the Spirit Caravan with the junior girls. Bridget didn't even have to check with them. Her friends loved Lisa, babied her. They wouldn't mind her tagging along.

But instead of being grateful, Lisa muttered "No, thanks," marched out, and got their parents to drop her off at the football field.

When she came home a few hours later, Lisa went right to her room.

Bridget still doesn't know which team won.

Lisa leans forward to spit in the sink. When she straightens back up, she notices Bridget in the mirror. Lisa's entire expression changes from happy to pissed off. "I'm in here," she says, and kicks the door to close it.

Bridget's grip tightens on the doorknob, and she pushes against Lisa to keep the door open. "Do you want me to help with your hair?"

Lisa narrows her eyes. "No."

"Are you going to curl it? Or wear it up?"

"I don't know, Bridge." Lisa pushes harder.

Bridget uses her foot to keep the door from closing. "What about your makeup? Did you want to borrow my lipstick again? I have a lip liner that goes with it. You really should wear liner. Otherwise it'll rub off after a few minutes."

"God, can't I have some privacy?" Lisa shouts and lunges for the door, pushing against it with both her hands.

Bridget moves her foot and the door slams shut.

She wants to scream about how Lisa could have hurt her, but Lisa switches on the hair dryer. Bridget turns and leans her back against the closed door. From inside, the whirling vibrations send tingles through her body.

She hates you.

She thinks you're a terrible sister.

Bridget slinks the rest of the way to her bedroom. If Lisa did think she was in trouble, did she have to be so horribly mean? Why wasn't she trying to make Bridget feel good about herself, instead of worse?

Anyway, it's over. For better or worse, the dance is here. She's going to put on that dress and face the music.

The red dress is hanging in the closet. She sheds her robe, sets it on her bed. She exhales all the air inside her, hoping to collapse herself. She pulls the dress up over her chest, slides the zipper up.

No problem.

Yay, Bridget!

Her lip quivers and the tears fall. She pitches forward so they won't drop on the fabric. She did it. She is even smaller than she'd been this summer. Smaller than that enormous bikini. The smallest she's ever been. She doesn't have to lose any more weight.

It's over.

Bridget lifts her arms up in victory. And when she does, the red dress sags low. Dangerously low. So low, her strapless bra peeks out.

This thrills her.

She sneaks into her mother's room and finds a box of safety pins in her sewing kit. Then she peels the dress off, lays it on her bed, and starts pinning it tighter, along the back, like she'd seen done to the mannequin at the department store.

Bridget catches sight of herself in the mirror. In her bra and underwear. Hunched over the bed, over the dress, making small even smaller. She looks like the bugs they'd been studying in Bio II. Like an exoskeleton, ribs and bones protruding little nubs and ridges underneath her skin. She smiles.

And then her stomach growls.

You're disgusting.

Can't you enjoy this for one minute without thinking of food?

You're not even that thin.

With trembling hands, she quickly finishes pinning the dress and puts it on. Then Bridget twists her hair up, adds a bit of lipstick. She gets ready without looking in the mirror.

Bridget doesn't need to see herself. She already knows.

She will never be pretty.

CHAPTER FORTY-THREE

Candace is in the bathroom, sitting on the closed toilet seat, her eyes shut. Her mom puts the finishing touches on her makeup for the dance. She can hear the girls in her bedroom, and all the talking and laughing makes her giddy. Though they'd shown up later than she'd hoped, and no one seems to be eating any of the appetizers she and her mom had made, her plan is still working.

Her only concern is that they don't drink all the rum before Candace gets a chance to have some.

"Are you finished?" she asks her mom. "I feel like we've been in here forever."

"Almost. You are so beautiful!" A brush dabs gently at her lip. "Okay. You can look!"

Candace opens her eyes and stares at the girl in the mirror. She almost doesn't recognize herself.

Her eyes are deep and smoky, traced with liner and shadowing that only makes them an icier blue. Her lashes are extra thick and long, courtesy of the fake ones glued along her lids. Her face has been spackled and powdered, and it would be lighter than her normal skin if not for the bronzer and the blush. Her lips are lined and stained a deep winey red. And her face and chest have been dusted in a light glitter.

It is, in essence, a mask.

"Remember, it will look different in the gym with the lights down. I took that into account." Ms. Kincaid turns the bathroom lights off and opens the bathroom door to let in light from the hallway. "Do you like it?"

Candace isn't sure if she does. But her mom knows what she's doing. She makes people beautiful for a living. Hides their flaws. And that is exactly what Candace wants tonight.

She walks into her bedroom.

"Whoa, Candace. I almost didn't recognize you."

"It's a little much," Candace says quietly. "Isn't it?"

"No! Not at all. You look gorgeous!"

"Like a model!"

They all compliment her. The only one who doesn't is Lauren. She just sits on Candace's bed in that weird witchy dress, her legs swinging. She's drinking from her cup, tipping it all the way back. After the last sip, she swallows and lets out a big *ahhh* like a soda commercial.

"You've seriously never had rum and Coke before, Lauren?"

"No!" Lauren cries. "But they are so good!" She holds out her cup for a refill.

Candace steps in front of Lauren and tries to intercept the bottle. "Maybe you should slow down."

"Come on, Candace. Let her have more," one of the girls says with a devilish smile.

Another adds, "She needs a drink! She's had a rough day."

"Look at her dress. She's in mourning."

There are more snickers.

"It's true. I am." Lauren pouts, and lets someone refill her cup. "My mom is pulling me out of Mount Washington."

Candace perks up. "What? Why?"

"She found the list. And then she told me that I couldn't go to the dance. So I snuck out."

Oh, god. This is bad. Lauren's mom is going to freak. "Lauren —"

Lauren leans around Candace and beams at the girls. "I am so glad to be here with you," she says, her voice quivering with emotion. A few of them laugh. Her eyes fill with tears. "No, seriously. This is all I've ever wanted. Really."

The girls giggle at each other.

Lauren tries to stand up, but her feet catch the hem of her dress. She falls forward into one of the girls and seizes the opportunity to hug her.

"Whoa! Lauren!" the girl snips and guides her off. "Take it easy."

Lauren hits the carpet and then pops up onto her knees, like some kind of planned tumble. She kisses another girl, one sitting on the floor, on the cheek, and in the process sloshes the girl's rum and Coke onto her dress.

"Lauren! What the hell?"

Lauren eases onto her back and lies in the middle of Candace's room, like she is making a carpet angel, and grins up at the ceiling fan. The rest of the girls stare down at her, lips curled.

"Don't give her any more," Candace says, pulling the empty glass out of Lauren's hand.

By the time pictures are taken and the girls have done their last-minute primping, Lauren is completely drunk. The two girls with their permits pack their cars up with bodies and drive over to the school. It is decided that Lauren should walk to help her sober up.

The other girls who can't fit in the cars walk briskly. Candace ends up falling back with Lauren, keeping her from drifting into the street.

"Your mom is so pretty, Candace," Lauren slurs.

"I guess."

Lauren stops walking. "My mom hates me."

"She doesn't," Candace says, grabbing Lauren's hand and pulling her gently along. "She thinks she's protecting you."

"I'm not going back to school."

"You can talk to her, Lauren. You —"

Lauren shakes her head. "I know it. She's not going to change her mind."

Candace, unfortunately, believes her. "I'm sorry." But she also realizes that Lauren leaving Mount Washington changes things. Her friends are warming back up to her. With Lauren gone, they'll most certainly let her back in the group.

When she looks at Lauren, Candace sees that she's started to cry. "I don't think the girls like me anymore. I don't know what I did wrong."

"They still like you. Don't worry." Lauren cries a little more, then stops walking again. "Are you going to throw up?" Candace asks her. "If you think you have to, do it. You'll feel better."

Lauren looks at her with watery eyes. She blinks a few times and says, "I don't like you with all that makeup on. I think it looks bad. You don't need any of it. You're so pretty, Candace."

"Whatever." Candace tries to keep it light.

When they finally arrive at the school, the girls are standing around impatiently. Candace can hear the music inside the gym leaking out of the windows.

"Candace! Come inside! Hurry up!"

Candace looks at Lauren. She is puking down into the storm grate. "We can't bring her in. She's wasted."

"So leave her in the car."

One of the girls opens the door to her backseat. Candace helps Lauren get inside.

"Don't puke in my car," the girl cautions. "If you need to puke, you go outside, okay?"

Lauren rolls on her back and whispers, "Okay."

Candace watches the girls run into the gym. When she looks back at Lauren, her face is pale and she can tell another wave of puke is coming. Candace drags her back out of the car, gets her over to the curb, and holds her blond hair back.

When Lauren stops retching, Candace says, "We'll hang here until you're puked out, and then I'll walk you home."

"No. You should go dance, Candace. Go be with your friends."

But Candace has already gone back to the front seat of the car, looking for tissues. One for Lauren to wipe her mouth, and one for Candace to take off her makeup.

CHAPTER FORTY-FOUR

Sarah stands naked before her full-length mirror. The edges are masked with stickers and pictures of the bands she loves, but enough glass is exposed for her to see herself from head to toe. Her skin is dull and chalky except for the hundreds of thin red scratches from her nonstop itching. They give the appearance of her having been attacked by a pack of angry stray cats. She lifts her tangle of necklaces and sees a green shadow of oxidized metal staining her skin. Her hair is wild and it hangs in her face in heavy clumps. She pins a little of it back, so the word on her forehead can be seen. It is mostly faded. She could retrace it, but decides not to.

In the top corner of the mirror, she's wedged the two homecoming dance tickets. Milo's, a waste of ten dollars. At least it was his cash, not hers.

She sits on her bed. Her uniform for the week, and now her homecoming dance outfit, hangs on the back of her chair.

The dance is about to start. She is late.

Hurry up, she tells herself. *Hurry up! Get dressed right fucking now, Sarah!*

Though she is in the homestretch of this anarchy, she does not want to put the clothes back on. She'd taken them off the second she came back from the Spirit Caravan.

Sarah had positioned her bicycle between two vehicles decorated to the nines. One behind her had fluttering streamers taped along the body and soap-caked white words scrawled on the windows, proclaiming allegiance to their class, to the team. The girls in the truck in front of her were dressed in mountain-eer outfits. She watched them all dance, cheer, and laugh together. One was that homeschooled girl from the list, Lauren, who had become the darling of her sophomore class. Lauren had looked so unabashedly happy to be standing in the bed of the pickup truck. She kept hugging the girls she danced with, hug-ging them after every song. Like a twelve-year-old. Her hair was so shiny and blond, and she whipped it around to the music. Sarah watched the other girls on the truck give Lauren funny looks. Her school spirit was a touch too much for them.

The people of Mount Washington came out on their lawns with cups of coffee and waved. The people who watched the spectacle didn't seem to notice how clearly Sarah didn't belong. Probably because they couldn't smell her. Sarah didn't wave, she didn't smile. She set her eyes on the bumper in front of her and pedaled down to the football field. And when other cars were looking for places to park, she spun around and rode home.

All the celebratory honks and cheers and fight songs gave her a headache, and she spent the rest of the afternoon in bed.

She thinks about how different her routine is from that of the other girls around town. How primped and perfumed and well lotioned they'd be. She puts on screaming noisecore to motivate her. She thinks of all the people she would disgust, fuels herself by imagining their horrified faces.

Finally she puts on the clothes, and it's awful. Like someone else's skin. A horribly stinky cloak.

There's a knock at her bedroom door. She opens it and at first sees no one. But peeking out into the hall, she sees Milo a few steps down, looking at an old picture of Sarah. One from seventh grade. It's a horrible picture. She'd tried to curl her bangs like the other girls, but of course it looked like ass. And that grody blouse she'd bought at the mall because everyone else was wearing them.

"Hey," he says, but doesn't take his eyes off the picture.

"I was just leaving." She pushes past him, but he grabs her arm. She tries to pull away, but he won't let her until he's slid something on her wrist.

A corsage. White daisies.

He is the only boy to ever buy her flowers.

"I said I didn't want a corsage," she says. She rips it off and presses it into Milo's chest. A few petals fall to the floor. God, he is going to make her cry.

"I don't know how many different ways I can try to prove how beautiful I think you are. It's killing me to watch you do this to yourself. I talked to Annie —"

"For fuck's sake, Milo!" She darts into her room and slams her door right in his face. She wants him to go. She needs him to go. She *cannot* fucking deal with this right now!

But Milo calls to her through the wood. He says, "And Annie said that it doesn't matter what I do. I can't make you believe me. It has to be something you feel."

"God, Annie knows *everything*, doesn't she? Someone should give her a talk show." Sarah lies down on her bed. She stares at the ceiling. Her eyes are watering. She desperately wants to scratch.

Milo opens the door. Sarah hides her face with her sheet.

"Come on," Milo says, and reaches for Sarah's hand.

"Where are we going?"

"Into the bathroom."

"No. I'm making a statement, Milo. You need to respect it."

"I have. I've let you take the list and basically turn it into a self-fulfilling prophecy. So now you need to respect yourself and take a fucking shower. You'll feel better, Sarah. Please."

He pushes her down the hall. And though Sarah protests a little bit, after a few steps she goes limp. Milo opens a few doors until he finds the linen closet. He picks a fluffy blue towel, hands it to her, and then shuts her inside the bathroom.

Sarah stares at the closed door. Milo's right. Mount Washington was never going to see her as anything other than what they wanted to see. As ugly. It didn't matter what she did. It didn't matter if she didn't shower for a week, or if she got into the fanciest homecoming dress money could buy. She couldn't change other people's opinions. She couldn't teach any lessons they didn't want to learn.

Milo sits outside. Once the water is turned on, he opens the door a crack and talks to her. About nothing, really. What he says doesn't matter. Sarah is just glad to hear his voice underneath the falling water. And he can't hear her tears.

It takes three lather-rinse-repeat cycles to cut through the buildup of grease and grime. And as much as Sarah hates to admit it, it feels so good to be clean.

She walks out with a towel around her, steam billowing.

"What now?" she says.

He shrugs. "We go to the dance."

"I'm never putting those clothes on my body again."

Milo kicks the pile with the toe of his sneaker. "Me, either. We should burn them."

"Yeah."

"Do you have a dress you could wear?"

"I am NOT wearing a dress."

"Fine. Wear whatever you feel beautiful in."

She ignores that part and settles on another T-shirt, her hoodie, and a fresh pair of jeans.

And the corsage.

When they get to the dance, Sarah lingers outside the gym door. She can hear the music inside. "I feel like a failure. Everyone expects me to show up and do something."

"Who cares about their expectations?"

"I never did want to go. If I hadn't been on that stupid list, I wouldn't have come here."

She walks off, circling around the school until she's at their bench. Milo sits next to her. Sarah opens a new pack of cigarettes and lights one up. It's been almost a week since she's had one, and the smoke is extra strong and thick in her lungs. She coughs, hard, and throws the cigarette to the ground.

When the smoke clears from her lungs, she asks, "Can I tell you something?" Her lip quivers. She bites down on it. "I don't know if I've ever felt beautiful."

"Sarah . . ."

"I'm serious."

Milo wraps his arms around her and holds her tight. And Sarah lets him. She lets herself be vulnerable for a second, lets him see her real, true, ugly self. It is a beautiful moment, and Sarah lets herself be a part of it, and that, at the very least, is a step in the right direction.

CHAPTER FORTY-FIVE

The gym is dark, shadowy. The only brightness comes from the white crepe paper strung between basketball hoops, the iridescent balloons tied to the bleachers, the disco lights affixed to the DJ table, and whatever trickles in from the hallway. It smells of pizza, fruit punch, and the flowers on the wrists of the girls Jennifer is dancing beside.

Margo, Dana, and Rachel wear matching corsages — miniature red roses that haven't yet begun to open up, interspersed with baby's breath, a few perfectly oblong lemon leaves, and springy curls of willow wood.

Jennifer's wrist is naked, light, and it lifts unrestrained to the beat of the music. Her other hand, the one holding her clutch, hangs heavily by her side.

The Mount Washington embossing stamp is tucked inside it. It takes up so much room, she couldn't pack her pocket comb or the Band-Aids for if her new heels gave her blisters.

Jennifer has kept her end of the bargain.

Not that Margo even bothered to check.

Jennifer shimmies behind Dana and positions herself so she's dancing directly in front of Margo. She's tried this a few times already. She wants to get Margo's attention so she can lift up her bulging purse and show that, yes, she'd brought the stamp as promised. But as soon as Jennifer positions herself, Margo does a half spin and turns away.

There are exactly twenty little green buttons climbing up the back of Margo's dress. Jennifer's had ample opportunities to count them.

As annoying as Margo's cold shoulder is, it is no colder than it's been the rest of the week. So she continues to dance merrily, because it appears that Margo has kept her end of the bargain, too.

Neither Rachel nor Dana have treated Jennifer any differently tonight. There's no indication that Margo's told them what she managed to figure out. Both girls are friendly and polite to Jennifer. They've made room so she can dance with them, split a Coke with her during a slow song, even posed with her for a picture that Jennifer took with her arm outstretched.

There'd been only one moment of palpable discomfort. It had come when the girls arrived to the homecoming dance, about thirty minutes after it had officially started.

Jennifer, on the other hand, had arrived to the gym thirty minutes early. The student council kids were hanging up the decorations. Jennifer offered her help, volunteering to sit at the front table, tear tickets, make sure all votes made their way into the locked ballot box.

It wouldn't be necessary, she was informed. There were already two freshmen assigned that duty. Jennifer was told to go have fun. Enjoy herself.

Instead, she hung near the doors and greeted each and every student as they arrived. "Vote Queen Jennifer," she'd said again and again and again, pointing to the sticker on her dress that said the same thing. It was not the one Rachel and Dana had given her. That had lost its stick. She'd made herself another one. A bigger one.

Jennifer could tell which students had voted for her. As they slid their tickets into the ballot box, they smiled and wished Jennifer luck. The ones who didn't say anything, who avoided her eyes, picked Margo or someone else.

When Margo, Rachel, and Dana arrived, Jennifer was there to greet them, too, in the same way she had all the others. Campaigning.

They gave her the strangest looks.

Margo, well, she could understand her reaction. But Jennifer never said she wasn't going to still give homecoming queen her best shot. Jennifer had just as much right to win as Margo did. List or no list.

But Jennifer had expected Rachel and Dana to support her. Obviously. Like they'd been doing all last week. Only, the girls seemed a bit taken aback by her forwardness. Which didn't seem to make much sense to Jennifer. Rachel and Dana had been spearheading this whole 'Vote Queen Jennifer' campaign from the beginning. If Margo hadn't told them, what had changed?

The next song the DJ plays is another fast one. Jennifer alters her moves just slightly, so she is still in sync.

And for the next few songs, Jennifer dances fast and hard. Out of fear, of nerves, of everything. There is so much riding on this night, and she feels like if she stops, she will have to think about the embossing stamp weighing down her clutch purse, the things that Margo said to her weighing down her insides.

She needs this. She needs to win, to prove to herself that she is beautiful. That she'd made the right choice.

As a slow song comes on, she exhales.

"I need some air," Rachel announces.

Dana and Margo follow her.

And Jennifer, too, a few steps behind.

Jennifer sees it first. Matthew Goulding, coming up from behind. He passes by Jennifer and slips his hand into Margo's. She turns fast, sharp, maybe because she thinks Jennifer is grabbing her. But she softens when she sees it is him.

"Do you want to —"

Margo does. Of course she does.

Jennifer doesn't expect Ted to come looking for her. She's tried to catch his eye a few times tonight, which he does anything to avoid. Turn his back, stare at his shoes.

So it ends up being Rachel, Dana, and her in the corner, where a door has been propped open to expose a slice of parking lot and let in cool air. They all watch Margo.

Jennifer can see the happiness. The joy of Margo's perfect night coming true right before her eyes. It is too bright in the dark, shining on her face, showing all the cracks.

Now that she is standing still, her feet begin to throb in her new red shoes. She slips them off and stands in bare feet behind them.

"She's loved that boy forever," Rachel says.

"I'm glad they're dancing. It gives her something good tonight." The way Dana says it, Jennifer hears the subtext. The thought that Margo will not be homecoming queen, even though she deserves to be.

That the thing they wanted for Jennifer is now the thing she's taking away from Margo.

"You both really do look beautiful," Jennifer says. She has said this so many times tonight. It just comes out of her mouth, filling the awkwardness.

"Yeah, you, too," the girls say again. They sound tired.

Jennifer smiles at her feet, the red shoes she'd bought, like Dana had said. When she looks back up, the girls have started talking about something else.

"Did you see that I got the red shoes, like you said?" She steps back inside them.

This time, Rachel and Dana pretend not to hear her.

Jennifer again wonders if Margo said anything. She promised she wouldn't, but Jennifer thinks Margo will tell people. Maybe not tonight. But eventually. After Margo gets the stamp. She just has a feeling it will come out.

She excuses herself and finds a seat alone on the bleachers. Another fast song comes on, but she doesn't feel like dancing.

Danielle DeMarco is surrounded by a huge group of kids. There's a boy, a cute tall boy, doing a funny break-dancing move right in front of her.

This boy is not Danielle's boyfriend.

Andrew is with his friends against a wall. He is watching Danielle, but trying not to watch her.

Jennifer flicks the hair off her shoulders. One boyfriend to the next. Classic slut behavior. It was part of the reason Jennifer had picked her in the first place. Having had to see Danielle suck face with Andrew in the hallway, every single morning. Flaunting the fact that she had a boyfriend.

Jennifer has little reasons like that for everyone.

She picked Abby because she'd heard Fern making fun of how stupid Abby was to her friends. Because she knew deep down that Fern thought she was better than everyone, even though she'd been on the list last year.

She picked Candace because she knew that if she did, a hundred girls in the school would say a silent thank-you for telling Candace the hard truth — that people have been secretly calling her ugly for years. Maybe she'll be a different person now that she knows. Jennifer doubts it. It's not even the point. She didn't put Candace on the list to teach her a lesson. She didn't do it for the gratitude. She did it because she wanted to.

She picked Lauren because she was unlike any pretty girl Jennifer had met before. She wasn't trying at all. And she knew that would drive Candace crazy.

She picked Sarah because she'd wanted to call her out. Sarah was full of crap. The tough act. The bad girl. It was all a cover. And tonight proves it. The fact that she didn't show up to the homecoming dance, after all that talk, those threats of ruining everyone's good time. Jennifer laughs at herself for ever letting Sarah's shtick get to her.

She picked Bridget because —

Bridget walks over and takes a seat on the bleachers, too, a few rows away.

"Hi, Bridget," Jennifer calls to her.

Bridget looks at Jennifer over her shoulder. "Hey, Jennifer."

Jennifer scoots down a few rows and says, "I want to let you know how glad I was that you were on the list. You deserved it."

Bridget watches a girl walk across the dance floor. It's Bridget's sister, Jennifer realizes. Anyway, the two girls catch eyes with each other, but both quickly look away.

"I wish I wasn't on the list," Bridget says. "The list has been nothing but trouble for me."

Jennifer's face wrinkles up. "How can you say that?"

Bridget is holding a plastic cup of soda. She lifts it to her mouth and takes the tiniest sip. "Oh, don't listen to me." She turns and smiles weakly. "I don't want to ruin your special night. I hear you're a lock for homecoming queen. Congrats."

"Thanks," Jennifer says, watching Bridget get up and walk off.

Margo might never think she's a good person. Margo might never understand why she did what she did. Both the list and the reading of Margo's diary. It was a hard thing to admit, but she didn't lie about it. And she could have. She could have never told Margo the truth. And she never told any of Margo's secrets, all the things she'd read. Jennifer kept them all inside her, like any best friend would.

She wasn't a bad person.

Really.

Principal Colby arrives at her side. "Are you having fun, Jennifer?"

Jennifer picks up her clutch from next to her and holds it in her lap. "Yes."

"Good." Principal Colby looks out at the dance floor. "Jennifer, I feel terrible that I wasn't able to figure out who made the list. I really wanted to give you that. I'm going to keep trying for the rest of the year, keep my ear to the ground. If I'm still unsuccessful, so be it. But I'll work twice as hard next year."

Great. Just great.

"Thank you," Jennifer says, quietly.

Principal Colby's smile sinks. "All that said, I came over here to tell you something very important. You didn't win homecoming queen tonight."

Jennifer feels all the blood drain out of her face. "Are . . . are you sure?"

"I wanted you to be prepared. I'm going to go up there and call a name, but everyone in this gym is going to be looking at you. They're going to want to see your reaction."

"Thanks," she mutters. It is freshman year all over again. Only this time, Jennifer won't be blindsided. This time, she knows she's the ugliest girl in the room.

"I know you're disappointed. But unlike what happened on Monday, and for the last three years, you'll have a chance to decide how you want people to see you."

Jennifer glances out onto the dance floor and finds Margo. Her arms are up around Matthew Goulding. Her head is on his shoulder. Her eyes are closed.

Principal Colby continues, "None of this matters, Jennifer. Years from now, no one will remember this dance, no one will remember who made homecoming queen, no one will remember the list. What people are going to remember are their friends, the relationships they've made. Those are the things to hold on to."

Jennifer's eyes brim with tears. Everything goes watery.

"Is it Margo? Did she win?"

Principal Colby doesn't answer her. Instead, she says, "You're going to be fine, Jennifer. Just take a minute to collect yourself."

Jennifer sits on her hands.

Maybe Principal Colby is right, but she hopes not. Because there's nothing left for Jennifer to hold on to. Except, maybe, a tiny piece of her dignity.

And she's not even sure she deserves it.

CHAPTER FORTY-SIX

When Margo hears Principal Colby say her name into the microphone, the entire gym becomes a vacuum. Everyone sucks in one collective breath, removing all the air.

Everyone looks for Jennifer.

Margo, too. Her eyes go to the bleachers, the snack table, the dance floor.

No one can find her.

So the crowd turns back to her. A few people clap. Then more. Soon everyone is cheering. Rachel and Dana both swoop her up into hugs. Despite their campaigning, they are thrilled for Margo. They are her best friends.

The students step back, clearing a narrow path for Margo to make her way to the DJ booth. Matthew is already there, wearing his crown. He's smiling, reaching out for her.

Margo's legs are shaking, but with each step, they begin to work better, feel stronger. This is the moment, the one she's been dreaming about.

It is coming true.

Principal Colby sets down the microphone and picks up the tiara. Margo nervously steps up to her.

"Congratulations, Margo," Principal Colby says, patting her on the back.

Margo looks behind her again. Searches the faces in the crowd. Is Jennifer here? Is she watching?

"Jennifer's gone," Principal Colby whispers in her ear.

It is exactly what Margo had hoped for.

Margo should feel relieved, but she doesn't. The stamp. Jennifer still has the stamp. And, now that Jennifer hasn't won, she's not sure if Jennifer will honor the bargain they struck.

Margo should go find her. Right now.

Then again, there will be time to get it. Later, after the dance. When things settle down. She will track it down. She will get the stamp and end the tradition forever.

But for right now, Margo is able to breathe, finally. She tells herself to enjoy this moment. Her moment.

Principal Colby puts the tiara on Margo's head.

She's surprised by the weight.

Obviously the rhinestones wouldn't be diamonds, but Margo had always assumed the tiara would be metal.

It isn't.

It is plastic.

ACKNOWLEDGMENTS

David Levithan, the countless ways that you nurtured, influenced, encouraged, and championed this book can be summed up by simply stating: It would not, could not, exist without you.

Emily van Beek of Folio Literary, I am beyond grateful for the wise advice, the fierce advocacy, and for your unwavering belief in my ability.

There are many wonderful folks at Scholastic who work hard on my behalf. Thank you all, especially Erin Black, Sheila Marie Everett, Adrienne Vrettos, Elizabeth Parisi, Sue Flynn, and Charlie Young.

Love also to Nick and the entire Caruso family, Barbara Vivian, Daddy, Brian Carr, Jenny Han, Lisa Greenwald, Caroline Hickey, Lynn Weingarten, Emmy Widener, Tara Altebrando, Farrin Jacobs, Brenna Heaps, Morgan Matson, Rosemary Stimola, and Tracy Runde.

Oh, and you, too, Bren, for being the most beautiful thing in my life.

Smart Girls in the Real World from Siobhan Vivian

Ruby and her friends tell each other everything…until secrets, lies, and boys get in the way…

Emily leaves the burbs for a thrilling art program in the city, but what happens when her worlds collide?

Natalie's life gets turned upside down by a school election, disloyal friends, and a very hush-hush romance.

An intense look at the rules of high school attraction—and the price that's paid for them.

Available in print and eBook editions

■SCHOLASTIC

www.thisisteen.com/books

SIOVIV3